BENEFITS RECEIVED

BY
ALICE GRANT ROSMAN

BENEFITS RECEIVED

By ALICE GRANT ROSMAN

MINTON, BALCH & COMPANY
NEW YORK
1932

TO

MABEL, CHARLES AND JENKS

CONTENTS

BENEFITS RECEIVED

.

BENEFITS RECEIVED

CHAPTER ONE

BIDDY AND SHOLTO

BIDDY KERLIN turned in her dreams, half wakened by the September sun pushing a long gold finger through her window as the curtains moved. She had been walking down a country road through a green tunnel of trees with the wind in her face—she could feel it still, cold and lovely—when some one had tucked her arm in his and she had turned with intense gratification to find that it was the postman. There was something so deliciously absurd about the dream that she tried to continue it, but consciousness had broken the spell, she was very nearly awake, waiting drowsily for Taylor to come in with her morning tea and snap up the blinds.

"A snappy woman, Taylor. It would be a brave postman who tried to take *her* arm," thought Biddy with a sleepy smile. "Even when she turns on your bath, she does it fiercely like Jove releasing a thunderbolt.... Now old Simpkins, if she turned it on would do it by stealth, the lamb, not a sound, not a swish, but the thing would be done. Simpkins is what you would call a survival, I suppose.... I like them ... genuine antiques...."

A church bell began to ring and a gust of wind swept the curtains and sunlight into the room together, so that

3

Biddy opened her eyes. The next moment she was sitting up in bed, contemptuous at her own dismay and saying to herself indignantly:

"You poor lunatic!"

This was no lofty, sumptuous bedroom in her grandmother's house where Taylor would presently bring tea and snap up the blinds, but a shabby room in a shabby street from which the Taylors of this world had long departed. The rug on the floor was old and faded, the walls of that serviceable brown beloved of thrifty landlords, and a stout iron contraption wearing a padlock sat beside the gas-fire, devouring shillings with a savage gusto, should the tenant wish to warm her toes, cook her breakfast or have a bath. The few pieces of furniture had been chosen with care, however, and the orange curtains at the windows and the orange coverlet that would presently convert the bed into a divan for the day, gave promise that it would be a home.

"I've seen far worse," said Biddy defiantly to the room. "Oh, dear, what a heavenly day for the country, and I've got to paint your poor walls.... There! that's what living in the lap of luxury does for you. It makes you soft. I ought never to have stayed.... I should have gone directly I was twenty-one."

Her cheeks burned and she rubbed them indignantly. She hated this propensity to blush, quite as much as the humiliation which in this instance had brought it about. Almost forcibly her grandmother had taken her into her house and after a year had turned her out of it. That she had done nothing to deserve such treatment had no bearing whatever on Biddy's anger. It was merely her sense of independence that was hurt. She had outstayed her welcome and actually believed that her grandmother cared for her in her own fashion and would be distressed if she went away. What a soft fool she had been!

"Well, don't sit there moaning, get up and have your bath," Biddy ordered herself, and obediently jumped out of bed.

The bathroom and the cupboard containing a small cooking stove, gave her new quarters the dignified title of flat, but it was something other than these which had brought her to Wincey Street,—an unexpected alcove window looking on a plane-tree. Biddy, who loved a storm, could hear in fancy the wind tossing its faded leaves on autumn nights ahead; and later there would be the charm of bare boughs against the sky till spring tufted them with feathery green again.

She pulled the window curtain aside and smiled briefly at the morning on her way to the bath. Then she lit the pilot light and watched with satisfaction the water steaming into her snowy tub. The geyser was the patriarch of all geysers, liable to blow up in unfamiliar hands; the bath had been used as a coal-hole and a beer cellar and a boot cupboard during successive tenancies; but the girl's roving life which had taught her the æsthetic value of a tree outside her window, had also endowed her with certain practical qualities. Aged geysers had no terrors for her and three coats of enamel had soon restored the virgin purity of the dilapidated bath. Running her finger over her handiwork in search of flaws, Biddy fell to thinking of other baths she had known—in cheap schools and boarding-houses, in furnished apartments and palatial hotels, in the "Meteor" sailing towards Arctic waters, in her grandmother's house in Portman Square. Stained, battered, impersonal, intimate and pompous, they appeared before her mind's eye in an orderly row, transient symbols all of them, but not to Miss Kerlin at twenty-one, on a September morning, a subject for dismay. They seemed to amuse her and as she tumbled into her bath, she sang derisively to herself:

> "I dreamt that I dwelt in marble halls,
> With vassals and serfs at my side...."

"Just as well I always knew it was only a dream," she thought and recalled with comfort her incredulity that first night when she had walked down an old Georgian staircase between treasures that caught her heart to the family dinner party assembled by her grandmother to meet her. To believe that this was really her home had seemed as fantastic as to be claimed by all these strangers as a member of a clan. The possession of a grandmother had been odd enough in itself and to behave as a polite guest in old Mrs. Devonshire's house the only response she had been able to make to the unlooked-for kindness suddenly showered upon her.

Perhaps this incredulity had been visible in her face, for her grandmother, looking her up and down as she came into the drawing-room, had inquired:

"You are feeling alarmed at the ordeal ahead of you, no doubt?"

"Oh, no, thank you," Biddy had replied. "Not in the least."

"I see! brave as a lion, but of course that is the attitude of your generation. Afraid of nothing and nobody." The old mocking voice had held a challenge to her youth as well as her courtesy. Biddy on the defense had hastened to admit:

"I am terrified of mice and black beetles."

"Ah, then you must take care this evening," Mrs. Devonshire had retorted, and in a flash the relationship between them had been proved, the girl dissolving suddenly into delighted laughter.

They had been unsworn but none the less certain allies by the time the other members of the clan arrived, Devonshires, Dawnays and Fenwicks, bewildering to the girl, who had heard of none of them three weeks ago. She knew that her mother, Brigid Devonshire, had walked out of this house one morning to marry David Kerlin at a registry office, and never came back; knew too that the marriage, so disastrous from the Devonshire point of view, had been an intensely happy one. But Brigid Kerlin had died in Biddy's eighth year, and by the time the girl was old enough to companion her father between his scientific expeditions, he was too much absorbed in his work to remember much about the family which had ignored him. Biddy herself indeed had felt little curiosity on the subject. The circumstances of her childhood had made her self-dependent, and sitting, bright-eyed and silent among the distinguished but often odd men who had sought her father, she had come more than ever to see life impersonally as they did.

The Dawnays had been the first arrivals at the dinner party, Mrs. Dawnay (once Gwen Devonshire), fluffy in a youthful gown of flowered ninon, and clearly afraid of her mother.

"Your aunt and uncle, Biddy," the old voice had instructed her crisply as she was introduced. Uncle Richard Dawnay, harassed and a little bald, was in the Home Office, and her grandmother had engaged him at once in a political argument, but he was no match for her... perhaps very few people were. She had towered above him and swept his arguments aside with suave amusement under Biddy's fascinated eyes.

Gwynneth and May, the two Dawnay girls, who were pretty and fair, had fallen upon the new cousin with an enthusiasm which had embarrassed her, anxious to be bosom friends in a moment, to instruct her, carry her off.

Their brother Herbert on the other hand had greeted her with languid condescension, and seemed to feel his presence there a concession for which the company should be duly grateful; as soon as his cousin Jane Devonshire arrived, he drew her aside and monopolized her for the rest of the evening.

Jane was thin and small with geranium-colored lips, an Eton crop and a long jade cigarette-holder, rarely out of her mouth. She looked at her relatives through half-shut eyes, saying little, and Gwyn and May confided to Biddy that she led a marvelous life, living in Chelsea and acting for the films. She and Herbert Dawnay referred to themselves as "we of the younger set." Since they were clearly the eldest grandchildren by years this had puzzled Biddy, unfamiliar with the society columns of the sensational press. Jane, it turned out, had a mother and brother, but did not live with them as it cramped her individuality.

The brother, James, at nineteen was rather a peevish youth, like his mamma. He had inherited the Devonshire place "Highways" in Sussex after the death of his father, following that of his uncle Hugh, the elder son, during the War. The property was let now owing to taxation and bad times and his side of the family seemed to think something should be done about it, by old Mrs. Devonshire for preference. They were always hinting that Hugh Devonshire had mismanaged the property and seemed to cherish a deep grudge against his widow and daughter, whom they had supplanted. The widow, moreover, had married again, a man of no particular family named Fenwick, who was in trade.

"Fenwick's Jam, you know," May Dawnay had chuckled instructively in Biddy's ear. "Granny was positively livid about it."

It had seemed a preposterous adjective to use about old Mrs. Devonshire even then, in Biddy's eyes, but May, rushing off from time to time to hang about her grandmother's neck, had had the air of being both knowing and privileged, and her sister Gwynneth had looked on admiringly as though anything May said must be accepted and believed.

The Fenwicks, three in number, had arrived last at the dinner party, and Biddy remembered thinking them a cheerful trio, without yet being able to place where exactly they belonged to the family. Sholto Fenwick, in fact, had enlightened her later in the evening, seeking her out with a box of cigarettes and remarking confidentially:

"I'm an interloper and no relation whatever, so if you are fed to the teeth with cousins and aunts, I'm your man. Sholto Fenwick's my name. Try it over once or twice and you'll get it."

Biddy had tried it obediently.

"But how do you come to be here then?" she had asked.

"By sheer snobbery. Being an upstart, I love fine, fierce aristocrats and great houses, so I act as hanger-on to my stepmother and sister who were born to the purple, and left it for vulgar commerce. Don't say you haven't heard of the scandal? It's our proudest boast, my father's and mine, that we married a Devonshire once removed.... There she is, talking to your grandmother over there, Edith, we call her, Freddy and I.... Freddy is the tall lassie with the large mouth, Edith's daughter. Now I think you know us all, and I hope you approve of us."

"Must I decide at once?" Biddy had enquired.

Sholto had handsomely agreed to give her three months.

Biddy, as she began to dress, smiled at the thought of Sholto, but she knew that her impressions of the family that first night had been really far less sharp than this; had had a vagueness she could never recapture. Occasionally she had been lionized as her father's daughter, that was reasonable, but this sudden assault upon her friendship by complete strangers had had no bearing on her father, and embarrassed her.

"Well, what do you think of them?" her grandmother had asked in her sudden way when the last guest had gone.

"They are all very good-looking, aren't they?"

"Looks, looks, handsome is as handsome does, so they tell us."

Smiling to herself, she had looked at her visitor brightly after this brisk platitude, and nodded her head, but given no information whatever. That was so like her. She had launched her granddaughter into the family but she would not pilot her, leaving her to find her own way through the shoals of that unknown sea.

The things Biddy knew now or sensed she had learned with not even a hint from her grandmother; the friends she had made among the relatives had been her own free choice, and neither approval nor censure had been forthcoming. Perhaps because throughout that year in Portman Square no battery had been brought against the privacy of her mind by the majestic owner of the house, the girl would always see her as some one set apart in splendor, and her own association with her as a dream which, like all dreams, had come to its appointed end.

"It is high time, anyway, that I set to work," she said to herself, as she tied on a white overall and began to make the coffee for her breakfast.

The episode of Portman Square was over and she would not think of it again. It had been great fun while it lasted, so utterly different from anything she had known, and yet unreasonable from first to last. Why had her grandmother taken her in and why had she turned her out?

"Life is so silly," thought Biddy, "and yet you can't help liking it. This is the best coffee I've had for months.... I always was rather good at it. I wonder how long it will take me to do the walls."

2

Sholto Fenwick looked at the windows of Number 25, Wincey Street, saw that two were wide open at the top of the house and decided to make a dash up the dubious-looking stairs. It was nearly eleven o'clock and church bells all over London were proclaiming it to a golden morning, but their persuasive tones seemed to be wasted in this quarter. Wincey Street slept late, insensible alike to dim cathedral aisles and the wider lure of grass and trees.

Sholto feared no such barbarous behavior from the tenant he was seeking. She would be up and about, gay as the morning, he felt sure. Whether she would shut the door in his face, however, was another matter, and when at the top of the last flight he reached that innocent-looking portal, his usually buoyant spirits dropped a little.

Touching the newspaper in his pocket to hearten his courage, he rapped loudly, then waited, feeling a fool and longing to turn and run.

The door was flung open and Biddy in her white overall, the draught blowing her short hair about her head, confronted him.

"Well!" she said in complete amazement.

"Oh, hullo!" Sholto, who had expected fireworks at the very least, went in, took the door gently out of her clasp, and stood with his back against it, perhaps in self-protection.

"But how did you get here?" Biddy asked, still struggling with her astonishment.

"I saw you in Regent Street about six last night and followed you here, but I wasn't game to come in then."

He held his hands above his head and Biddy laughed.

"But why the melodrama, my poor lamb? If I cut you in Regent Street you must have known I didn't see you."

"You didn't cut me. I was behind you, as a matter of fact. But as you had chucked the family I thought you might also be chucking the hangers-on, and I couldn't have a brawl with you outside Liberty's. We have shares in the place."

"You needn't try to spare my feelings," said Biddy to that. "It was I who was chucked, as you know very well. As to the family, I don't recognize the term... it is only a term, after all, but I don't chuck my friends."

"Oh, cheers, then we'll go into the country for the day. Come along," cried Sholto joyfully.

The girl reluctantly shook her head.

"I can't, Sholto. I am going to paint my palace walls."

"Good God, girl, on a day like this? You can't do it. I'll come round and do it for you in the evenings.... Wall-painting is the secret passion of my life... striped, spotted or plain, all lines kept in stock, friezes to curdle the blood. ...I say, Biddy, I like this room, all shapes and not cramped and cubish."

"I have a tree, too," said Biddy eagerly, pulling the curtain aside.

"Lovely... this was a wood once and he's the last survivor, poor old boy. There now, he's bowing to you. He likes a friendly word.... What's this—a window-seat even?"

"No, it's a trunk put in there out of the way. I shall get rid of it," said Biddy, a hint of storm in her face.

She hesitated a moment, then flung off the covering and opened the lid.

"Just look at it," she said indignantly.

"Corpses?" enquired Sholto, a wary eye on her face.

"More or less! Frocks and so on. My grandmother gave them to me so I naturally left them behind. They were sent to my bank and the bank forwarded them after me here.... I nearly pitched them out of the window. Old Simpkins wrote a note. You can read it if you like."

Sholto took the letter from old Mrs. Devonshire's maid, smiling at the precise, neat handwriting, so like Simpkins herself with her pursed lips and stiffly pleated hair.

"The mistress found the gowns you left hanging in the wardrobe, Miss, and ordered me to send them to you at once. If you do not wish to wear them, she says, you will please give them away to the poor, which if you'll excuse me, would be most unsuitable. Hoping this will find you in good health,
                    "Yours obediently,
                              "P. SIMPKINS."

"P. Simpkins ... it can't be Priscilla. That would be too perfect."

"I called her Pet," said Biddy, "and that was most unsuitable too, she said."

"Still, she's right about the frocks. Unkind to the poor to hand them a trunk of white elephants."

"Not at all, they could pawn them, idiot."

"Yes, but you get so little on elephants ... and I say, Biddy, here's that autumn-tinted one simply bursting for a day in the country. Nip into it, there's a sport, and come along."

Sholto, sitting on the edge of the trunk, held up the sleeves of a soft woolen suit in its paper wrappings clasped in an attitude of prayer, but the girl shook her head.

"Not today. I really must do the walls."

"Oh, by the way," Sholto patted the pockets of his coat,

knowing the value of a red herring across the trail, "I saw this in the paper. I wonder if you have come across it."

"Thanks," said Biddy briefly after one glance at the heading, and carried the newspaper to the window, turning her back on him.

"THE KERLIN FUND"

"Sir Neville Willesden, treasurer of the Kerlin Fund, informed the meeting of the Royal Society yesterday that £2,576 had been subscribed towards a memorial to the late David Kerlin in recognition of his distinguished services to the cause of science. The form of the memorial will be discussed at a meeting of the committee in the near future."

Sholto watched her, a still, tall, white figure between the orange curtains. He longed to take her in his arms and comfort her, but now that the moment had come he did not dare.

Did she need comfort? He could not tell. They had played together for a year but he knew that it had been only play. They had none of them, he thought, touched more than the surface of Biddy's mind, unless perhaps old Mrs. Devonshire, for how much she saw or knew, you could never be sure.

Last night this paragraph in the evening paper had seemed to him heaven-sent, but now he was not so sure. Her composure disarmed him, and the remembrance of her easy welcome made all his guile absurd. It would have been easier to deal with indignation or dismay; they would have been a better augury, he felt.

During the two weeks since Biddy's departure from her

grandmother's house Sholto's naturally care-free spirit had been disturbed by emotions entirely new and astonishing, fury, fear and, above all, a wild hope. Hitherto Miss Kerlin of Portman Square had been safely unattainable to a young man of no importance earning three hundred a year. Certainly he had had his dreams of winning the Irish Sweep or making millions overnight on the Stock Exchange, and flinging them at her feet, but meanwhile life was good, since Biddy seemed in no hurry to bestow her affections elsewhere, and he, as Frederika's step-brother, was a handy escort for dances and shows.

Biddy, thrown out into the world, alone, perhaps even penniless, was another matter. Sholto, for all his rage against this indignity and his terror for her safety, had known that it was his chance. He would find her, beg her to marry him, work, for the first time in his life, really work to care for her and make her happy, and old Mrs. Devonshire and all her clan could go to the devil. He almost included Edith and Freddy in the holocaust, much as he liked them. Their calm at Biddy's disappearance had shocked him so much.

She would be all right, they said; Biddy knew how to look after herself; she would be sure to let them know her plans as soon as she had decided what she was going to do.

Sholto, revolted at the callousness of women, had secretly engaged a detective to find the girl and even lurked in Portman Square of nights, hoping to bribe one of the servants for information, but chance alone had helped him in the end and here he was.

And here was Biddy herself, in a poor street certainly,

but gay as a lark and unconcerned, getting ready to paint her walls and evidently quite equal to the task.

Sholto sat abashed before such efficiency and courage. Even if they were mere bravado, some sensibility within him made him aware that this was no moment to spoil her gesture by an offer of his poor three hundred a year.

"Good, isn't it?" remarked Biddy in a casual tone, turning round from the window and handing back the newspaper, "especially in these bad times."

"Oh, rather! But keep it, Biddy. I mean you'd probably like it, wouldn't you? Only I daresay you knew all about it already."

"No, I haven't seen Sir Neville for ages. Naturally, knowing I was in grandmother's hands, he didn't bother." Biddy put the newspaper away in a drawer and whirled round suddenly. "I *will* come into the country and wear the brown frock, too. After all, she gave them to me if she did turn me out of the house."

"Old harridan," said Sholto glaring. "She'll find there are thousands of people who would give their ears to take you in."

"Not really? Well, I hope the queue won't block the street." Biddy, amused and unbelieving, went off to the bathroom to change, quite unaware of the delicate application. After a moment she put her head through the door to say: "Let's tramp! You did mean to tramp, didn't you?"

"For miles," agreed Sholto fervently. "For ever!"

The last phrased cheered him a little even though she had shut the door.

3

The morning wind had blown every cloud out of the
sky and gone away; the day was glowing and still, warm
in the sunlight but chilly in the shade, as though the old
summer and the young autumn walked hand in hand.
On the commons the heather had laid down a purple
carpet; blackberry leaves, hiding the ripe fruit, were already
turning russet and red; yet here and there a buttercup
patched the grass with gold, or a wild rose unfurled its
petals on the top of a hedge. A few leaves fell, but softly,
from quiet trees.

Sholto and Biddy had caught a passing coach into Surrey,
found an inn on a neglected by-road and lunched on the
usual mid-day Sunday dinner of such places—roast beef
and boiled potatoes and apple tart. Sholto, ashamed to
offer her such fare, was cheered at her appetite, and then
worried lest she had been starving all these weeks.

If so he had to admit her looks and tone belied her, for
Biddy, swinging along the deep-hedged Surrey lanes, was
a spirited sight, her blue eyes brilliant and her cheeks
aglow. She had no actual beauty of features and yet, he
thought, she was the loveliest thing. Sometimes it was the
quick turn of her head that enchanted him, and then again
her amazing stillness as she marched on beside him, gazing straight ahead.

Driven at last from the winding lanes by the rush of
cars from town, they wandered into a beechwood where
the sun fell through a silver screen and the whistle of birds
filled the high air.

"Nice of you to come and save me from a solitary omelette and bring me to heaven for the day," remarked Biddy. "Thank you kindly."

"I say, Biddy, how do you manage about food in that place of yours? Where do you have it, I mean?" asked Sholto.

"In the palace, served by the royal chef, of course."

"Is it a kind of service flat then?"

"My poor lad, do you take me for a millionaire? If you will have it in vulgar prose, I cook my own meals. Don't look so incredulous. I've made omelettes for bigger men than you. Father's friends were an absent-minded lot and used to forget their meals as often as not."

"I suppose you knew that Sir Neville What's-his-name awfully well?" remarked Sholto disconsolately.

"Um; bushy eyebrows and very untidy. Did you ever see him? He used to embroil me with all our landladies by burning their mantelpieces with his cigarettes. I kept a pot of paint handy at last to touch up the spots before I went to bed.... Sholto, I think I'll color my walls green to cheer the poor old plane-tree. He must miss his friends."

Biddy grew absent-minded, her eyes on the silver-green, shimmering roof of the trees, quite unconscious that her little glimpse into the past had filled her companion with a new sense of disturbance. "She has had a wonderful sort of life for a girl," he thought; "why, that voyage to the Arctic alone.... We must seem a pretty poor lot to her, all of us."

"I suppose you miss all that, Biddy?"

"Oh, I don't know. Life's exciting rather. You never know what is coming next. My grandmother, for instance, swooping out of the blue and taking me home like a sack

of flour. Of course if I hadn't been ill, I might have resisted....I've never been able to make up my mind. It
was Fate, I suppose, and Fate that she threw me out again."

"But there must have been some dirty work at the cross-
roads. She didn't just point a finger and say 'Go!' surely?"

"She pointed all right, but was tired of me, and the dirty
work was an excuse. Some one told her I had been seen
lunching with a disreputable-looking man and clinging to
his arm."

"Oh, rot!"

"Not a bit of it. He was a man who had sailed with
father on one of his expeditions and he was down and
out—starving. He may have been a waster or just out of
luck, but I couldn't let him starve so I took him into the
nearest restaurant and gave him lunch. Then because he
was obviously ill I helped him into a taxi and took him to
father's doctor. He's in hospital now."

"But didn't you tell her?"

"She would not listen...she didn't want to hear."
Biddy's cheeks grew red as she spoke. "She said I was a
disgrace and ungrateful to her and various other things.
And then she talked about my upbringing sarcastically,
and said she had tried to do her duty by me for my
mother's sake."

The girl flung a stone down the track, watching its
flight with stormy eyes.

"That finished it. I told her nobody was going to work
off their back duty on me."

There had been triumph in that retort up to now, but
put into words again it rang rather doubtfully, and Sholto's
laughter was a relief.

"You see, she had never tried to do her duty by my mother," explained Biddy, "or think of me, until there was all that fuss about me in the papers after father's death. I suppose she merely wanted to put a stop to it but I was simple enough to think that she had done it out of kindness."

"The old hell-cat!"

"No."

Biddy knew suddenly that, quarrel or no quarrel, the glamour still remained.

"We can't sit here calling her names," she said thoughtfully. "It is so feeble and, besides, they don't fit."

"My mild disposition deceives you," said Sholto. "I can do better than that. Hell-cat was only a beginning. When I get to the climax you will be surprised."

"You like her," said Biddy smiling, "so don't deny it."

"The tense should be in the past, Miss Kerlin. Be tender with the English language. If a man may not change his mind, what becomes of the liberty of the subject, tell me that if you know what it is, which is more than I do."

"In other words," said Biddy, "the answer is in the affirmative."

"Not at all. I did like her, but owing to the scandalous behavior of the accused....Would you really like to hear my address to the jury, because I warn you it will blister if not blast the leaves at your feet!"

Sholto, stretched at full length, looked up at her hopefully, but she shook her head.

"Never you mind my quarrels. Now for the next round with Fate," she said.

"But how are you going to manage?"

"I shall be all right. I'm not penniless, my dear. I have about a hundred a year."

"Look here, Biddy, it isn't enough. I have three hundred—"

"And three and one make four and two into four make two ... you see how good I am at arithmetic. ..."

"But you can't possibly live on a hundred a year," expostulated Sholto, avoiding her eye lest he had given himself away in spite of all his good resolutions.

"Bless you, I wouldn't try. I mean to go in for antiques— a thing I have always meant to do some day. I have a kind of flair for it," said Biddy grandly.

The boast was true enough. During holidays in her fifteenth year she had stayed with her father in rooms over the shop of an old dealer, and spent hours there almost daily, learning much from him because he recognized that sense in her. In her grandmother's house she had learned more and read every book on the subject she could lay hands on. She knew that "going in for antiques" was not quite the simple matter she had seemed to suggest, but had no intention of admitting as much to Sholto at present.

It had been gradually borne in upon her that there was a change in him, that the old happy ease of their friendship was missing and she wanted it back. The Fenwicks had been good to her and she was fond of them. She could not allow them to be embroiled in her quarrel as they certainly would be if she did not handle Sholto with care.

"Oh, hang the family," thought Biddy, filled with a sudden forlorn nostalgia for the old simple days in her father's life-time in which these human complications had had no place.

She shivered slightly and Sholto, with his eye upon her, exclaimed:

"You are cold. We must get out of the wood."

The phrase was so apt that it cheered her, in spite of Sholto's anxious tone, and she agreed to the necessity with a twinkle in her eye.

"Down this track.... I'll race you."

Speeding through the bracken between the old trees, they came out upon an open road looking across country to the gold rim of the downs. The wind and the clouds had come back and purple shadows ran over the fields; the air was sweet with the scent of hay and grass and the damp mold under running water.

"You should have brought Freddy, Sholto. She would have loved this."

"Yes, I know, but I couldn't be sure you would let me in, or wanted any of us to know where you were."

"Have I committed a murder then? Am I a fugitive from justice? I should have written to Edith as soon as I was settled, as a matter of course, and you may advertise my address through the B.B.C. if it will ease your mind. But don't call at Portman Square and hand it in, will you?"

"Do you think I'd go near the dam' place?" exclaimed Sholto.

Biddy turned and faced him.

"If you don't, Sholto Fenwick, you are no friend of mine. You must for Freddy's sake...you always have gone...long before I was heard of, and besides, my grandmother likes you."

"Not she."

"Yes; you talk to her as one man to another and don't mind what you say. She's fond of bandying words." Biddy's face broke into a reminiscent smile as she recalled a voice which even in anger and impatience had never lost its quality, and in moments of delight had charmed her beyond measure. Sholto had been an entertainment to her grandmother, and so few members of the family were that.

"She would miss you," she said urgently, "and I won't have it."

"You speak now as though you and she were bosom friends," expostulated Sholto.

"Call me smug if you like, as long as you do as I ask. It is no good," said Biddy, "I am not used to families and am better out of it. I tried hard enough to get away but she wouldn't let me go, and certainly I am not going to be the cause of a family row. If you don't promise to treat her as usual I'll move from Wincey Street and leave no address."

"I'll promise," said Sholto.

"She's not going back," he sang to himself, "she's not going back. She's only thinking of Frederika, bless her heart."

CHAPTER TWO

THE BIRTHDAY STAKES

OF OLD Mrs. Devonshire's family, her daughter Brigid only had chosen poverty. The others had had it thrust upon them by all those forces which of late years have been so busy robbing Peter to pay Paul. Since no one likes to be robbed their resentment was perhaps natural, though to Brigid's daughter, young Biddy Kerlin, when she came upon the scene, the condition of the entire family seemed one of incredible affluence.

Biddy, however, with no experience of country estates, mansions in town and a large staff of servants behind her, was not a fair judge. She and her father had always just managed to have enough money for the needs of the moment, and their chief anxiety about it had been a purely extraneous one—whether sufficient funds would be forthcoming for some impending expedition.

Naturally the unlooked-for year in her grandmother's house had seemed to the girl a rosy dream, a kind of fairytale interlude. She had enjoyed it enormously, but now that it was over she was ready and eager to begin the serious business of living.

She had said to Sholto that the word "family" was merely a term and she had been quite sincere. The Fenwicks were her friends. Under the old eyes watching her, she had chosen them and discarded the rest as people of no great interest to whom she found herself related by ties of blood—a phantasy these ties to Biddy at twenty-one.

To them, however, though she did not know it, she had a very definite significance. Old Mrs. Devonshire all these years, taxes and bad times notwithstanding, had continued to live in Portman Square, quietly, yet in much of her accustomed state. Her fortune was her own, the house part of her marriage settlement. None of the family knew the extent of her means, and open speculation on the subject was not indulged in, by the elders at least—the decencies must be observed—but thought and hope are free. The presence of a granddaughter, hitherto neglected, in Portman Square had been disquieting; her departure, its reason and its consequences were translated according to the different temperaments of each household, but discussed by each and all.

2

The Fenwicks lived at Buckingham Gate in one of those inconspicuous but substantially-built blocks of flats with spacious room which preceded the barrack-like modern structures with their groups of cells. Here Edith Fenwick, once Mrs. Hugh Devonshire, mistress of Highways and ten indoor servants, kept a cook and a house-parlormaid, and ran her home with equal grace and probably less fatigue.

A woman of breeding and good sense, she had remained part of the family, merely as Frederika's mother, aware of their scorn at her second marriage but indifferent to it.

Freddy Devonshire had been nine years old at the time;

now she was a tall, hardy child of nineteen and a coming tennis player, a fact which her aunts were disposed quite unjustly to ascribe to the Fenwick connection. They thought it distinctly queer. The girl was like her father, an outdoor person by inclination and heredity. She had no imagination, no nerves, no girlish graces, a quick eye, a blunt honesty of speech and mind.

"I suppose you don't know any one who wants some genuine antiques?" Sholto asked his stepmother at breakfast a morning or two after his excursion with Biddy.

"I do," said Edith, "I need a tallboy for the hall, but short of burglary, I don't know how I am going to get it."

"Oh, good, Edith, I'll tell Biddy to look for one for you, shall I?"

John Fenwick glanced over his newspaper.

"I have always known this popular word 'Modern' was only another name for 'Mediæval,'" he said. "You perceive, Edith, knight-errantry in the home!"

Frederika, a belligerent ally, deserted her grapefruit in defense of Sholto.

"Well, somebody has got to do something, John," she remarked in her slightly husky voice. She and her stepbrother only used parental titles when their elders were obstreperous, not often, as they handsomely informed them from time to time.

"I don't want to damp your ardor, Frederika," said her stepfather, "but England is full of people who sit down and make such profound statements as that, and all too lacking in those who get up like Biddy and do it."

"But you know I am afraid it is going to be harder than Biddy thinks," interrupted Sholto.

"It always is," retorted his father dryly.

"She is very independent," Edith pointed out, "and would probably scorn orders from the family in her present state of mind. Give her time, Sholto."

"And devote your knight-errantry to Fenwick's Jam," pleaded his father, "just to keep your hand in meanwhile. I wouldn't press it for any other reason. As a parent I know my place."

"I'll get an order from Portman Square if you'll undertake to put a pint of poison in it," returned Sholto.

"And I'll pay for the poison," added Freddy darkly.

Mrs. Fenwick called them to order. She was an elegant woman with a beautiful voice and a cold manner, which made many people dislike her intensely. Freddy, her direct antithesis, admired her mother helplessly without understanding her in the least. Sholto, more intuitive, knew that Edith's reserve was inherent rather than acquired, and while he loved to upset it in moments of deviltry, he trusted her judgment and generally took her advice.

"Don't forget Thursday is your grandmother's birthday, Freddy.... Sholto, do you hear? You should get your presents today."

"I'm not going near the old villain," swore Freddy, scowling.

"Then," said her mother, "you will only get Biddy into further disgrace."

"I don't see it. If I give her a present when I hate the sight of her I'm a hypocrite. And these birthdays, as if she were the Queen of Sheba, are so absurd. You don't really want me to go, Edith. It's just a fetish."

"Obligation is the word you mean," put in her stepfather. "Obsolete, I know, but look it up in a pre-war dictionary."

"You have both been going there constantly all the year and if you stay away now and neglect her birthday she will blame Biddy for mischief-making, which would be most unjust."

"Something in that," agreed Sholto, much to his family's surprise. "You are playing in a match on Thursday, Fred— a good excuse to wait till after dinner when I can lead you by the hand. We'll beard the dragon together, our swords between our teeth."

"Oh, all right," said Freddy. Sholto could do the talking, he was good at it, he could talk all night, but *she* never did know what to say at Granny's and felt a fool. "If she asks me where Biddy is," planned Freddy, "I'll say, 'Starving probably,'—that'll show her and I hope she'll like it.... Meet me at Woolworth's, Sholto, to choose her old birthday present," she requested.

Mrs. Fenwick followed her husband into the hall and they exchanged a glance as a burst of laughter followed them from the dining-room.

"I hope they will behave to her, they must," said Edith, "though it is a fetish in a sense. I know how I dreaded those birthdays when Freddy was small and I had to take her, but then Mrs. Devonshire always has disliked me."

"Any woman would," said John smiling.

"No, it was because I married her son. If I hadn't done that we might have been quite good friends. Biddy is rather like her."

"Yes, but a girl can afford to forgive a beautiful woman where an old woman can't, my dear. You are right about

Biddy, I believe. She has a touch of her grandmother's manner, now I come to think of it, but she does not alarm me to the same extent. She has been less softly bred."

"Alarm you indeed? What a myth." Edith smiled at him. "You think Mrs. Devonshire is arrogant, but you are wrong. She is old and disappointed, but she would never admit it. She lost her sons and she did care for them. I know."

"She has lost more than that—her world," said John Fenwick. "Tell those young devils if they don't behave to her they will have to reckon with me." He put his arm round his wife and kissed her rather as if she were something very delicate and liable to break at a touch.

"Now then, Sholto, no loitering in there! You will be late," he called to his son.

"Late?" echoed Sholto, appearing from the dining-room with a look of bland surprise. "What ingratitude for my perfect tact."

3

Jane Devonshire strolled into the crowded restaurant, steaming with hot food and cigarette smoke, and looked about her in disgust. A nice place Herbert had chosen, so like a relative, to consider his own convenience rather than her comfort, she thought. Suppose it *was* near his chambers, there was no need for Herbert to keep up the fiction of work with her.

She was ten minutes late, but even so before him, which did not improve her state of mind. Jane disliked being first at a rendezvous. She had an impression that punctuality was a sign of unimportance, and even at a theatre would invariably arrive late for fear of being mistaken for one of the multitude, to whom such things were a treat.

She enquired languidly whether Mr. Herbert Dawnay had engaged a table, found that he had at least conde-scended to remember that, and sat down ready to stare haughtily at any man who looked at her, yet infuriated when they did nothing of the kind. Geranium lips were common enough in that quarter of London and leisure scarce. A real tiger might have moved the gathering, per-haps, but no mere amateur like Jane.

"Well, this is a nice hour to turn up, Herbert, and what a place! Really, I hardly liked to come in," she said storm-ily when at last he arrived.

"My dear old thing, I was too simply rushed, so don't be harsh with me. You'll find the food quite tolerable. Well, how's life?" said Herbert.

"Dam' life!"

"Too many late nights. I know. We of the younger set live too hard, but somebody's got to do it, Janey. You thank your luck you're a girl and can take a rest now and then. I've not been in bed much before five this month. Give you my word."

"Girl indeed!" A sudden misery flamed in Jane Devon-shire's eyes. "You have your profession at least and a father behind you. What have I?"

"What! Tired of being a film star?"

"Star? They kill you...work you to death and string you on with promises, and then turn you down for some vulgar little upstart with baby curls. Herbert, I've got to have some money. Lend me twenty pounds for a month."

"Twenty what? Wish I had so much."

"Well, if you are so busy, you must be making something and you know I'll pay it back."

"Jane, I'm on a new stunt. You can't make money at the Bar, but I've met a chap and we are getting out a play that will bring us a fortune. Noel Coward stuff but stronger—much stronger. It will knock London and New York silly. Ask me then and I'll lend you forty pounds. Just now I couldn't lay hands on a spare fiver," declared Herbert. "Sorry and all that. Why not touch Granny ... after all, now the bright Brigid has been shown the door ... I always thought she was a shade too bright. What's the true story, d'you know? Mother had some gory tale about a wicked night-club or some such thing.... Jolly good for the rest of us anyway."

"Well, if you realize that, you owe it to us. Mother, for once in her life, had her eyes open. Biddy was going about with some shady-looking man and Mother thought it her duty to let Granny know.... Dirty trick all the same," added Jane unexpectedly.

"What? You have got 'em badly ... quite too sportsmanlike for words, my dear old thing."

"Oh, I know, beggars can't be choosers, and that's what we are, beggars at Granny's gate. But she will live to be ninety, you'll see. Why shouldn't she with that great house and everything she wants?"

"Thursday's the ancestral birthday, Jane. Be tactful with your present and then drop a hint at the right moment. She can hardly do less than disburse."

Herbert was not quite as convincing as he would have liked, but he hoped to divert Jane's demands to a more suitable channel. Granny ought to provide for the poor girl. Fair was fair, and Jane was getting on. Her cousin in the last few moments had been startled to notice it. And on the tiresome side too....

Jane, turning from giving her order to the waitress, grew more tiresome still.

"How can I buy birthday presents when I haven't a bean? Herbert, you'll simply have to lend me a pound. I can't afford to offend Granny.... I'd clean forgotten Thursday."

"But surely your Mother can spare you something for that? Good Lord, Granny's birthday is a kind of convention. The world would come to an end if any of us dropped out...."

Jane frowned and stuck a cigarette in her jade holder impatiently.

"You know very well Mother doesn't care whether I offend Granny or not. She cares nothing about me. She only thinks of James and Highways," she retorted bitterly.

"Oh, all right." Herbert hunted ostentatiously in his various pockets and grudgingly produced the loan. "But it's going to put me in a hole, I can promise you, Jane, so stump up as soon as you can."

"Of course." Jane, feeling better, let her mind stray to less contentious topics. Herbert was generally kinder than this, and she strove for a return to their old footing of allies in a hostile world.

"I didn't know there were night-clubs in the Biddy-fracas. How too naughty-naughty. Wonder which night-clubs.... Let's dance somewhere tonight, Herbert. I feel I want a little cheer."

"Can't possibly. Sorry, but I'm full up for nights ahead."
Herbert took out an esoteric notebook and turned the
leaves briskly. "No, not a hope . . . I'll write you. . . . Well,
here's luck to the Birthday Stakes. . . . That's a good one,
by Jove! Wonder if I could work it into my play?"

"That's what it is . . . the play," thought Jane with relief. "Silly idea, but he'll get over it. There's nothing else,
it's only this play."

She had had a sudden dreadful fear that Herbert was
being snatched away from her, and she could not afford
to lose him. For the rest of the meal she listened to his
rhapsodies about the play and applauded at the right
intervals. Applause being all that Herbert required of her
at any time, they parted on excellent terms.

4

Thinking it over later in the afternoon, one of the
tenantless, unprofitable afternoons which she found so
difficult to bear, Jane Devonshire decided that there was
something to be said for Herbert's view that her mother
should provide the present. After all, her favorite James's
interests were involved. It was at least worth trying.

Jane rarely went to her mother's crowded little house
in Knightsbridge if she could help it. Mrs. James Devonshire considered a good address imperative for the owner
of Highways and paid a high rent for ugliness and inconvenience in consequence. In her more bitter moments Jane
suspected that the meagerness of the house had been an
attraction to her mother; it gave her such excellent opportunities for comparing the hardness of her lot with the

comfort of the Dawnays who owned a roomy house at
Lancaster Gate, and even the despised Fenwicks'.

Mrs. James Devonshire was a poor manager and extravagant in a hundred useless ways. Jane found the
crowded little drawing-room fitted with new lamps, all
disguised as something else, as though her mother had
suddenly discovered a light that was boldly a light to be
highly immodest. One grew out of a China vase and was
chastely covered with an umbrella; another sprang from
the wall in the shape of a monstrous fan without visible
means of support; a third appeared to be a long alabaster
paper-weight of cubist design which had inadvertently
sprouted a cord tail.

"I needed more light, I could bear it no longer," said
Jane's mother defensively, seeing her eyes upon these inno-
vations. "I can deny myself, but I cannot ruin my sight.
Well, Jane, this is an honor. You do not often favor me
with your society."

"I've been working," said Jane in the interests of peace.
She knew that her mother had both disliked her living at
home, and going elsewhere. "I ran in to see what is being
done about Granny's birthday."

"Ah yes, her seventy-fifth birthday, wonderful! We
must make it a great day for poor darling Granny."

"I don't see anything particularly poor about her,"
snapped Jane, irritated by this habit of talking to her as
though she were a stranger to be impressed. "However,
what are we going to give her? That's the question."

"Oh, James and I have her present already," said her
mother with satisfaction. "The dear boy has had his photograph taken by that firm in Bond Street, ruinously ex-

pensive, but it is only right that his Granny should be considered. She ought to have a portrait of the head of the family, the only Devonshire left.... I have had a really brilliant idea, Jane; I have made her a nice warm bed wrap in gray wool with touches of black, so suitable for an old lady. You'll be astonished. Miss Jenkins, who comes in sewing by the day, said she had never seen anything like it. She was greatly impressed and could hardly believe it was my own work. People never," said Mrs. James Devonshire complacently, "think I can do anything. I don't know how it is."

Jane knew. Her mother's words seemed to jangle against her mind, to be as empty as the bright day without. She said hastily:

"What have you got for me to give Granny?" and when her mother began to expostulate and argue she let the sound flow over her head unheeded. There was no need to listen. You just had to hold yourself in and bear it, she thought.

"You must have something, Mother," she said mechanically, meanwhile racking her brains for some news or gossip that would make the other responsive. Perhaps Herbert had said something at lunch...yes, of course he had....

"Let us go up and look in your room, you have so many things.... By the way, I heard a further installment of the Biddy scandal.... Night-clubs."

Jane was already out the door on the way to the staircase. Her mother followed avidly, calling staccato questions, barely waiting to draw breath.

"Night-clubs?...What did you hear?...Who told

you?...What did your Granny say?...Who took her to night-clubs?..."

Jane knew that for the moment she was safe to open drawers and cupboards, letting catechism and comment flow on unheeded. The bedroom was an amazing place. The money her mother spent on useless things because they were cheap or took her fancy would have kept the girl in clothes, but it was too late to alter that, it had become a passion. Three clocks, two grotesque hat-stands, for which there was no room, an evil-eyed glass dog, a doll intended to conceal a telephone, but fallen over limply because there was no telephone in the house, and three photographs of James in babyhood, occupied the mantel-piece. Every kind of decorative handicraft ever invented for making money in the home was represented in the innumerable candlesticks, trays, little boxes and powder-bowls which over-ran the dressing-table, window-ledge and even the floor.

How could any one choose a present for an old woman who had everything in the world? Jane wondered, disconsolately surveying six pairs of elaborate bedroom slippers, size three (always so cheap at the sales) and therefore never destined to be worn in this household.

"...sly, as I said to James at the time, and now my words are proved. I could have told you, Jane, I never liked Brigid Devonshire, her mother; and the same dreadful man, I suppose? Was she turned out of the night-club ...was her name in the newspapers...how did you hear?"

"No, I don't think so...of course not," said Jane, suddenly becoming conscious of her mother's words. "Mother,

Granny has a telephone and this thing can't possibly be
of any use to you. They are quite expensive too, I know."
She took down the doll, shook out its Victorian skirts and
found that the head was loose. "It's broken but I can stick
that...."

"Yes, do ... a good idea, but tell me, Jane, who *was* the
man? What did your grandmother say?"

"I don't know anything about it really, mother. It may
all be just talk, and you'd better not mention it either.
Biddy's gone, which is all that concerns us. And now I
must rush.... I'm dreadfully late already."

The high voice followed her all the way downstairs.

"Very wise of your grandmother to turn the girl out ...
it has been a great relief to me. I have to consider poor
James, and with a designing, naughty girl like that you
don't know where you are."

Jane hurried down the street, carrying the telephone
doll. The sun had fallen behind the tall roofs ahead of her,
rimming them with gold; a false twilight touched the
housefronts kindly and seemed to have brushed the day's
dust from shrub and tree; a pigeon walked grandly in
the middle of the road.

Jane saw nothing but the barren emptiness of the world.
She had succeeded in her errand, the borrowed pound was
safe and that was good. But beneath her mechanical re-
joicing she was aware of a nagging sense of disquiet.
Biddy and the night-clubs ... her mother, of course, had
embroidered the story, but she had provided the thread,
clutching at Herbert's vague rumor and throwing it to
her mother as a bribe.

Well, she had warned her that it was probably just talk,

and what was a night-club to cause such excitement? Everybody went to them so why not Biddy? There was nothing to worry about. Whatever tale her mother chose to make of it, it couldn't do Biddy any harm. A silly story...people would merely laugh, and besides the girl had already left Portman Square, the mischief had been done. Jane had had no responsibility in that and mentally shook herself into a more sensible mood.

What did anything matter? You had to look out for yourself in this world, or get nowhere...hard as nails, that's what you had to be.

She remembered Herbert's jibe, "quite too sportsman-like," and felt that it had been just. It was always the same when she was alone, it made her low in the mind. Loneliness terrified her, she needed crowds, noise, gayety.

Jane quickened her steps, saw red buses rushing past the end of the street and sleek, black cars full of lucky people going somewhere in a hurry, while she was isolated and alone, missing everything. She ought to marry, but none of the men had any money nowadays...not permanent money...perhaps it would be Herbert in the end. They understood each other...they would get on.... Herbert had been odd this morning, but it hadn't been anything, it couldn't be....

Jane saw a telephone-box and in a panic entered it and caught up the book. She must do something, see somebody, ask some one out to dine. There was Herbert's treasury note and she owed hospitality all round. People dropped you out if you hadn't money to spend. Beastly, the world was....

5

"I wonder if Biddy-the-Bad will give Granny a present," said May Dawnay, with a bubble of laughter at her own wit.

Such as it was the wit, strictly speaking, belonged to her sister Gwynneth, who laughed too, quite accustomed to having her occasional inspirations purloined by the lively May, and bearing no malice.

May was a soft, fair, pink and white little creature, a born flirt, utterly brainless but so high-spirited and good to look upon that she was never without an admiring court. Gwynneth followed in her younger sister's train, providing a leaven of common-sense, retrieving bags and wraps, pacifying outraged partners evaded by the scatter-brain, keeping her eye on the clock, and enjoying a reflected glory.

The two girls had been into Kensington High Street with their mother to buy a bedrest for old Mrs. Devonshire's birthday, and were now admiring this object, which had just been delivered.

"I wonder what Aunt James was confiding to Mummy?" said May. "From her nodding and becking in Barker's it was something juicy, not fit for our young ears. Come on, I'm going to worm it out of the parent."

Mrs. Dawnay was struggling with her household accounts, an abstracted eye on a worn spot in the drawing-room carpet which always worried her. It was so difficult to hide, and the hope of buying a new carpet seemed to grow more remote every day.

"Mother, do you think Biddy will produce a present

for Granny ... ? What was it that Aunt James was saying?
I know it was about Biddy. You could see it in her
eye."

"Nothing. I can't tell you children. Biddy ought to be
ashamed of herself."

"Really?" May curled herself up on a chair arm, bur-
bling. "Come on, Mummy, tell us the worst."

Mrs. Dawnay looked at them weakly and with pride.
There could never be a whisper against her girls, so pretty
and frank and sweet, she thought. She did not wish to be
unkind about poor Brigid's daughter, but then Brigid herself had always gone her own way, so what could you
expect? Surely Mother would see the contrast now; she
must see it. It was all very well for poor James's wife to
talk about her boy's claims, but, after all, Gwynneth and
May were the daughters of their grandmother's only surviving child.

"Daughters-in-law's children are different," she said to
herself, getting a little mixed in her genealogy but happily convincing herself.

"You must be very sweet to your Granny, darlings,"
said Mrs. Dawnay. "It is so sad that she has been so
disappointed in Biddy. You must just love her the more
to make up. We don't want her to think all her grand-
daughters the same."

"Be a sport, Mummy. What did you hear?"

"Well, as Biddy is your cousin, perhaps I had better
tell you," agreed their mother who, like most weak people, always produced a reason of some kind when she
changed her mind. "Your Aunt James tells me there has
been quite a scandal. Biddy was turned out of a night-

club...it is all very sordid, children, and I am merely telling you so that you may be on your guard and know nothing if you hear the matter mentioned....She was turned out with a man."

"Why, was she drunk?" enquired May reasonably.

"Really, *darling!* What a dreadful idea! And what an unpleasant word."

"But I can't think of any other reason why they would turn her out."

"No, dear, fortunately you are too innocent," said Mrs. Dawnay, at which her daughters naturally exchanged a pitying smile behind her back.

"And if not, why sordid?" enquired May.

"Hush, children, that is quite enough!" Mrs. Dawnay, unable to answer this pertinent question from sheer lack of experience, reverted to nursery tactics, but the imagination of her daughters was equal to the occasion.

"I wonder if the man was married?" remarked May as soon as they were alone.

"He must have been, I suppose," returned Gwynneth slowly, "or why all this fuss?"

Next time they saw their brother Herbert they told him in strict confidence that from things their mother had not said they gathered Biddy-the-Bad had been caught playing about with a married man. Herbert, not recognizing the legend which his hint to Jane had started, merely said, "Poor fellow!" At dinner that night, however, the story recurred to him and he enquired of his parents:

"So I hear the bright Biddy has been breaking up somebody's happy home. Who is the man in the case?"

"That is not the kind of subject to discuss before your sisters," he was informed by his father shortly, and Herbert subsided with a faintly superior smile.

He went out immediately the meal was over, so it was impossible to question him, but Mr. and Mrs. Dawnay agreed in private that the whole affair was evidently worse than they had supposed and poor dear Mother in Portman Square was well rid of the girl.

An old lady getting on in years, said Richard reasonably, was not perhaps the best judge of young people. It was hardly to be expected.

"No, dear," said his wife, "that is what I have felt from the first. Poor Mother is very easily taken in, but then I am afraid she was always the same, a little obstinate. Now perhaps she will see her mistake at last...our girls are so bright and open, they must comfort her for her disappointment in Biddy. I have told them so."

"Er...quite," returned Richard, not without discomfort. He glanced at his wife, hesitated and finally went off to his study, saying nothing more.

Mrs. Dawnay sighed a little, her eyes instinctively seeking the worn place in the rug. Life was so difficult nowadays; poor Mother could have no idea how very difficult it was, with Richard's retirement coming nearer every year and two girls to think of. "Why, at Gwynneth's age I was already married," thought Mrs. Dawnay; "but how can I afford to give my darlings opportunities? The world has so terribly changed since the War. Mother, of course, has no idea of that and it is so difficult to talk to her about important things. She catches you up. My daughters, I am glad to say, will never feel it impossible to talk to me."

She felt that she had come upon an illuminating truth. She had been a good mother, a good wife, a good and dutiful daughter too, not walking out of the house like her sister Brigid to marry against her mother's wish, but choosing a suitable mate and a wedding with six of the season's prettiest bridesmaids at St. George's, Hanover Square, as society expected of a Devonshire...a great occasion and *everybody* there.

Mrs. Dawnay was not vainglorious about it, but the consciousness of having done her duty lit a warm glow within her and restored her spirits. She could not doubt that these modest but none the less solid virtues would be rewarded in the end. Dear Mother was an old lady and a little unreasonable at times, which was to be expected, but her dismissal of that naughty Biddy proved that she was not blind.

Perhaps the carpet could be turned round again and a couch moved to cover the wear. There was no need to worry. Things would straighten out in time.

Mrs. Dawnay was not consciously hoping the carpet would survive her mother. Such a thing would have shocked her to the soul. Putting her trust in Providence, she turned her back on the offending worn patch, and settled herself to her novel like a sensible woman.

6

Biddy, curled up on the trunk under the open window, with the plane-tree outside, very green in the fading light, for company, was reading a letter from Frederika, begging her cousin to meet her for lunch next day and help her to choose "a beastly birthday present."

It had occurred to Freddy that thus cunningly she could kill several birds with one stone, see that Biddy, that ninth wonder of the world (Sholto long ago having monopolized the eighth place), had a proper luncheon, obtain ideas, always difficult to find for Granny's present, and at the same time assure Biddy of her undying hatred of the recipient-to-be. Frederika, a fierce partisan, was even ready at the merest shadow of a frown on Biddy's brow, to defy the family, drop the present and ignore her grandmother for the rest of her life.

Biddy, ignorant of these deep-laid plans, wondered whose birthday could be in question and after a moment noticed the date of the letter and understood. The busy days had rushed by and she had forgotten. On Thursday her grandmother would be seventy-five.

The girl's mind took in the fact of those accumulated years mechanically and did not dwell upon them. Of all the members of Mrs. Devonshire's family this one alone did not think of her as an old woman whose race was nearly run. Their meeting perhaps had been too sudden, their association after all too brief and too close.

Fresh before her eyes as though it were yesterday, Biddy would always have her first sight of the other woman, a dazzling, magnificent figure who might have walked out of a play, standing in her bedroom at the nursing-home, and saying in the courteous, cool voice of authority: "My car is waiting, doctor. Send a nurse with her if you consider it advisable, but I am taking my granddaughter home."

Biddy, letting the note slip to the ground, folded her
arms on the window-ledge and gazed at the plane-tree, her
eyes alight in her mobile face, as she recalled the last birthday at Portman Square a year ago.

She had not known of its approach until the day before
when Simpkins had dropped her a tactful hint. "There
will be visitors all day tomorrow, miss." The idea had
surprised and amused her, it had an Arabian Nights flavor,
she thought, princes and potentates arriving with tribute.

While Mrs. Devonshire rested after luncheon she had
sped out, wondering how she could buy a gift that her
grandmother would like and be safely back when she came
downstairs again; above all what she could take to such
a treasure house that would not be utterly out of place!

"Sweets," she had thought sadly, were the only thing,
and then had remembered the old glass box. She had seen
it in a pawnbroker's window on one of her early morning
walks, an octagonal box, deep rose in color, the tone of
her grandmother's bedroom, she recalled. Her knowledge
of glass was small, but as soon as she had found the shop
again and held it in her hands, she had known it was
beautiful and suspected it was rare. The pawnbroker, with
his eye on her clothes, had asked her a pound for it, which
she had paid at once. Wasn't she rich for the moment with
dividends in her purse and so little need to spend anything
at all?

The best confectioner she could find in the district had
filled it with his most expensive sweets and tried, unsuc-
cessfully, to persuade her to have it tied with a rose ribbon.
The lovely box had been given to her grandmother at

breakfast next morning guiltless of adornment, while
Biddy, unused to giving presents to magnificent people,
had waited, scarlet and embarrassed, lest it should be all
wrong.

Mrs. Devonshire had lifted the lid with interest.

"Ah, sweets? How delicious! That is very kind of you,
Biddy."

She had made no other comment and all day the old
box had glowed, small and unnoticed among the rapidly
accumulating presents from the family, nearly all of which
excited extravagant praise from one or other of the visitors who came and went. The box had been carried away
that night and Biddy had seen it no more.

Since then she had learned something of old glass, and
she knew it had been a find, but her grandmother, living
among treasures all her life, did not care for them perhaps.
She had certainly enjoyed the sweets, however, for often
since then Biddy had been commissioned to buy her the
same kind again.

"That's an idea," said the girl suddenly to the plane-tree.
"I'll persuade Freddy to buy her some really special sweets,
she'll like them."

She smiled at the thought of Thursday's ceremonial, the
gifts that would be brought and her grandmother's courteous and impassive face; the afternoon tea for which the
cook would surpass herself; the dinner-table set with the
crystal and Crown Derby of a ceremonial occasion; and
then she caught her breath, wondering whether this year
her grandmother would dine alone. There was something
so desolate in the thought that she jumped to her feet,

turned on the light and dismissed such fancies with derision.

"What did she do before you came on the scene?" she said to herself. "The conceit of you!"

CHAPTER THREE

IN PORTMAN SQUARE

" AND I wish you many happy returns of the day, I'm sure, 'm," said Simpkins.

Mrs. Devonshire eyed the thin, neat figure before her with grim amusement.

"My good woman, your intentions are excellent, but your sentiments absurd," she said; "unless of course you were referring to another sphere.... Now don't stand there looking sentimental. Just give me my dressing-gown, will you?"

Simpkins brought the robe of old rose satin and enveloped her mistress in it carefully. The deftness of long use was in her movement, for it was characteristic of Mrs. Devonshire, who had kept so many graces fast vanishing from the world, that Simpkins had been with her for forty-five years. She had, it might almost be said, grown into the fabric of the house, quiet, inconspicuous, attaining a quality that set her apart from the household in general. Not only below stairs, but among certain members of the family, how much old Simpkins knew was a matter of frequent discussion. She kept her own counsel, close, or possibly stupid, but which they found it difficult to decide.

Simpkins brought the rose slippers and put them ready beside the bed, kneeling down to see that they were well in place, then sitting back neatly on her heels like some devotee before a shrine. The pose was instinctive, however. Just so had she knelt in merrier times, to adjust the folds of a gown or fling out a train. Whatever else Simpkins might know, she knew that her mistress disliked fuss, disliked unnecessary aid, could not endure more than the merest touch of a ministering hand, even hers, even now, as though the independence of her spirit had spread to every fiber of her body.

Simpkins' attentive eyes were fixed on the slippers at Mrs. Devonshire's feet, ready to move them if necessary, but her mind was not engaged with this familiar ritual, and perhaps the prescience that comes of long intimacy conveyed as much to the tall figure above, for she said briskly:

"You have no need to worry, you know. You are provided for."

"You are very good, 'm, but I don't like change," muttered Simpkins stubbornly.

Mrs. Devonshire laughed.

"Oh, there I can be no help to you, I am afraid. You will need to apply to a Higher Authority.... As for goodness, don't talk such nonsense to me. You have worked for me and I have paid you. Anything further is between friends."

She slipped her feet into the slippers and stood upright, a tall woman with a fine carriage still and keen eyes under straight brows. Aware of Simpkins, rising like a shadow in her wake, she turned to an old glass box which stood on the table beside her bed.

"I shall be self-indulgent this morning," she remarked, taking a sweet. "You had better follow my example, Simpkins. We shall need sweetening before the day is out, you and I.... A pretty thing this... eh?"

She held up the flat, octagonal lid of the old box and the morning sunlight turned it to a glowing rose, yet not more glowing perhaps than the embarrassment it was intended to disperse.

"I have always thought it a very nice color for the room," admitted Simpkins, with the careful reserve of one who knew the giver of the rose box to be under a cloud.

"Valuable too," continued her mistress. "I suspected as much, and let Herkomer's man see it when he was here the other day. Curious how these things happen.... H'm! Well, I don't think we shall see much that will interest Herkomer on this occasion.... The bath... the bath, woman. Don't stand dreaming there...."

The accusation was unjust and meant nothing. Simpkins, the towel warm from the radiator on her arm, opened the bathroom door. Mrs. Devonshire, before closing it upon her, looked back at her for a moment.

"This is a birthday, not a funeral. Be bright," she requested.

"You take no care," muttered Simpkins indignantly.

"Never fear. I'll splash," retorted Mrs. Devonshire, and closed the bathroom door.

Simpkins stood outside it, faded and shaken. Her mistress had seen through her as usual, for all her care, seen the terror she felt every time the other was out of her sight. She was ill, dying, but still unchanged, intolerant of fuss, herself, as she would be to the end.

"Between friends."

Simpkins would have wept if she had not lost the habit, tears being impermissible in Mrs. Devonshire's service. Even that ... had she sensed even that?

Simpkins: On such and such a date at 49, Portman Square, Patty Simpkins, for so many years the faithful maid and friend of Mrs. Frederick Devonshire ...

Simpkins for some reason had always expected to die before her mistress and how often when reading *The Times* in her spare hours, had some such notice stirred her with a trembling hope? And the years of her service had gone on, forty—forty-three—four—five. It might be fifty yet ... a good number, half a century. It had not troubled Simpkins or perhaps occurred to her that she would not be there to read that glorious obituary. Now, luckier than most people, she had been given, living, what she had only asked for dead. Her emotions recorded it but not yet her mind as, silent and efficient as usual, she opened wide the window, and set ready her mistress's clothes, one ear turned from time to time to the faint but reassuring sounds behind the bathroom door.

The first touch of autumn was in the air, she felt it sharp on her face, the trees in the square were faintly veiled as on misty mornings at Highways long ago when young Mrs. Frederick Devonshire went out to ride. Clearly, as though it lay before her eyes, Simpkins could see the voluminous riding habit, such a terror at first to her unskillful hands under the mistress's eyes. Quick in everything she did, Mrs. Devonshire had had no patience all her life with the clumsy and the slow. But Simpkins, obstinately determined to better herself, in the phrase of the time, had mastered the riding habit, and presently been promoted to standing in the bright cold air to see her mistress mounted and set the long skirt decorously in place.

"A fine seat on a horse," that's what they used to say, Simpkins remembered with proprietary pride, and who should have known better than the folks of a hunting county.

If at that moment she saw before her mind's eye the majestic sweep of the Downs, and the beauty of the old gray Sussex house, looking out on the ever-changing panorama of flowers and trees; if she felt again the excitement of the hunt breakfast, the gentlemen in their pink coats as they liked to call them (though Simpkins knew better ... red as a turkey-cock, they were), the ladies arriving on horseback, and more timid ladies in carriages driving up; and everywhere voices, laughter, the stamping of horses, the impatient clamor of the hounds—all these things, the majesty, the beauty, the clamor were but a background for that one magnificent being whom she, Patty Simpkins, had been appointed to serve.

She had not seen Highways for fifteen years, had not lived there for almost twenty-five. Absence and time as they have a way of doing presented the modest country house to her memory as a vast and splendid mansion, fit for the first lady in the land. Indeed to Simpkins in this moment she was almost that, for there had been three Queens of England in that period to whom she owed allegiance, and only one Mrs. Devonshire.

The long years through which she had borne impatience, sharp reproof, deserved and undeserved, hard work

and scanty praise, borne them and held her tongue in the
stubborn determination to keep her place were swept away,
and Simpkins saw only the glories at which she had
assisted, country houseparties, London seasons, balls, pres-
entations, dinners, weddings, christenings, deaths. Of the
family all but her mistress were as shadows to her, the
master long since passed away, the young master too and
his brother lost in the War—they had been children in the
nursery when she knew Highways first. And their sisters,
Miss Gwen, the eldest, pretty and docile, and little Miss
Brigid, quick like her mother and with a temper of her
own and a will of her own, but minding her own business
which was more than you could say of Miss Gwen as she
grew up.

Simpkins would have been surprised to know that "minding her own business," as she called it, really meant making no demands upon the one person whose comfort, rest
and peace of mind, no less than whose magnificence, it
was her jealous concern to guard and tend. She had
dressed the two young ladies for their presentation and
Miss Gwen on her wedding morning, and could concede,
since they were their mother's daughters, that a finer and
prettier sight it would have been impossible to find in
the length and breadth of Europe. She had also endured
the aftermath of her mistress's quarrel with Miss Brigid,
which had preceded the departure of that impetuous
young lady to the registry office and out of her mother's
life; but having preferred Miss Brigid of the two girls, it
was easy to convince herself that her mistress secretly had
shared this predilection; for why else had she gone out
that day, months ago, and without a word of warning to

any one, even to Simpkins, brought Miss Biddy home?

A great state and a fine fury Simpkins had been in about it at the time, she remembered, after these last peaceful years with her mistress, to have a young girl come into the house to upset them all, a proper heathen too, from her photograph in the newspapers, sailing to Poles, of all the nonsense, with a parcel of men! It was not fitting in the mistress's granddaughter.

Simpkins had held herself severely aloof from the intruder for a good month, and after all had modified her views considerably. The young lady had behaved as a young lady should, had not once while staying in the house intruded into her grandma's room, and had kept herself to herself, familiar with none. Certainly she had called Simpkins a pet and a treasure, but that was just her way of rewarding some little service, all young people being more free-spoken nowadays than when we were young.

Simpkins smiled as she recalled the first occasion. She had found the pretty lace dance frock which the mistress had bought the young lady, torn and had set to work to repair the damage, in no good temper either. Miss Biddy had caught her at it and protested in real dismay.

"Well, miss," Simpkins had told her shortly, "somebody has to do it."

"But of course I can do it myself. That's what I have just come up for. Why, I've made every evening frock I ever possessed till now, Simpkins. I am not accustomed to all this splendor."

Splendor! That was the word. Simpkins liked it, and a very nice sentiment too.

She had continued to mend the frock, however, and done many other little jobs for the young lady and quite enjoyed them after that. It was some time since she had had pretty things in her hands, and she had always been fond of needlework.

Yes, whatever the rights and wrongs of the mistress's displeasure with Miss Biddy, Simpkins was convinced it would blow over before long. Look at the glass box, for instance, and what store she set by it. And today was her birthday again and Miss Biddy not the one to forget.

A noise in the bathroom brought Simpkins' heart into her mouth; but it was only the mistress opening the door. In a second the window was closed and Simpkins ready; the past had vanished and the dreadful present was back again. The mistress was ill, had been ill for months saying nothing, even to Simpkins. Now only Simpkins knew —and the doctor, drat him! There was no hope and she was to tell nobody. The mistress had commanded it. She would have no fussing but would die decently and privately, and Simpkins was to see to that.

Simpkins would see to it. She understood the order and approved of it, and her own grief and dismay were subdued by this trust in her and a great pride. Between friends. . . .

2

Mrs. Devonshire walked down the stairs of this house which had been part of her wedding settlement half a century ago to celebrate her last birthday. A solemn occasion, no doubt, but that view did not strike her. She merely thought it rather tiresome that she had slept so badly with a fatiguing day before her. All this birthday ceremonial was great nonsense and she should have put an end to it long ago. However, it had amused her considerably in the past and might even now be at least instructive, so no doubt she could endure it with a little patience, she thought.

A William-and-Mary cabinet stood in an angle of the hall, glowing faintly in the subdued light. It was one of the finest specimens in the country, coveted by collectors and museums. She touched it gently as she passed, but the gesture was dictated merely by a private whim. The treasures in the house had been gathered haphazard by various generations, and hers was too restless a mind to concern itself with the hoarding of such things for their own sake, though for practical reasons she had made it her business to know their value and to keep them safe.

A few months ago, standing unnoticed at the head of the stairs, she had seen her granddaughter, Biddy Kerlin, touch the old cabinet as she had touched it now. The window above the girl's head had been open to the summer morning, the sunlight pouring in, and Mrs. Devonshire, an observant woman, had seen it was no random touch, rather the greeting of a friend.

The incident had roused her interest and her curiosity, for this child of her blood (and of so many other people's also, as she shrewdly remembered) had several qualities in common with her. Biddy was not given to vicarious enthusiasms. In spite of her evident zest for life and her enjoyment of a neat phrase, the girl was aloof and impersonal, her affections shy to emerge.

If Frederika had chanced to touch the old cabinet she

would have done it boisterously—for no reason at all, thought the old woman; as for those two girls of poor Gwen's, they would do it to impress an audience, gushingly—"so sweet"—but this was a secret touch and came from the mind.

Mrs. Devonshire had not betrayed her presence to Biddy or asked any questions. From the first she had accepted with secret amusement the attitude which consciously or not her granddaughter had chosen to adopt, that of a young girl accepting hospitality from an elderly woman who, for some mysterious reason, desires to give her pleasure.

In time certainly Biddy had come to call her "grandmother," though not too often, and more perhaps because some form of address was necessary for good manners than for any more intimate reason.

Mrs. Devonshire rather maliciously had watched her struggling with that problem, but provided no aid. Biddy from first to last had given more entertainment than she had received, though she would never know it.

Simpkins' romantic belief that her mistress had been moved to bring the girl home by preference for the older Brigid was as far from the truth as most speculations about human motives.

Mrs. Devonshire had cared little for her daughters. She was a woman of an alert and eager mind and, born into other circumstances or a later generation, might have made her mark in the world. As it was, her sons had engrossed her. As men they would have their definite place in the scheme of things, and work to do; she could feel little interest in girls whose province was in those

days merely to please the eye and marry a suitable mate.
She had seen that they were well-dressed and well-behaved
and had the kind of education considered requisite, but
she had made no secret of her preference for their brothers.
She did not pretend to be what the Victorians called a
womanly woman, and for all her brains had no idea that
she was an unreasonable one.

The years had not changed her, but they had changed
the world before her eyes. When she was already old she
had seen the security of her own class swept away, but
she had not, like most women of her age, seen it with
bewilderment and distress. She was interested, watching
the new order and its struggles with irony and some regret
that she could not, in the nature of things, expect to see
the outcome of it all.

Apathy, however, infuriated her, and she saw it on every
side with increasing disgust. Her sons were lost to her,
her two grandsons were poor creatures of whom she was
ashamed. She would have sold the house in Portman
Square and its treasures and shouldered the burdens of the
family, had there been one among them worth the effort,
but she was convinced that there was not. Herbert Dawnay at twenty-eight with a profession, was still supported
by his father and playing the fool. His sisters giggled and
danced and waited for marriage in a society devoid of
suitable men, and their mother bemoaned their unfortunate lot. The boy James Devonshire had no aim, no
ambition, and would presumably go on living on the rent
of Highways until increasing mortgages swallowed it up.
He and his mother were waiting for his grandmother to
endow him for life, as she knew well; and even the girl

Jane, though she made a pretense of working for the films, did it with very little result, as far as any one could see.

Young Frederika Mrs. Devonshire dismissed from consideration as needing no help from her. This daughter of her eldest son had at least a mother with some self-respect, if it *had* only taken the form of marrying trade and providing for herself and child; a pleasant child enough, but tennis playing was hardly a constructive occupation, thought her grandmother grimly.

These irritations had been of long standing on that morning thirteen months ago when she had seen the photograph of another grandchild, as yet unknown to her, looking out from her morning newspaper.

Wireless news of David Kerlin's death at sea while he was returning from a successful scientific expedition to the Arctic had been announced a week before. Mrs. Devonshire had not read the details of his accomplishments for, like Simpkins, she had little sympathy with Poles and uninhabited Arctic spaces. She thought her unknown son-in-law might have been better employed.

His ship the "Meteor" had now arrived, however, bringing home the explorer's twenty-year-old daughter, Miss Biddy Kerlin, who, said the newspapers, "with characteristic British pluck had on her own initiative braved the Arctic seas to meet her father's expedition—thus being the first Englishwoman to set foot on those Northern wastes of snow and ice."

"Nonsense!" Mrs. Devonshire had said to herself, dismissing this journalistic effort and the headlines "Arctic Heroine" with contempt, but she had looked at the photograph sharply. That the girl was outlandishly clad in a

sou'-wester and, no doubt, trousers below troubled her not
at all; it was merely the face she saw, an alert and keen
young face, entirely strange to her, yet answering some
need within herself. Vulgar the girl might be for all she
knew to the contrary, but at least she possessed initiative
and possibly spirit and a mind. Here was one of her own
stock, not bred in luxury like the rest, and conceivably the
better for it. Mrs. Devonshire had admitted that it would
be extraordinarily interesting to know for certain.

She had had no idea of the girl's whereabouts, connections, or circumstances, however, and would probably not
have moved in the matter but for Sir Neville Willesden's
announcement in *The Times* some weeks later that Miss
Kerlin had been removed to a nursing home suffering
from influenza brought on by exposure and the strain of
nursing her father through his last illness.

Sir Neville Willesden had been easy to manage in Mrs.
Devonshire's experienced hands. The girl had a bad cold
and needed rest from the newspapers and sensation
hunters, he had admitted, readily giving the address of
the nursing home.

If poor Kerlin's daughter had a wealthy grandmother
ready to take charge of her, so much the better, thought
Sir Neville, and relinquished his self-imposed responsibility for Biddy with a sigh of relief.

Mrs. Devonshire had had no intention of "taking charge"
of her granddaughter, though it had virtually come to that
in the end, partly because the girl was so politely incredulous and ready to depart, partly because it amused her
grandmother to have her stay. The uneasy amazement of
the family had had something to do with it too, Mrs. Dev-

onshire being maliciously alive to that and feeling a little fright would do the family no harm.

On this birthday morning looking back Mrs. Devonshire did not regret the experiment, quite the reverse. The child had been pleasant and amusing in the house, yet had gone her own way none the less, confiding in no one. She had not talked of her loss, displayed her knowledge of Arctic regions or shown any animus against previous neglect, all of which might confidently have been expected, and Mrs. Devonshire, grimly watching to see her grow slack and pleasure-loving, thought she had found out something else instead, unless she was very much mistaken.

The William-and-Mary cabinet had given her the first hint, though she might have thought little of it but for the remembrance of the old rose box which she had up till then imagined to have been chosen in happy innocence for its pretty color. Thereafter she had proceeded to lay traps for the unconscious Biddy, secretly putting rare things close to her hand and from time to time pointing out articles of no value as priceless antiques. The girl was polite about the latter and examined them carefully, but for the genuine treasures she had always a different attitude, a kind of breathless gentleness of touch.

It had not been difficult to discover either that the books in the library dealing with old furniture and glass were continually changing their places in the shelves.

"Do you read in bed?" she had enquired of the girl conversationally.

"I am afraid I do," said Biddy. "Do you mind?"

"Not in the least. It is said to be bad for the eyes but I know it is excellent for the temper. I have used the remedy

all my life. In my young days, of course, it was strictly
forbidden."

Biddy, laughing, had enquired:

"Did you forbid your own children?"

"Certainly. I had the same predilection as other parents
for passing on all the disagreeable precepts of my own
youth."

"I wonder if they obeyed you?"

"I am afraid they did, my dear. They were such blame-
less creatures. Now you, I suppose, read thrillers—is that
the term?"

"Sometimes, but not very often."

"Too exciting perhaps. I shouldn't advise you to study
in bed either. That I am sure is not wise," Mrs. Devonshire
had remarked with an air of benevolence.

"Then I won't," the girl had promised at once.

"Telling me exactly nothing at all, the rascal," thought
the old lady, recalling this conversation with an approving
chuckle.

She went into the long drawing-room and sat down by
the window looking on the Square. On a marquetry table
at her hand the morning letters and an ivory paper-knife
were waiting, but she did not attend to them at once. She
was tired after her sleepless night and the many sleepless
nights that had gone before, and of the continual dull pain
of which she had become uncomfortably aware months
ago and ignored, impatient of it as of so many things. She
did not want letters or the burden of answering them,
letters had never amused her; she preferred to go on thinking of Biddy who did. She wondered what the child would
do with her life, then remembered with the grim humor

which she could still summon at her own expense, that she would not, whatever it was, be there to see.

Common sense told her that no girl of that age pores over books on antiques for mere recreation, and Biddy was no blue-stocking but as fond of gayety as any other young creature. The girl had some scheme in her head, one might be sure of that, not mere emptiness like some people, she thought.

She looked down the room with its old amber curtains of rich brocade and its air of spacious elegance, saw the faint glow of polished wood, the shapely beauty of a chair, the glitter of Waterford glass, and thought of her possessions, soon to be scattered, she knew not where.

It did not matter. The world had grown poor and the generations growing up must lead simpler lives which would do them no harm.... The rare pieces would do well enough in a museum ... cold places, however, and so instructive, she had always disliked them.

There would be a sale in the house, that was unavoidable. Mrs. Devonshire's face darkened as she heard in imagination the trampling of heavy feet and the shouting of men ... in short, intrusion, a thing she had fought all her life.

"It is just as well that I shall not be here to see it," she said with an indignant flash of her old fiery anger, and thought of a girl with alert eyes and a still yet eager body, touching the treasures with a gentle hand.

CHAPTER FOUR

BRINGING GIFTS

"MRS. JAMES DEVONSHIRE, madam. Mr. James," announced the parlormaid.

"Ah, I expected as much. In at the death," thought Mrs. Devonshire, carefully turning her back to the light and rising to greet her visitors as though merely half her years lay behind her.

"Dear Granny, we felt we must be first to wish you a happy birthday. As head of the family James said it was his right, too impatient he has been, fidgeting all over the house and urging me on, the tiresome fellow."

"Oh, rather," agreed James in a limp voice.

"Quite the champing steed," said dear Granny to herself.

"And such a lovely day we've brought you, haven't we? —as well as our little gifts. James, I must give place to you, I suppose, in spite of the rule about ladies first. You men have all the privileges."

"Oh, well, happy returns and all that, Granny," said James, pushing a large object into her hands.

"Open the parcel for Granny, you silly boy."

"Not at all," said Mrs. Devonshire, briskly taking up a small pair of scissors and snipping the string.

"He had it specially done for you in Bond Street, darling," said Mrs. James, "because we felt it was your right to have a portrait of the head of the family. I am sure you will think it splendid."

"A remarkable picture," returned Mrs. Devonshire suavely. "The man is evidently an artist (and no photographer)," she added mentally. "Thank you, James."

"Yes, a real artist...we must tell him you said so, mustn't we, James? He will be so pleased for he took no end of trouble....It does pay to go to an expensive man, though but for you, Granny, we should not have dreamt of it. If you knew now how close Mr. Crow is about money your heart would bleed for my boy. He talks of nothing but retrenchment and economy and quite behaves as though *he* were the owner of Highways. I wondered, dear, if you could do something, if only to speak a word to Mr. Crow. The man is simply pouring James's money away in taxes. It is really disgraceful."

"A jolly swindle," said James, brightening to a favorite topic. "Taxes ought to be abolished and these thumping death duties too. They get my back up."

"An impossible feat, I fear," thought his grandmother.

"Ah, but you can evade death duties," put in her daughter-in-law, "by just giving away your money before you die. Some one was telling me!"

"Yes, mater, but it must be three years before, remember," prompted James.

"So much?" His mother looked slightly dashed, but went on brightly after a moment: "Even so, such a splendid idea. If I had money I know that is what I should do."

"And live in penury for three years? How self-sacrificing," observed Mrs. Devonshire in evident admiration. "But surely you have forgotten your 'King Lear'?"

Mrs. James laughed, feeling that this was generally safest when you were not sure of the point of one of Granny's observations. Who was King Lear? He must be somewhere in the Bible, she imagined, but really it was so difficult to keep track of all those Kings. Still, Granny was looking very pleased and had called her self-sacrificing, which she had never admitted before, though it was certainly the truth. Mrs. James, glad that justice was being done to her at last, and that she had so delicately broached the subject of the money, hastened to present her birthday gift, explaining its virtues as attested by the sewing girl, Jane, and various other witnesses to her prowess as she did so.

Mrs. Devonshire unfolded the yards of gray and black knitting fastened together at each end like an unfinished bolster, and expressed a gratifying astonishment. "Never look a gift-horse in the mouth," she thought. "Politeness before pleasure, but what a revolting-looking object...and I never did like swaddling clothes."

She placed both presents carefully on the table while James and his mother watched her and exchanged a satisfied smile.

"You haven't seen that naughty Biddy, I suppose?" began Mrs. James presently. "I had no idea of all this scandal about the *night-club*. I don't wonder you were shocked."

"It was a restaurant last time you told me the story, Marion. Do be accurate."

"Oh, but darling, this is something much worse...turned out of a night-club, I hear, and I'm only relieved you found her out and sent her away before it was too late."

"Too late for what?" enquired her mother-in-law.

"Well—er—er—"

Mrs. James was saved from an embarrassing situation by the opening of the door.

"Mr. Herbert Dawnay," announced the parlormaid.

2

"Well, Gran, all the best and so on," cried Herbert heartily as the James Devonshires retreated. "I've dropped toiling for my bread and butter just long enough to say 'chin-chin.' Can only stay two minutes. By the way, I hope this little gadget will be useful to you. Rather large to carry so I had to blow the expense and treat myself to a taxi."

Herbert unfurled from a mass of wrapping paper a fur foot-warmer and put it at Mrs. Devonshire's feet.

"Tuck in your toes, Granny, and think of little Herbert when you are sitting all cozy and warm on cold evenings...."

"Thank you, Herbert. I'll have your handsome gift on the table if you'll be so good. Yes, there beside your Aunt James's present. The photograph is intended to represent your cousin James."

Herbert enjoyed this witticism.

"Now then, Granny, you're a bit of a wag, you know. You are really. Still, I'm glad you told me.... So young Biddy has been giving you trouble, I hear? Too bad.... Playing about with a married man, wasn't it?"

Mrs. Devonshire raised her eyebrows.

"This is the first I have heard of it," she said. "Biddy seems to have lost no time since she left me. First your

Aunt James tells me she has been ejected from a night-club, and now you say she is engaged in an illicit love affair. I am no judge of such matters perhaps, but I should hardly have thought there was time for both in a brief fortnight. You would not, I imagine, suggest these things happened while she was beneath my roof?"

Herbert was quite astonished at what he supposed to be the old lady's cunning.

"No, no, of course you can't be held responsible. Most unpleasant for you," he assured her in what he hoped was a legal manner. "You leave this to me. Aunt James, between ourselves, never had any discretion and I'll tell Jane to talk to her. Poor old Janey has the sense of the family."

Herbert took out a gold case and proceeded to light a yellow cigarette, unconscious of the attentive eyes of his grandmother upon both.

"Upon my word, that woman has no business to come here upsetting you on your birthday and I'm glad I barged in. I could see I was unwelcome by the glare she gave me. Of course I am unpopular in that quarter at any time—the only other grandson, eh, Granny?"

Eliciting no response to this modest suggestion, Herbert went on:

"Well, I must return to the daily grind.... Oh, before I go though—do you want to make some money? Of course you do ... every one in the world does, and I'll let you into a secret. I'm at work on a play ... joke that ... rather good, don't you think? ... It is going to knock London; it'll be what we of the younger set call a wow, and I'll let you in on the ground floor."

"Ground floor? You mean the stalls, you will give me

seats in the stalls?" said Mrs. Devonshire innocently. "How kind of you."

"No, no, no—at least, of course I will. But what I mean is we'll need backers to produce the play. You invest a bit of money in it and then take your profits.... Think it over, unless of course you'd like to give me a check for a few hundreds straight away...."

"Mrs. Fenwick," announced the parlormaid.

3

Edith Fenwick, out shopping, had seen some of the late cream roses of which old Mrs. Devonshire was particularly fond. She had not meant to come to Portman Square today, but here she was, the roses in her hand and already half regretting the impulse. She hardly knew what had prompted it, partly perhaps a suspicion that her mother-in-law had quarreled with Biddy in a moment of temper on both sides and was probably regretting it, partly a faint anxiety lest the partisanship of Freddy and Sholto, for all her warnings, might make Biddy's case still worse.

"I have just looked in with a few roses and my best wishes, Mrs. Devonshire," she said. "I am not going to stay for I know how many visitors you are sure to have. The children are coming in this evening. Freddy wanted to wait for Sholto."

"Thank you, these are very lovely.... Quite a long time since you have joined the—shall we say—procession," remarked Mrs. Devonshire blandly.

"I know. I have felt that you would naturally prefer to have just the family on your birthday," said Edith, "and now since Freddy has been old enough to go about alone..."

"Not a bit of it," interrupted the old lady. "You mean since you have had that rascal of a step-son to relieve you of a disagreeable duty...."

Edith smiled at her mother-in-law's triumphant face.

"Well, if I did, which I am not going to admit, I must have repented, for here I am," she said.

"Excellent! And not to be out-done in magnanimity, I'll confess it is a relief to be called Mrs. Devonshire and see a well-cut suit. Sit down, Edith, and talk to me for a little while."

It was the first time in her life perhaps that she had asked such a thing of any woman, talk had no interest for her. Conversation?...yes, and wit, if they had not vanished from the world, but she could not expect these miracles to flower suddenly from Edith, who had married her eldest son, across the barrier of twenty years.

This turning to Edith was due merely to the irritations of the morning, it was a turning to quiet and dignity, but she was still sufficiently clear-sighted to appreciate the irony of that; and to see in a brief flash the years stretched out behind her and the paths she had missed.

The parlormaid came in with a jug of water and arranged the roses in a rainbow jar, putting them at a gesture from her mistress on the Queen Anne bureau where the sun would reach them.

Mrs. Devonshire turned her back on the "swaddling clothes" and looked at these golden blooms instead, hearing Edith's pleasant voice telling her of a new play it might amuse her to see, the supposed identity of the characters in the last scandalous novel, and the new autumn fashions in the shops.

Fashions in the shops...Biddy in high disdain leaving all her clothes behind...

"Now I," said Mrs. Devonshire to herself, "did not hesitate to keep her gifts."

All this spiteful talk of Biddy, all this hardly concealed relief because she had gone....Not a word from Edith, however. And what did that mean, unless that she had seen the child?...

Mrs. Devonshire looked at her daughter-in-law out of the corner of her eye.

"Talking of clothes," she said, "I have just had to bundle a trunk-load of Biddy's out of the house. She left them behind—a polite method, no doubt, of flinging them in my face to relieve her mind. Waste being abhorrent to me, I sent them after her."

"That was kind of you. Good clothes are so important for a girl with her way to make in the world," said Edith.

"And how does she propose to make it?" enquired Mrs. Devonshire, catching her neatly up.

"I haven't seen Biddy myself," said Edith with some hesitation, "but the children tell me she has always wanted to go in for antiques and has been studying all about them in her spare time for some years."

"Indeed?" The old eyes looked down the room as they had looked once before that morning, but now with a triumph that beat with the rhythm of her heart. "But what an opportunity the girl has missed," she said. "She might have asked me to set her up in business."

She waved a hand about the room, then lifted her chin

in a way she had and looked down at her daughter-in-law with an air of assumed astonishment.

Edith met the look squarely.

"I can see that you are not very angry with her, Mrs. Devonshire."

"And I know you to be an impostor," nodded the old lady. "Ah, well, I suppose at my age I can hardly expect to be loved for myself alone.... Peacemaking, that's what you came for."

"I hardly know why I came," admitted Edith, "but it was certainly not premeditated. I saw the roses and suddenly thought of your birthday and bought them, but I *was* slightly worried. We all like Biddy and the children are her friends. If they show it too plainly please don't blame her."

"Her," repeated Mrs. Devonshire thoughtfully, leaning back with her fine old hands on the arms of the chair and looking into space. The word gave something to her which Edith Fenwick could not know, a sense of decency perhaps, in a sordid world. A unique member of the family, this, who asked nothing for her own children.

"Very well," she said briskly at last. "If they show any temper to me, I'll disown the pair of them."

Edith laughed at her "obliging" face.

"I'd almost rather you did even that," she said. "They have parents to look after them. Biddy has nobody but you."

"And a quite capable aunt, apparently."

"Oh, aunts. She isn't easy to know, Mrs. Devonshire, and I don't think she would be easy to help."

"And where I have failed, how can you hope to suc-

ceed?" finished the other. "But that may be just your
modesty....Go home, Edith, and don't argue with a
woman twice your age. I shall not ask you to lunch for I
am dieting, and you would be horrified at such a meal.
Thank you for coming and telling me about the fashions."

There was a twinkle in her eyes and Edith laughed
helplessly, but went away feeling glad she had come, not
more so, however, than the woman she had left behind.

Night-clubs and married men, forsooth! Lies, all of it,
and such incapable lies!

Simpkins, entering fiercely with a medicine glass, found
her mistress looking over her birthday gifts with an air of
rich enjoyment and apparently delighted beyond measure.

"We only need a feeding-cup and a pair of bed-socks
for a complete invalid outfit, Simpkins," she said.

"Well, 'm, I've never known you to wear such things as
bed-socks yet," declared Simpkins, scandalized.

"No, my girl, and you never will."

4

"Mrs. Dawnay, madam. Miss Gwynneth and Miss May."

It was an understood thing that on her mother's birthday Mrs. Dawnay and the girls should come for tea. This
ritual the only surviving child considered her right, and
every year she took care to remind what she called the
more distant branches of the family to choose some other
hour for their call.

Mrs. Devonshire was ready for them beside the tea-
table. Since luncheon she had slept for two hours, deeply
and well, and her fatigue had dropped away. The trophies

of the morning were still spread out in the window behind her, but Edith's roses were on the table with the Crown Derby tea-set and Georgian silver. The roses were no birthday present but an extravagant impulse, a thing Mrs. Devonshire had always liked.

The two girls came in carrying their parcel between them and bubbling with laughter which they tried to suppress. May's eyes flashed to the tea-table with its foie gras and asparagus sandwiches, cream cakes, pastries, crumpets and scones.

"Oo!" she thought, "fancy Biddy giving up all this for any man. I wouldn't. Granny does do herself well."

Gwynneth thought: "Granny looks ill, but I suppose any one would at seventy-five. It's terribly old. . . . I hope she'll really like our present, it would be awful if she didn't care for it. I have a feeling we might have got something nicer with all that money . . . it's so useful . . . and perhaps she has one already."

May was hanging round her grandmother, swinging her end of the bed-rest gleefully.

"Oh, Granny, what a perfect birthday! Doesn't it all look scrumptious? Wait till you see what we've brought you, Gwyn and I. We've carried it between us all the way, jabbing the passers-by. You should have seen the black looks that we got. Poor Mummy really grew quite agitated."

She flopped at Mrs. Devonshire's feet, seizing the parcel and standing it on end to be undressed, taking the center of the stage from long custom and confident of approval. She flirted with her grandmother as with all the world, screening the present from her gaze till the last moment, while Mrs. Dawnay and Gwynneth looked on at these antics with fond, admiring smiles.

"Well, I suppose some one will marry her for her pretty face and empty head," thought Mrs. Devonshire, "and regret it ever afterwards."

"Don't look, Granny, no peeping now.... There! It's done."

"Dear me, what a gigantic present," said Mrs. Devonshire. "A game is it?...But of course a new game."

"*Granny!* It is a bed-rest, angel. You clap it on to the side of your bed, whisk it round and it holds your breakfast or your newspaper and your novel or your morning tea, and nothing can wobble or spill on it. Isn't it marvelous?"

"Spill," echoed Granny, concealing a fastidious shudder as she gazed at this object of fumed oak, so reminiscent of a hospital ward, and no doubt so excellent for poor creatures in the habit of spilling. She had not come to that yet, she hoped, nor to being clamped into her old carved bed like a child into a high chair.

"Complete invalid outfit," she thought with a gleam in her eye. "Coincidence?—or has that fool Simpkins broken her word to me?...There they sit, the lot of them, waiting for me to die, and I am bound to oblige them."

She mastered her fury, agreed that the gift was quite extraordinary, and sent her granddaughter to place it among the presents from their cousins and aunt.

"Darling Mother, mine is a very small gift but I hope you will find it useful," said Mrs. Dawnay, unfolding a spectacle case of black moiré and silver braid. "I thought the long cord was such a good idea ... you put it over your

head, you see, and then you can never mislay your glasses.
... Like this...."

"Thank you, Gwen, but we'll lay it with the other
presents, please. I don't like things dangling when I am
pouring out the tea," said Mrs. Devonshire, lifting it off
again.

(Or at any other time. As for glasses, when have you
known me to mislay them or anything else, I should be
glad to learn? This thought was directed to her daughter's
back. A little too plump, poor Gwen, and inclined to lum-
ber as she walked. Fluffy ... and no sense.)

Mrs. Devonshire sat more upright than usual, thanking
Heaven that at seventy-five she could still walk down a
room and hold herself erect.

"Now, you must let me pour out the tea for you and
save your poor arms, just for a birthday treat," said her
daughter coaxingly, as to a child.

"Nonsense, Gwen! I trust I am still capable of presiding
at my own tea-table. I am not a centenarian by a quarter
of a century, remember," said her mother.

The Crown Derby cups were filled and passed; the girls
chirruped and devoured sandwiches and quantities of
cakes; May ogled her grandmother; Mrs. Dawnay was
patient with "poor mother" and proud of her darlings,
meanwhile wishing she could afford a good cook, as well
as a new carpet. These cream cakes, for instance, were
light as a feather, she would have another and presently
she must try one of those delicious pastries.

Mrs. Devonshire ate a finger of dry toast with her strong
tea, looked at the roses, more golden now in the milder
tone of the afternoon, and thought she would have a

cigarette presently to annoy Gwen, who still thought smoking a vice in women, poor thing, but a nice, manly virtue in men.

"I am so vexed, Mother, my drawing-room carpet is wearing into patches. Of course it is twenty-two years old, but really it looks too dreadful," said Mrs. Dawnay.

"This has been down fifty."

"Yes, dear, but we cannot compare our poor ramshackle home, can we? And then this room has never had the wear and tear...."

"Tear? Certainly not. Rowdyism was never permitted in my house. Wear, of course it has had wear. You are losing your memory, Gwen. I suppose this room has seen as many guests in a night as yours in a year."

Mrs. Dawnay sighed. Her mother was so unreasonable, but then she had never suffered. She did not know what lack of money meant with two dear girls to marry and a carpet wearing out. All this great house and rooms shut up, carpeted rooms! Gwen felt the full weight of a justified grievance. It was true a carpet from one of the closed bedrooms would have been a poor consolation to her, but it was the injustice that rankled. Still, now Biddy had gone, she thought....

When at length tea was over and the parlormaid had cleared away, she sent the two girls to look at Granny's china cabinet with a mysterious air of disclosures to come. Mrs. Devonshire, smoking her cigarette, was aware that it was more than a gesture of defiance now, it was a positive need, if she wished to keep her temper.

"I didn't want to discuss this before the children, dear," said her daughter, "but I wondered whether you saw what a large sum had been subscribed for the Kerlin memorial?"

"I see nothing unsuitable for the girls' ears in such a subject," said Mrs. Devonshire. "Memorials to scientists are quite respectable, as far as I know."

"But it is about Biddy, Mother. After all, as Richard says, these funds generally make provision for a man's dependents, and he knows Sir Neville Willesden personally, and could say a word to him. We thought it would relieve your mind to feel poor Brigid's daughter would be provided for."

"Will you kindly mind your own affairs, Gwen, and tell Richard to mind his?" exclaimed Mrs. Devonshire testily. "Do you propose, the pair of you, to beg charity for Biddy? You might show a little instead. If the girl chooses to apply to Sir Neville Willesden, that is her own concern. She knows him far better than Richard—the man was her father's intimate friend—and so do I know him."

"I see," fluttered Gwen. "Of course we didn't realize that, Mother darling. We were only thinking of you, for she's a very naughty girl, making such a scandal with men and night-cl—"

Her mother loudly rapped the table.

"*Will* you be silent! I am tired to death of all these hints and innuendoes and tittle-tattle about the girl. First one and then another of you, all day long, and I'll have no more of it! She is of age and has her own life to live like every other human being. It is not your business and it is not mine. As for night-clubs, do you think I am in my second childhood to be frightened by a booby? Do you expect me to believe no other grandchild of mine has ever entered such a place, and that it is a sign of depravity? Upon my word, if I hear any more of it I'll leave everything I possess to a home for the weak-minded, where the majority of my family ought to be. The girl has been a guest in my house for months. Do you suggest that I don't know how to look after her? I consider all these insinuations the greatest impertinence."

"You are most unkind," wept Gwen. "I am only trying to be helpful and you talk as though I had invented the story. Why, it is all over the place."

"What place? Are you referring to Lancaster Gate or a cottage in Knightsbridge or both?" enquired her mother. "I am not interested in the gossip of either. And don't sit there crying and making yourself ridiculous, Gwen. You had better concern yourself with your own children in future and leave Biddy alone. Don't mention the girl's name to me again. I will not tolerate it."

"Silly of me, but I get so upset," said Gwen, wiping her eyes, and quite unjustifiably seeing in the last sentence a great light. Biddy's name was not to be mentioned to her mother ... all was well then ... the break was final.

"Come, children, poor Granny is tired and we must be getting home," she cried brightly. "Such a lovely party."

5

"Miss Jane, madam."

Jane Devonshire, unlucky as usual, came in just after the storm, and well before the thunder-clouds had cleared from her grandmother's brow. She had had an inspiration and came not only with her birthday gift, but with a fair

offer, but Mrs. Devonshire only saw a jaunty manner
which she disliked, and too much paint on her granddaughter's face.

"Sorry I couldn't get here before, Granny, old thing.
How's the birthday? Congrats," said Jane, presenting the
doll.

"Playthings at my age?"

"No, she's for the telephone, hides it with her skirts, the
hussy. Shall I put her with the other loot...? You've had
a good day, haven't you?"

"I have had an extremely tiring day, and in five minutes
I shall be obliged to turn you out, or possibly it will be
sooner. That depends upon you," said her grandmother
acidly.

"Oh, I say, fair is fair. What has little Janey done?"

"Be good enough to speak your mother-tongue, Jane. It
is not what you have done, but what you are probably
intending to do, to which I refer, judging from many
experiences today," said her grandmother. "I may tell you
at once that if you mention your cousin Biddy's name to
me, you will go out of the house or I shall go out of the
room."

"Biddy *has* done it," thought Jane, not unnaturally, and
assured her grandmother:

"Of course I won't then. But you must miss her a bit
all the same, don't you, Granny?"

"Miss her? Certainly not!" said Mrs. Devonshire in astonishment.

"Oh well—I always get the pip if I'm alone," admitted
the girl rather desperately. "I thought you might. I was
wondering if you'd like me to chuck my studio and come

along here for company? I'd be out working in the day-
time, of course, but I'll do it in a minute if you say the
word."

"You are too kind."

"Not a bit. Works both ways, Granny. I'd save on it
and I'm not pretending that I wouldn't."

"A handsome admission, and I regret I cannot accept
your offer, Jane," said her grandmother. "We should not
see eye to eye on a number of subjects. It is not to be
expected and, to be perfectly frank, I want my home to
myself. Selfish, no doubt, but there it is."

"Righto, Granny, . . . just as you say." Jane knew how
to accept defeat, though how she was going to pay her
overdue rent, she did not know.

With a smile that was not without a kind of jaunty
courage in the face of adverse fortune, she patted her
grandmother's back and kissed her cheek.

"I'll be off and let you rest," she said, "and if the family
come talking bilge and bothering, send for me. I'll settle
them. Toodle-oo."

<h2 style="text-align:center">6</h2>

"Miss Freddy and Mr. Fenwick, madam."

Mrs. Devonshire was playing The King Bars the Way,
the only Patience she could tolerate because it required
some alertness of brain and rarely offended by coming
out. She wore her horn-rimmed glasses, which was unnecessary and contrary to her custom. In fact, it might be
said that she had dressed the part and staged it. Her last
birthday was nearly over, the procession at an end, an
irritating, a maddening day, but the evening should re-

deem it. She was determined that if any one were maddening on this occasion it would be she.

As her last two visitors came in, she looked up and nodded to them briefly, then bent over to seize a refractory King and sent him to guard his consort at the end of the line.

Freddy and Sholto tiptoed to the card-table and watched these manœuvres with deep concentration.

"Seven of hearts," cried Freddy involuntarily.

"Will you be good enough to let me play my own game?" said Mrs. Devonshire, looking up fiercely through her glasses. "You young people of the present day are all alike. I don't know what the world is coming to, I don't indeed."

With an inward chuckle and a gleam of the eye for this well-worn platitude, she pushed the cards into a heap in the middle of the table, and sat back to demonstrate that they had ruined the game, while Freddy and Sholto exchanged glances.

"Sorry," said Freddy gruffly. She held her present behind her back and produced it and her birthday wishes with evident reluctance.

Sholto laid his parcel on the table beside it.

"Since you are so kind you might cut the string for me, Sholto," remarked Mrs. Devonshire, with the air of a tyrant who will shortly pronounce the order for execution.

Sholto unfolded a handsome box of chocolates and presented them with a flourish.

"Dear me, Frederika, what can have made you suppose I would eat sweets at my age?" said her grandmother, lifting the lid and peering inside.

"I was told you liked them," muttered Freddy. "If you want to know who told me, Biddy did."

"Indeed? A mine of information truly."

"Biddy's a friend of mine," said Freddy, shooting her thunderbolt.

"Birds of a feather, no doubt. Allow me to offer you one of these delicious chocolates," said her grandmother.

"No, thank you."

"You refuse? Ah!"

Mrs. Devonshire was aware of a pantomime behind her, Sholto perhaps calling Freddy to order.

"If you don't like the chocolates I'll change them," offered Freddy cautiously, "but I'm not going to eat your present."

"Naturally," said Granny in a sinister voice, "and then you must consider your digestion no doubt, being a public character. However, perhaps Sholto will oblige me?"

"Thanks awfully, Mrs. Devonshire."

Sholto took a chocolate, and the old lady having watched anxiously for fatal results, and seeing none, followed his example and pronounced Frederika's choice excellent.

"And did Biddy also give you the benefit of her advice?" she inquired sweetly of the young man.

"No, worse luck." He produced a locked diary. "To write your memoirs in," he explained.

"Memoirs ... memoirs, but of course. You hope to see yourself in print at last?"

Sholto gave a shout of laughter, and even Freddy's expression of unnatural severity widened into a grin.

"And a fine character I'll give you," said his hostess.

"A lazy rascal, waiting to marry a rich girl and live in idleness for ever after. I know you."

"Oh, rather, but I haven't a hope," said Sholto sadly. "There are no rich girls in the market, and if there were they'd boot me out."

"So that is your view of the modern girl, is it?"

"Ancient and modern. You'd have done it yourself, Mrs. Devonshire."

"You presume to call me ancient, young man?"

"In wisdom you are pre-Sphinx," he said after consideration.

"It is fortunate," said Mrs. Devonshire severely to this impertinence, "you are not a member of my family."

"Time yet," said Sholto to himself, but did not dare to put that hope into words. His levity departed and he left the victory with Mrs. Devonshire, who noted the abrupt transition and the twinkle in his eye, and drew her own conclusions. So he was fond of the child Frederika, was he? Well, why not? She liked the boy, she had always liked boys, and there was no need at her age to deny it. As for Frederika, bringing her chocolates, and announcing the source of that idea with a fine gesture of defiance, the girl was blunt but no sycophant like some others one could mention.

"Freddy wants to wait and come with Sholto."

Edith had said that (Edith and her roses and her pleas for Biddy!). Ah yes, she saw it all.

"You are in love," she said, turning upon them suddenly, "so don't deny it."

Freddy had chosen that moment to get herself a chair,

and it was Sholto who met the attack and started with appropriate astonishment.

"There, you've found me out," he said. "Of course from the first moment I saw you.... Freddy, quick, come and defend me! The only rich girl I know is going to boot me out."

"You are an insolent boy," she informed him, but she smiled none the less. She had been called "a wag," she recalled, by one young man this morning, but had not melted to that compliment as to this lad's fooling, which was native to him and disinterested, and had a courtesy of its own to a woman of her years. "Ring the bell and don't waste your blandishments on me," she requested him.

She cast a look at her granddaughter, who was gazing after Sholto, with an admiring grin. The girl would never have Edith's looks and poise. She was like her father... like Hugh.

Mrs. Devonshire caught up that thought and locked it away. Even now she could not remember her elder son without a dreadful darkening of her mind, and suddenly she had a glimpse of the bewildering pattern of all life, fine threads and coarse, dark threads and bright, spun out at last, but now with a new thread of the same texture joining on. Hugh's thread...Frederika's...and hers...?

Biddy.

"Bring champagne and glasses, will you?" she said to the snappy Taylor who answered the bell.

"Whew!!"

"*Granny!*"

Aha, so they could be impressed, these young lords of creation—of both sexes, for it had come to that!

"You will permit me to celebrate my own birthday, I hope?" she retorted to their exclamations. "Not for the first time in this house ... the fiftieth."

"A jubilee, Freddy, think of it. And in another ten years a diamond jubilee. Mrs. Devonshire, say we're invited ten years from now, and I'll begin saving up for the best diamond in London."

"Ten years? You will have something better to do with your money, if you have any, which I doubt—children to clothe and educate, and see that you teach them to mind their own business, both of you," said Mrs. Devonshire peremptorily, flashing her glasses upon them.

"I haven't decided to have any yet myself," said Freddy with calm.... "But I expect it'll mind its business if I do," she added consolingly. "We do rather in our family. Sholto, do you think I'll be able to walk home after this?"

Taylor had brought the champagne, silver bucket, ice and all. Sholto was preparing to officiate and Freddy looking anxiously over his shoulder.

"You'll have to, girl. You're much too hefty for me to carry," Sholto informed her brutally.

"Pig!... It still goes to my head a bit," she explained to her grandmother.

"Well, thank heaven for that," returned the old lady crisply.

"Mrs. Devonshire, your health and happiness!" said Sholto, not without grace.

"Here's luck, Granny." Large-eyed and solemn, Freddy clutched her champagne.

"Thank you." Mrs. Devonshire looked from the amber liquid to the two young faces. "You drink to the old order," she said. "I drink to the new," and lifted her glass.

7

They had gone, her last visitors...the new order. The chocolates and the locked diary "for her memoirs" still lay on the table beside the cards, she would not lay them yet with that chamber of horrors, the complete invalid outfit, under the window.

So Biddy had suggested the chocolates, had she? But no old rose glass on this occasion, to betray her hand. Mrs. Devonshire could see her, impersonal, amused, alive, assisting the giver, yet for all her independence and her pride, the recipient too a little, since she had chosen something she knew well that her grandmother would like... instead of some silly trifle...taking a neat revenge.

Biddy was out in the world and not afraid of it, quite the reverse. An old woman of seventy-five who could still feel that same zest, believed that when she could feel it no more, it would still beat on through the pulses of this younger life that she was leaving behind...and she was content.

The girl had friends...those two young fools who had just gone, for instance...in love in the casual manner of their generation.

"But that is just assumed to deceive the eye," said Mrs. Devonshire, "and small blame to them. Love had too little privacy when I was young."

She was too delicate a woman to lift the blind and peer

after the departed "lovers," which was just as well perhaps.

Released from the comedy and drama with which she had provided them, uneasy under a faint sense of solemnity behind her, Freddy challenged Sholto to a race, and they sped down Portman Square, overtook a 'bus, mounted it at a leap, and clambered up the stairs.

Sholto mopped his brow.

"A dizzy evening!" he remarked.

"My word!"

"Can't help liking her, can you?... sort of grand panjandrum."

"All the same I'm glad I gave her one about Biddy, and you needn't have kicked my shin either."

"Well, of all the ungrateful young hounds! Wait till I save your life at the peril of my own again. In another moment you would have been thrown out on the pavement, and Biddy would have had the blame for that. See that you teach your children tact, Frederika... send 'em to their Uncle Sholto for a course of lessons at an early age."

"They'll be an 'it' or nothing," returned Miss Devonshire. "You'll have to have three, an Edith and a George, and a something Frederika."

"Here, is this my family or yours you're so busy christening off?..."

The argument took them merrily all the way to Victoria.

CHAPTER FIVE

A BLUE MOON

BIDDY DRESSED hastily, for it was nearly midday, and a note from Sholto giving her no time to refuse had come by the early post asking her to meet him for luncheon at one o'clock.

Her brown walls had been transformed to green, she had finished coloring them this morning, in spite of Sholto's command during their Sunday walk to leave them till Saturday afternoon for his more accustomed hand. Painting walls, his tone had suggested, was his life-work, but Biddy doubted it. Her orderly mind required a settled and orderly habitation, and before she began looking for a post in her chosen profession the flat must be as cheerful as she could make it.

She had squandered a pound to have the ceiling whitened as soon as she moved in, but the walls had cost her little and she was pleased with them. The little odd-shaped room was now full of light, and the orange curtains glowed against the pale almond green of the walls.

The physical work had given her busy mind full play to consider and plan her position. Her father's small legacy had been left to her unconditionally, but she did not intend to touch her capital if this could be avoided. What she hoped to do was to find some antique dealer who would take her in as a pupil without premiums and of course without salary, except a small commission, on the strength of what she already knew. Her knowledge at present was partly instinct, partly gathered from books and observation. During her father's last absence, until the moment of her impetuous determination to sail on the "Meteor" when it went North to meet him, she had spent her time at Christie's and minor sales-rooms, and prowling in the Caledonian Market or among the hundreds of antique and secondhand shops scattered over London.

Her father had not discouraged her bent, though it had surprised him. The girl must have some career and science made no appeal to her, alas. After the embarrassment of her continual growth and continual needs in clothes and schooling from term to term had ceased to trouble him, the two had become excellent friends in a silent fashion. Her unobtrusive capability had occasionally struck him as amazing; these modern schools, he supposed. For the first time since his gay and lovely Brigid's death, David Kerlin had enjoyed some comfort in his domestic surroundings, fleeting and makeshift though these often were.

Now he would come home no more, and Biddy was making a home of her own. As she pulled her little russet hat in place and collected her bag and gloves, her mind was still engaged with her palace walls rather than with Sholto whom she was going to meet.

The clock on the church spire lifting its slim spire at the end of the street struck twelve as she went out, ponderously, but to her ears not without melody. It was no harasser of mankind, but an indulgent, elderly clock, slow of speech, and beginning its announcements with a hoarse chuckle.

"Come .. on, come ... on, come .... on," said the old clock above the noise of the traffic as she walked down the street; but at night when the world was still, he would sing like some benevolent watchman of the past: "All's well! All's well!"

Biddy was glad to be out. As she reached the Bayswater Road and saw the traffic racing, she hastened her own steps in sympathy. The doorway of the Tube yawned in her face, like a hungry monster. She saw people go in and the iron jaws of the lift devour them. Red 'buses caught up still other people and hurried them on, but she walked free, her eyes on roofs and spires and an occasional flag against the sky above the misty outline of the Park.

She turned in at the Victoria Gate and walked under the trees where the first leaves were beginning to fall and happy dogs chased them in the grass and growled. The bright air stirred her youthful hunger and then, for the first time, her thoughts, up till now random and busy with a dozen things, turned to Sholto and the rendezvous ahead, unconscious of the cunning with which he had devised this chance to see her, but aware that it was a lark to be going out to lunch, and she was ready for it.

A dandie dinmont approaching her with great dignity on his short legs, paused as they met and sniffed her shoe, then lifted a pair of speaking eyes that suggested friendship. She wished he was hers, she would have liked a dog, but it would have been unfair to him and to the visiting cat, she thought smiling, a black one, and therefore not to be denied admission. This masterful creature the last few days had rattled her door-handle of a morning and then stalked in, swishing his tail, and taken possession until his fancy carried him elsewhere. He said nothing and food was not his object, for he refused it with disdain. He merely sat, his haunches wide as a Victorian gown and watched her with an inscrutable gaze, occasionally jumping on the windowsill to cock an ear at the plane-tree, where game might be lurking for all he knew. Biddy rather enjoyed V.C., the visiting cat.

Oxford Street was crowded and the traffic crawling. She eventually succumbed to the temptation of riding at ease and entered a 'bus, which promptly took flight, pushed ahead of its brethren in a highly unsporting manner, and leapt past one green-eyed signal after another. Biddy, the only passenger on top, was tossed and bumped and delivered at her destination ten minutes too soon, while the 'bus, very red in the face and growling, rushed on. Quite content, she betook herself to the nearest shop-window, and discovered Sholto there before her, earnestly peering in. She put a cool hand into his coat pocket, he whirled round and grasped it, discovering her with a shout of delight.

"Biddy, bless you for coming so soon. I've been kicking my heels and moaning at the slant-eyed siren in the window. Come on, quick, before we starve."

"I'll come quietly," promised Biddy, releasing her hand. "I don't want to make a habit of hauling or being hauled by men in and out of restaurants. These things get about."

"Dam' their eyes!" muttered Sholto pleasantly to that, as he opened the door for her.

"Sholto, you are encouraging me to eat beyond my

income, it won't do," protested Biddy, looking about her with dismay.

"Only for once," he assured her. "Jam's doing well at present, I felt I ought to celebrate."

She laughed, wondering whether he liked his work; he had never mentioned it to her before that she could remember. After a moment's hesitation she asked him.

"Yes, I do." He was charmed at the question, at her interest in his daily round, at her remonstrance over his extravagance, indeed for the moment at everything in the world. "I like handling people," he explained, "not that I have a hope at present. I am just a minion, learning the whole thing. It sounds simple and dull enough, doesn't it, making pots of jam and selling them, but I've been on the spot nearly two years now since I came down from Oxford, and I still get a kick out of it and want to know more. Of course John is unique in his way. I could have had a profession, he offered that, and then casually invited me while I was thinking the matter over to help him once or twice during the vac. when he was short-handed. All my eye, of course. Fenwick's is never short-handed. That was John's low cunning."

"And then you went into the firm of your own accord?" said Biddy. "He must have been pleased."

"Oh, John didn't go into any transports," said Sholto, grinning. "He presented me with a complete list of all the disadvantages and argued against it for hours. He even suggested I might find it a social drawback. I didn't know John at that time nearly as well as I do now—until he married Edith I was benighted among a flock of aunts, and then of course away at school and so on—but the social drawback did it—from John of all people, who had snaffled a wife like Edith! I laughed in his face. I said I'd go into the firm if I had to make the dam' jam, or even the pips.

"That reminds me, we are forwarding you a box of our little sample jars, in the hope of obtaining your custom, Miss Kerlin," added Sholto with due solemnity.

"Oh, you mustn't do anything of the kind," cried Biddy. "My custom wouldn't pay for the samples in twelve months."

"Ah, but your recommendation would be above price. Besides, the head of the firm ordered it to be done and I have no influence with the man. It's the best jam, I can assure you. . . . Now what hour do I turn up to do those walls tomorrow?"

"I finished them this morning," said Biddy, casual because she was suddenly nervous of making this admission, though she did not know why. "Don't pretend to look reproachful, Sholto. You couldn't suppose I was going to let you spend your only free time in the week podgering for me."

"Ha," said Sholto, endeavoring to rally from the blow, "you thought I couldn't do it. I know I haven't an artistic face, but that's a blind, that is. However, since they are finished we can do a matinée tomorrow instead."

"Thanks awfully, but I have to be out all day."

"Oh, Biddy, have a heart."

"I didn't mean to mess up your Saturday," said Biddy, suddenly contrite. "I didn't really."

"Never mind. But if you tell me you are going out all Sunday I shall die on the spot, and you'll have an inquest on your hands. Edith wants you to dine with us and then

Freddy and I thought we'd get another chap and all go somewhere to dance."

Biddy felt perturbed. Sholto on Sunday, Freddy on Wednesday, Sholto on Friday (and Saturday too if she hadn't put her foot down), and now Edith on Sunday. It was too good of them, but it would not do.

"I should love to come to dinner on Sunday," she said, "but I'd be terribly grateful if you'd let me off the dancing. I have to begin work seriously on Monday, and you don't understand. I don't belong to the idle rich, I never did. I have been poor all my life and used to doing things for myself. You have quite the wrong idea of me, seeing me only with my grandmother.... That was a sort of interlude, rather unreal, but now it is finished and I must give up dancing and expensive lunches and all this, except once in a blue moon—at least until I am beginning to make a living."

She looked so urgent and anxious that he smiled at her.

"But there is a blue moon on Sunday. I saw it in *The Times*. Still, we won't dance, we'll stay at home and pray for the Royal Family. You can't have any objection to that," he said. "As for the idle rich, you are as bad as John with his social opportunities. Is a poor jam-maker's seventy-ninth assistant one of the idle rich? Aha, I've got you there, Miss Kerlin."

"I can see there will be a brawl if somebody doesn't change the conversation. Tell me about the birthday," said Biddy.

Sholto, feeling he had scored about the idle rich, gave a spirited account of their evening in Portman Square in his best manner.

"She must have been in good form."

"Oh, rather! Walked all over us. You know, though I hate her like poison for treating you as she did, I've always had a sneaking admiration for Mrs. Devonshire," admitted Sholto, "and somehow you are rather like her, Biddy."

"I?" exclaimed the girl incredulously. "Do I bow or wilt?"

"She bows. . . . It isn't her looks," he added, a searching eye on the amused young face across the table, "but a kind of look . . . a kind of vim."

"She certainly has vim. . . . I believe I am terribly flattered on the whole, but of course you are talking nonsense," said Biddy thoughtfully. "She is the most entertaining person really, not like any one I've ever met, very acid yet not spiteful in the least, interested in everything but people, I think. She isn't like my idea of a grandmother—anybody's grandmother, too live-and-let-live-ish. Irritable though and determined."

"You talk as though you were quite fond of the hell-hound," expostulated Sholto in a disconsolate voice. "You wouldn't go back there, Biddy?"

"Oh, no, I wouldn't go back," said the girl flushing suddenly and with that sinking of the heart the subject always brought her. To have outstayed her welcome in a stranger's house—for that was what it came to—to have been turned out with ignominy. . . . "I suppose I should have to go and see her if she sent for me, but she never will," she said. "She was tired of me and caught at any pretext to send me away. But why couldn't she have told me frankly? I had so often wanted to go and she wouldn't hear of it. It was insulting, and then I lost my temper as much as she

did and was rude. She is not likely to forget that, and probably thinks me an ungrateful cub....All the same," said
Biddy hardily, "she brought it on herself."

"Very well then, hell-hound it is," offered Sholto, but
she went on without heeding him:

"I don't pretend she wasn't good to me. I had a marvelous
year, but it couldn't have gone on. There's my work and
you don't know what a thrill there is in getting down to
it at last."

"Oh, by the way, that reminds me," interrupted Sholto
eagerly. "Edith was moaning about wanting a—what's the
thing?—tallboy. If you come across a good one I wish you'd
let her know."

Biddy laughed in his face.

"And John is wanting to start an antique shop in con-
junction with the jam factory and needs a girl to manage
it, and Edith is rather wanting to adopt a daughter," she
finished for him.

"Put two more words on to your last one," whispered
Sholto, "darling!"

"What are you muttering?" said Miss Kerlin suspiciously.

"Me? I never uttered or muttered a word! Crushed, that's
what I am."

2

Sir Neville Willesden, waiting for Mrs. Devonshire to
appear and explain her sudden summons, looked about
him. An imposing room this, he thought, for these days of
straitened incomes and depression. Some of the old families
still had money evidently; the country wasn't done yet,
in spite of the politicians. Queer to think of Kerlin marry-

ing a wife from such a house all the same, unworldly to the last degree, and caring as much for pomp and circumstance as for the moon. Queer too that he had never mentioned the mother-in-law. No love lost perhaps. However, she must have relented, the old lady, to take Biddy, and what could this summons mean but a check towards the fund?

The door opened and Mrs. Devonshire swept into the room, followed by a maid bearing tea. Sir Neville, an awkward man in women's company, bowed stiffly, shook the delicate old hand held out to him, and sank into a chair which his hostess suggested. In a few moments he was enjoying an excellent cup of tea under her solicitous eyes as though he had dropped in for a pleasant chat and nothing more, as an old and valued friend of the house.

Mrs. Devonshire chatted to him and received his brief observations with evident delight. It was not until the tea-cups had been taken away that she remarked:

"Well, Sir Neville, I must explain my reason for troubling you."

"Pray don't mention it, Mrs. Devonshire," said Sir Neville with confused courtesy.

"It is very good of you to spare me a few moments of your valuable time," continued Mrs. Devonshire. "It seemed simpler to ask you to come here at your convenience rather than to venture to disturb so busy a man."

"Not at all," said Sir Neville. "As treasurer of the Kerlin Fund, I am only too happy to give you any information. We have, as you may have learned from the newspapers, been able to collect something over £2,500 ... one moment and I can give you the exact figures."

"Please don't trouble...an excellent sum in these bad times, and reflecting the greatest credit on your powers of persuasion. Have you decided what form the memorial is to take?"

"Probably a scientific scholarship, at one of the Universities if we can enlarge the fund sufficiently."

"Magnificent!—and so much better than putting up another statue. I congratulate you," said Mrs. Devonshire suavely. "However, I must not take up your time like this, but come to the point. Sir Neville, I want to speak to you in strict confidence."

Sir Neville, very much bewildered, bowed again.

"You have not—or have you—seen my granddaughter lately?"

"Biddy?...dear me, no. I have not seen the child since I wound up her father's affairs and handed her the securities."

"And you can, I imagine, hold your tongue?"

"In a good cause, certainly."

"Very well, this cause should satisfy you. I have sent the girl away. If any fools come applying to you to help her from this fund, be sure they do it without authority and refuse them."

"But I understood—forgive me, Mrs. Devonshire—that you had taken charge of your granddaughter," expostulated Sir Neville.

"My dear man, can you really suppose it possible to take charge of any responsible human creature?" Mrs. Devonshire raised her eyebrows in astonishment at such a notion, and then continued reasonably, "I took her into my house for a time certainly, but I am not immortal. If you must have it, I am a dying woman, but that I emphatically command you to mention to nobody."

"Dear me, I am greatly distressed, I..." stuttered Sir Neville, knitting his bushy eyebrows in a way he had in moments of embarrassment.

"Not at all," said his hostess calmly. "We must all come to it, but you will see, I am sure, that the house of an old dying woman of seventy-five was no place for a young girl. Biddy has had her own sorrows and held her tongue about them, to her credit;... moreover, I am not the woman to care for an audience in my last days, which are unlikely to be any credit to me," finished Mrs. Devonshire.

"I see. You sent her away then on account of your health?"

"That was my real reason, but not to be divulged to Biddy while I live. God bless my soul, do you think the girl would have gone for any such reason as that—having lived in my house all those months? The young even nowadays have their high notions—most of them wrong. Biddy, unless I mistake her, would have stayed in spite of me if she had had an inkling of the truth.... I picked a quarrel with her," explained Mrs. Devonshire, looking pleased with herself. "We had high words, oh, very high.... How else could I be sure she would stay away?"

Sir Neville mopped his brow. These tactics were beyond him; his mind was in a turmoil. An extraordinary woman, no wonder poor Kerlin...

"Then I have your word that you will keep my disclosures to yourself, Sir Neville, and refuse suggestions of help to the girl that may come from outside? I have reason to think some members of my family who have no authority in the matter may think fit to do so. Of course if Biddy herself asks for help that is quite another matter."

"Certainly. I think it unlikely from my knowledge of your granddaughter, Mrs. Devonshire. At the same time," said Sir Neville, "if I thought she was in any want I should certainly feel it my duty to see that she was provided for."

"She is in no want. That I know. She has friends and, I understand, an intention of taking up work to augment her income. There is a possibility she may fail, of course, and find it necessary to apply to you. In that event, Sir Neville," said Mrs. Devonshire, "I should be obliged if you will say nothing to the girl, but immediately communicate with me, as I should feel it my duty to reimburse the fund which the public has so generously subscribed."

"That is very good of you, very, and I greatly appreciate the delicacy of your offer," said Sir Neville. "I am not a rich man, but I feel some responsibility for my old friend's daughter.... You may rely upon me, Mrs. Devonshire."

Somewhat later he went away, without his subscription, but hardly conscious of it yet.

Mrs. Devonshire, out of the world these ten years, had not lost her touch. She had entertained him, alarmed him about Biddy, shocked him about herself, utterly bewildered him, and then provided her antidote, sending him away grateful for something which she would in all probability never be called upon to do.

As for her, she had made certain of learning what seemed to her in these last days of her life the one thing that mattered any more, something further of the girl who had intrigued and interested her, and perhaps, though she was not the woman to admit such a weakness, very nearly won her heart.

3

"And if you please, 'm, would you wish me to put the presents away?" inquired Simpkins.

Mrs. Devonshire glanced at the tallboy in her bedroom, on the top of which reposed the complete invalid outfit, Sholto's diary and Freddy's chocolate box.

"Certainly not," she said. "Leave them where they are. I like to look at them."

From her expression it was clear that Simpkins did not. She disliked what she called clutter, and there was no way of making the tallboy look orderly with bed-rests and gray woolen wraps and telephone dolls—the nonsense—all over the place. And the mistress such a one for order too, fidgeted by a mere thread on the carpet! The silly doll was forever falling over and there was another thing, that book or diary or whatever it was, standing against Mr. James's portrait, hiding the young gentleman up to the nose. Simpkins had put it down times out of number, yet whenever she looked, there it was back again.

"Seven presents," remarked her mistress, counting them. "Ah! a lucky number."

Simpkins produced the nearest thing to a sniff that her gentility would permit.

"There should have been eight," she muttered in an indignant tone.

"Then it is just as well there were not," returned Mrs. Devonshire.

"Well, 'm, ingratitude is a thing I don't understand and never did."

"No? But I understand it perfectly—revenge for benefits received, and gratitude the expectation of benefits to come."

Simpkins, intent upon her own private grievance, paid no attention, knowing from the tone of satisfaction that this was a remark which she was neither expected to understand nor required to answer. It meant that the mistress was in one of her pleased moods, pleased with her presents, no doubt, though Simpkins could not say much for them, and trouble enough they had brought her, what with the mistress thinking she must have broken her sworn word and let out to Miss Gwen or Mrs. James Devonshire that her lady was ill. She, Patty Simpkins, tell one of them? Not she, not if wild horses tried to drag it from her, she wouldn't.

Wild horses had been Simpkins' standby all her life, her last word. From the variety of misdemeanors into which these strange and ferocious beasts presumably wished to drag the defenseless woman they must have been closely related to the cockatrice, or even the more familiar person with horns whom she would not have felt it quite nice to mention by name.

Mrs. Devonshire commanded.

"Don't glare!"

"You would think she had forgot," said Simpkins doggedly, "not being so long used to our ways as you might say. But not a week before she went she spoke of it, when I asked should I put out the new gown for Miss Freddy's party. 'No,' she said, 'that's for dinner, Simpkins, to wear on my grandmother's birthday....' I'd have staked my life she'd have come...."

"I shouldn't do that. You are more used to me alive and, who knows, we may see her yet."

The mistress's tone was suddenly sharp.

"Which just shows," thought Simpkins, with that magnificent capacity for misinterpreting the being nearest to us which is common to us all. "She's hurt and no wonder. She's hankering for the child. I couldn't have believed it of Miss Biddy—no ... wild horses wouldn't have made me believe it."

Actually, that cry, "we may see her yet," had been merely a challenge to Fate, a subconscious insurance against something feared, for Mrs. Devonshire, though having no fabulous monsters to constrain her, could still believe anything of anybody.

Simpkins was a good soul but a fool. She made no allowance for temper and pride, would probably, poor creature, see fit to disapprove of both, though her mistress could have taught her better. A poor world we should have without them!

There were two other reasons (besides the best of all) why Biddy might not come back—assistance from outside, or a too easy success. Well, Mrs. Devonshire had seen to it that she should be informed of the one. Now for the other....

"Telephone Dawes for me, Simpkins. Ask for Mr. Dawes himself and see that you get him. Say I shall be obliged if he will find time to call as soon as possible—in person. I don't want any underling. The matter is private and important."

Simpkins departed. Mrs. Devonshire rested in a deep chair near the window because sleep evaded her this afternoon, and she had become impatient of lying down, a practice to which she had come reluctantly only in the last year or so.

The Dawes idea was an inspiration and she was pleased with it. Mr. Dawes would come to oblige her, as he had come before, knowing the house and what it contained. He would come hopefully and she must see that he did not go empty away—not quite empty—some little thing, some pretext...he could tell her so much.

Mrs. Devonshire looked out the window and saw a gray sky against which the tree-tops in the square stood deeply green. Suddenly rain broke from a cloud and began to fall, tapping the glass like a stealthy hand.

"Why can't you storm and be done with it?" she apostrophized the rain. "I dislike drizzle."

Apathetic, that was what it was, like so many people in the world today, whining and complaining, instead of falling into a good round temper and getting things done.

"I shall get up and go downstairs. This resting is a farce," she thought, throwing aside her rug impatiently and rising to her feet. "Rest? I have never rested in my life, why should I submit to it now?"

"Mr. Dawes will be pleased to wait upon you on Monday at four o'clock, ma'am," said Simpkins, returning.

4

Across the dinner-table from time to time Edith Fenwick glanced at the young, eager face of her guest and thought

a little incredulously of the lonely house in Portman Square
from which this bright presence had gone. Incredulously,
because Mrs. Devonshire had been always self-sufficing, and
alone for many years; yet the sense of loneliness remained
with Edith and with it a disquieting feeling that some key
to the situation lay in her hands.

She was reluctant to admit this thought. Though Biddy
had been in and out of the flat for a year or more, she
knew her chiefly through the chatter of Sholto and
Frederika, which, she was shrewdly aware, was probably
not at all. She did not subscribe to the theory that relatives
are privileged by the mysterious ties of blood or marriage,
or think that the middle-aged have some divine right to
counsel the young. Very rarely indeed, she believed, had
the two even a common speech. If she had any plea to
make to the girl (which her inclination denied) it was
from neither aunt nor elder, but from friend to friend.

But that denoted a degree of friendship in Edith's code.

Biddy was in blue of a shade that brought out the much
deeper blue of her eyes. She had none of the vivd beauty
of her mother, the other Brigid, and yet there was a fire
about her. Even in stillness, and she was often still, her
face was alight. Edith, who had not greatly liked Brigid
Devonshire, knew that she had felt from the first an increasing kindness for the girl.

There was a good deal of banter at the table, Sholto setting the pace, but how little that told you of any of these
young things, thought his stepmother. Perhaps it was so
popular among them for that very reason—a barrage—
wasn't that the old war term? Sholto himself, for instance,
with his airy manner and pleasant impudence, how slowly

and how seldom he had revealed himself during the ten years of their acquaintance! She remembered the school holidays after her marriage to John Fenwick when the boy had come to the flat for the first time. Accustomed hitherto to gardens and plenty of space, with convenient schoolrooms where the young could be entrenched, she had found the problem of a schoolboy in the flat alarming, but the sight of the lad awkwardly tiptoeing about like a repressed and unwelcome visitor, had shown her that young Sholto Fenwick already had had problems of his own.

Freddy, following this new and exciting member of the family doggedly from room to room, had said to him one morning:

"Why do you walk on your toes? Is it to make a squeak?"

Edith, from the study, had heard him reply in a loud whisper:

"My boots make such a row."

"Do they? How lovely! Let's hear."

"No, your Mother wouldn't like it."

"Why?"

"Oh, I don't know ... women don't."

"*Don't* they?" It was news to Freddy, but she was a literal child and accepted it round-eyed.

When luncheon-time came she led the way into the dining-room with a hushed air, on the tip of her toes.

"Is this a new game?" Edith had inquired.

"No, we're being quiet," explained Freddy in a hoarse whisper, "in case you have a headache. Have you one?"

Edith, denying any knowledge of such afflictions, had been conscious of her daughter's disappointed face.

"Well, Sholto's aunts always had," protested Freddy.

"Really? Poor things! However, Sholto is at home now luckily, and needn't be afraid of disturbing them, and if he can make more noise than you, Freddy, I shall be astonished."

A reckless invitation this, as the afternoon had proved, various thuds and yells suggesting that Freddy was endeavoring to settle the interesting question once and for all. Sholto's response remaining cautious, Edith had said to him rather shyly after breakfast next morning:

"I haven't done anything much to your room, Sholto, until you came home. You probably have all sorts of things you want to hang up and stow away, and if you think a set of bookshelves would be handy, we'll go out some time and you can choose it. You will find a hammer and nails here in this drawer."

"Oh, thanks."

An hour later she had found Sholto hovering at her elbow.

"You didn't mean I could put nails in the walls, did you?"

"Why, of course."

"Oh! ... I thought it might make a mess of the room."

"I don't think it need, and it's your room, so naturally you must do as you like with it."

"Do I keep it then? ... I mean always, in term-time and everything?" the boy had inquired in so incredulous a tone that Edith had had some inkling of what his previous holidays must have been.

"Oh, dear, yes," she had said lightly. "The men of the house must have their own rooms and there are locks on everything, so you can be sure your treasures are safe when you go back to school."

"Thanks awfully."

Sholto, during the following years, had done many fan-tastic things to his room, but term-time and holidays alike, the keys had stayed in their locks. They had not even been lost, though in general he was as disorderly as most of his kind.

Some days after this interview he had said to her awk-wardly:

"I say—er—what ought I to call you?"

Edith, seriously considering this delicate question, had suggested:

"How would Edith do? After all, I'm a member of the family now, and Mrs. Fenwick would sound so odd."

For the first time she had heard the sudden infectious shout of laughter that belonged to the normal Sholto then as now, and was always forthcoming in moments of relief.

Edith, looking at the sleek dark head and mischievous face of her stepson, reflected that, good friends as they were, he and she, most of her real knowledge of him had been gleaned from such slight incidents and her own conjectures, to which the dry comments of John and the transports of Freddy had added an occasional flash. The boy had a good deal more in him than he chose to reveal. Freddy was transparent to the point of absurdity; but what Biddy might be how could one know?

The young people decided after dinner to push back the drawing-room chairs and dance, and leaving John Fenwick to make a fourth, Edith retired to the study with a novel. Fifteen minutes later Biddy came in search of her.

"Oh, Edith, I wonder if you have a pin," she said. "I caught my heel in one of these flounces."

Edith found a needle and thread and tacked up the torn frock temporarily.

"You seem to have treated it rather badly, Biddy. There is another mend here, isn't there?"

"Yes, Simpkins has done it twice for me."

"What fine stitches, and she must be quite old," remarked Edith. "By the way, I was over there the other morning."

"On the birthday?" inquired Biddy.

"Yes. . . . I suppose you didn't join the procession, as your grandmother called it, this year?"

"Oh, no." The girl's tone was quick, and Edith saw her flush suddenly. "Just fasten it off anyhow. I didn't mean to give you all this trouble," said Biddy.

Edith, conscious of a kind of withdrawal and desire for flight, fastened the flounce and let her go. "I was quite right," she thought, returning to her novel, half-regretful, half-relieved, "there is nothing I can say."

She took up her book again, but her attention wandered and she found herself listening to the music and the rhythmic movement of the dancers, thinking of the past year and how curiously it had brought her back into the orbit, as it were, of Hugh Devonshire's mother. They had never been friends, far from it, yet the other woman had not merely permitted Biddy's friendship with Sholto and Frederika, she had had them both constantly at the house, taken them about, sent the three to theaters, or out to dance, on many occasions alone. She had shown herself indeed, thought Edith, extraordinarily liberal-minded for a woman of her years and circumstances, and yet those three dancing away in there with the solemn quiet of their generation at this exercise, were probably not in the least aware of it. They would have been amazed at any other attitude. Suddenly Edith saw that alliance of Biddy and her grandmother as far more incredible than the quarrel which had ended it. It could not have been expected to last, their years were too far apart, and she had been a fool to think that she might intervene.

"Edith, come and use your auntly influence here," called Sholto at eleven o'clock, "and tell Biddy you insist upon my taking her home."

"Edith, you use your stepmotherly influence and tell Sholto that he is not to stir out of the house," requested Biddy.

"I don't know which kind of influence sounds the more sinister," returned Edith, dryly. "No—to both of you."

The two combatants stood in the drawing-room doorway, Freddy sitting on a table nearby, presumably to act as referee.

"But, my lamb, I am not used to being a clinging vine," protested Biddy. "I've gone about alone in London for years."

"Still, there is a blue moon after all," said Sholto reasonably, at which she laughed and gave in.

"There is no moon," remarked Freddy, looking out the window. "It is dark as pitch and raining. They'll have to get a taxi. If I had known that I'd have gone too."

"You think they can't be trusted in a taxi?" inquired her stepfather in mild astonishment.

"Of course. They are not driving, stupid. Taxis are as safe as houses, but I would have liked a ride."

"I must buy you a perambulator," said John Fenwick, retreating.

The taxi sped through the rain along roads where the lights ran together in golden pools and the swish of the traffic was like the sound of the sea. Biddy lay back and thought it was fun (just for the last time) to belong to the world that goes home at its ease after dancing to music from Rome and Paris and Czecho-Slovakia.

Sholto looked at her every time they passed a lamp, and wondered what she was thinking and wished he dared tell her his own thoughts. The taxi-driver said to himself, "I'll get out of this blasted traffic and go round, they won't care."

He was probably right.

As Biddy put her latchkey in the front door of Number 25, Wincey Street, Sholto, standing on the step below her, said:

"Look here, I don't like your going up those stairs and into a pitch-dark flat alone."

"Dark?" retorted Biddy. "Nothing of the kind. You've forgotten your moon."

CHAPTER SIX

GENUINE ANTIQUES

JOSEPH DAWES, of S. Dawes & Sons, Dover Street, knew more about period furniture and antiques in general than most people. A man of high reputation and conservative manners, he was familiar with many great houses and such treasures as they contained, as had been his father before him, rather more perhaps since of late years many people, wishing to avoid the publicity of the auction rooms and needing money, had parted with first one rare piece and then another through his discreet hands.

Mr. Dawes had disposed of various valuable but not very attractive things for Mrs. Devonshire in the past (the money had gone to help pay the death duties on Highways after the loss of her second son—fruitlessly, as she reflected in her more bitter moments). There still remained in her possession, however, one or two pieces in particular that made any summons from the old lady a matter which Mr. Dawes was not the man to neglect.

Mrs. Devonshire guessed as much. Poor Mr. Dawes, of course, was going to be disappointed, but there was no need to tell him so brutally once and for all. Indeed such a course would be foolhardy, since she might require his services again. At the same time it was not her habit to employ any tradesman without paying for his services. Dawes was no butcher or baker but an expert, and no doubt an artist in his line, whose sensibilities, since he was a courtly man in his way, it would be polite as well as politic to consider. Mrs. Devonshire, with her fondness for tactics, had spent an amusing Sunday considering her plan of campaign.

She was aware that her efforts might be wasted, that Dawes might be able to tell her little now and nothing hereafter of what she wanted to know, but she was not to be deterred.

She had come to a place where she needed some occupation for her mind, to spin out the days. It was nothing more than that, she told herself firmly. What were the troubles and fooleries of the world to her any more? She had found it impossible to read her newspapers the last few mornings. Disarmament, tariffs, India, they were words, mere words, futile words. As well pick up a dictionary and read it!

It was unlikely that the girl had ever heard of Dawes. If she had heard of him it would be as a man too important for any mere beginner to venture to approach. But Dawes knew all the dealers worth the name, would know the prospects for a young woman whose fancies lay in that direction, and the probable procedure. Biddy had no capital, but she must have some plans. Aha! little she knew that her secret studies in this very house had been observed.

Mrs. Devonshire summoned Taylor on Monday morning to open up the closed bedrooms on the second floor, and went slowly through them, lifting the dust-sheets delicately in search of a consolation to fling to Mr. Dawes. The atmosphere reeked of moth-balls, which she disliked intensely, and she scolded Taylor who was in no way re-

sponsible, because camphor had not been used instead. And
then she remembered that this was of no consequence
whatever and told the woman to go away and get back to
her work. She would ring when she required her again.

The rooms as she went from one to the other looked
at her with empty faces. They had lost their identity, they
were muffled up like fools afraid of the air. She had no
patience with them. All these things of wood and metal,
these possessions, meaningless and cluttering up her life,
fretting her mind, and all for what? Grandeur, luxury,
comfort? Words!

She had been married into this setting fifty years ago
and here she was, with nothing done.

If any ghosts walked beside Mrs. Devonshire through the
shrouded rooms, she brushed them impatiently aside. She
had something to do now at last; she was busy. If in the
depths of her mind she knew this, like all the rest, to be
an illusion, she let that go. For want of something better,
an illusion must suffice.

Simpkins, lurking on the stairs, could contain her anxiety
no longer, and followed her mistress.

"All these windows open! It's scandalous. You'll catch
your death," muttered Simpkins.

"Well, if I don't, it will catch me," retorted her mistress.
"Go away! I will not be watched and pestered and you
know it, yet day in and day out you follow me with your
long face....Go away."

"Now where was I?" asked Mrs. Devonshire, alone again,
of the muffled room. "What am I looking for?"

A sudden blankness of mind held her alarmingly for a
few moments, and she struggled back to complete con-

sciousness as from something horrible. She was feeling her age, but she would not admit that, putting it down instead to illness and sleepless nights. She must make haste, there was no time to lose. She began to move briskly from room to room, driven by this sense of having something imperative to do, something worth doing before she died.

2

Joseph Dawes, in morning coat and Edwardian beard, was ushered into the long drawing-room, and looked about him as he waited for Mrs. Devonshire. Crossing the hall, he had seen with satisfaction the William-and-Mary cabinet safe in its niche. The Queen Anne bureau too, there by the window—ah, an elegant piece ... very little change here yet, he noted. ... Ha!

Mr. Dawes's eye had caught a glimpse of the bait which Mrs. Devonshire had spread for him. With the leisurely step and polite admiration of a visitor to the house, he strolled across the room to look at something he knew he had not seen here before. He heard a footstep in the hall, but did not make the mistake of turning back hastily to his chair. Mrs. Devonshire found him gazing with interest at an old French work-table.

"Pretty, very pretty," he remarked when they had exchanged greetings. "Louis Seize, I should say."

"Foreign fripperies," said Mrs. Devonshire, dismissing the whole bundle of Louis's. "That belonged to my mother-in-law. I never cared for it and, as a matter of fact, it has been put away upstairs for years."

"Ah, that is why I have no recollection of seeing it when

you were good enough to show me some of your pieces," remarked Mr. Dawes.

"You have a good memory, Mr. Dawes."

He smiled.

"How else, madam, should I live? I believe I can say with truth that I never forget a beautiful object, and rarely a face. . . ."

"But infinitely prefer the former," finished the old lady, pleased with herself. "You side with my mother-in-law, I observe . . . perhaps, shall we say, because she was not yours?"

"Ah, very true, very true. Association. There we have it, something stronger than fashion and taste. Is there by any chance a signature or any history attached to the worktable?"

"Look at it, Mr. Dawes, by all means look at it," Mrs. Devonshire waved a gracious hand. "I know nothing of its history, though you will agree that if it has never been described as the authentic possession of the unfortunate Marie Antoinette, there must have been gross carelessness somewhere," she said with a gleam and lift of her chin.

"Yes, indeed, poor thing, a lady of many possessions. I have met some, if you will believe me, of a period even later than her own," smiled Mr. Dawes appreciatively.

He was at the little table, examining it with an inscrutable face, deciding it was after all, though genuine, an inferior specimen. Mrs. Devonshire knew it, but was unconcerned.

"These are strange times, Mr. Dawes," she observed conversationally. "And now, I wonder, do they affect such a business as yours? There are private buyers still, here and there, I imagine?"

"Well, madam, yes and no," said Mr. Dawes.

"I am curious for a somewhat personal reason. A young member of my family, a granddaughter, of all unlikely people, has developed an ambition to enter the profession. A preposterous notion, but you know the young people of the present day, they go their own way; they will listen to no advice."

"Indeed?" There was reserve in Mr. Dawes's tone, and Mrs. Devonshire, conscious of his quick glance, composed her frowns accordingly.

"I do not pretend to know how she supposes she is to bring this miracle about," she said, "or where she is to obtain the requisite training and experience. An orphan, with infinitesimal means. Well! ... I have washed my hands of her."

"Difficult, very difficult," admitted Mr. Dawes, looking sympathetic and faintly relieved. "In these days ... with staffs cut down to a minimum. One does not like to be too positive; there may be firms of decent repute where a premium would obtain an opening of sorts for the young lady, if she could prove her aptitude, but otherwise frankly I think she will find you are perfectly right."

"There is no question of a premium," said Mrs. Devonshire. "None. The girl is a daughter of Kerlin, the explorer. You may recall all the sensation in the newspapers at the time of his death. The foolhardy girl had gone off to the Arctic against all reason and advice to meet him. That expresses these modern young people exactly. There is no money, moreover, and the sooner she is cured of this craze, the better. If she should apply to you, Mr. Dawes ... which would be, of course, great impertinence, a thing

these young people never consider...I trust you will be
good enough to put a few of the difficulties clearly before
her out of consideration for me. Not that I wish you to
mention my name in the matter. Far from it. That would
be fatal. We are not on terms, as they say, but naturally I
feel uneasy."

"Most certainly, madam. Kerlin, you said, Miss Kerlin?
I will make a note of it," said Mr. Dawes, taking out his
pocket-book.

"Biddy Kerlin."

"Miss Biddy Kerlin. I will give orders that if the young
lady calls I am to be informed at once. And in the mean-
time if I hear anything about her, perhaps you would like
me to send you word? There are ways...things get round
to one in the course of business....Though if this Miss
Kerlin should bring me some object of vertu she has had
the cleverness to pick up, I don't promise that I shall send
her with it to one of my rivals," finished Mr. Dawes with
a smile. "I am but human."

"Ah, if she performs a miracle," agreed Mrs. Devonshire
dryly, "I could hardly blame you. In fact, I will go further.
I'll take the thing off your hands if the price is within my
means. You see how little faith I have in miracles....Well,
Mr. Dawes, and what is your opinion of my mother-in-law's
work-table—or shall we call it Marie Antoinette's?"

"Genuine of its kind, madam, but a poor specimen of
the period."

"Ah! What do you say to my taste now? There is a
market for such things, however, or is there not?"

"Oh, certainly—at a price I should no doubt find a
buyer in time."

"Give me ten pounds for the thing and take it out of my sight."

"My dear madam, it distresses me to believe you should suppose me a robber," protested Mr. Dawes, shocked.

"A little reflection might persuade you that in that event I should have held my tongue," retorted Mrs. Devonshire with her dry smile.

The two, well-matched, and now in excellent form, proceeded to business. Mr. Dawes eventually wrote a check and engaged to have the obnoxious work-table removed. He had made a good bargain and handsomely admitted as much, though not in so many figures.

"And you will remember that tiresome girl, Mr. Dawes, and let me have word if you hear anything that you think I should know. What do you suppose that old cabinet of mine in the hall should fetch in these bad times, by the way?"

"Ah! there now you have something that will always bring its figure," exclaimed Mr. Dawes, betraying eagerness for the first time.

"Well, well, we'll see. I mustn't keep you now. Good-by, Mr. Dawes. I am much obliged to you. Be sure I will send for *you* if I decide to part with it...."

Mrs. Devonshire had rung the bell and the parlormaid stood at the door.

Mr. Dawes was ushered out, consoled by that faint but meaning emphasis, and pleased with his bargain.

A reasonable lady, most reasonable—a rarity, alas, in these hard times—and one whom it was a pleasure to serve.

The reasonable lady, having given Mr. Dawes a keen

desire to keep in touch with her in that final and dishonest hint, and provided him with a means of doing so
in the question of her granddaughter, Biddy Kerlin, decided she would go to her rest.

"Objects of vertu," she said to herself as she went,
"excellent!"

3

"I am sorry, V. C.," remarked Biddy on Monday to the
visiting cat, washing his whiskers in the middle of the rug,
"but now to work."

V. C. ignored her and went on with his toilet, a serious
matter not to be lightly interrupted. Having polished one
side of his black face he began on the other, turning his
ear inside out and scrubbing it conscientiously.

"Haven't you a bathroom at home then?" inquired
Biddy, "or have you mistaken the door? The public baths
are further down the street, my boy."

V. C. with one paw in the air, seemed to consider this,
and dismiss it as unreliable information, for he proceeded
almost at once to wash his backbone, a knotty business only
to be accomplished by standing on three legs and turning
the head back to front.

"Of course if this is a theatrical performance," said Biddy,
"I have nothing more to say."

She took out her notebook and studied the list she had
made from the Post Office Directory at the Free Library.
Far down on this list was the name of S. Dawes & Son,
Dover Street, but she had marked it with a query as rather
too august for her to approach, except as a last hope. Its in-
clusion was perhaps a challenge to Fate to prove to what

lengths she was prepared to go, if the worst came to the worst.

As this possibility recurred to her, she turned to the back pages of the little book, reserved for financial items. One side contained her assets, £41. 2. 6 in the bank; on the other she had written blithely:

"Rent for 6 months................. £36
Lighting, heating & laundry........   5.   2.   6

£41.   2.   6.

"Wash all but bed linen at home.
Food, fares, clothes and extras must not exceed £2 a week.
Must make £40 within the next 6 months. Ought to be able to do it."

Now she looked at it, this seemed no very reckless boast, but even if she did not succeed in justifying it, she was not going to be cast down. She would realize some of her securities and live on her capital until she was able to earn a regular and sufficient wage, she decided.

"And then," she said to the visiting cat, "you shall have cream on Sundays."

V. C. yawned widely and jumped on the window-ledge as though to say cream meant little in his life. If she had said poultry now....

Biddy closed her book, put on her hat and gloves with an air of finality and took the visiting cat under her arm.

"Call again some time," she said as she put him down in the passage and locked her door. "Before nine or after six I shall always be at home to you. Good-by."

Fourteen days later she was walking slowly down Dover Street to her "last hope," S. Dawes & Son.

Fortune had not been kind to her, quite the reverse. A spell of rainy weather had set in, and almost every day she had returned to the flat exhausted from tramping through mud and rain and waiting in damp shoes and steaming clothes for interviews which led to nothing. Some of the places on her list proved hopeless at first sight; in others she found it impossible to see any one in authority without stating her business, and then was quickly shown the door. When she did encounter kindness and courtesy she also received the greatest discouragement.

"But people must begin somewhere," she argued with herself, lying awake over the problem night after night. "They are all so old and successful they've forgotten.... Still, what's a fortnight? If I haven't got in anywhere in six months, it won't really matter."

In this way she had been in the habit of talking firmly to herself of nights at school when a visit from her father was due and her shoes wearing out again. "After all, if I don't manage to tell him, I can put a thick piece of cardboard in." They were so terribly prone to wear out, and breaking the news to him always such an embarrassment.

The clothes which her grandmother had sent after her were a great standby to her now, for it was uplifting to know that at least she would not have to go shabbily clad for some time to come.

"Actually, I have never been so well off in my life," said Biddy to herself daily as she dressed, "and I can sell some of the evening frocks if I find it necessary."

The outside of S. Dawes & Sons had a conservative air, but her spirits rose to the adventure ahead because she felt it was rather a joke to beard such a lion as this in his den, even if dangerous. It would be fantastic to have any hope of success, but she had determined to leave no stone unturned, even the largest.

Biddy, having thus converted her lion into a stone, opened the door and went in.

Dimly carpeted rooms stretched before her, austere, uncrowded, one after another, filled with a beauty that made her catch her breath. This was no shop, it was a gallery, and yet less cold somehow, more human. She walked to an old glowing table and bent over it eagerly, her face alight, the interview for the moment forgotten.

"Good morning, madam. What may I do for you?"

An assistant hovered deferentially, believing her a customer. That was good. You had to be cunning, as the last two weeks had taught her.

"I want to see Mr. Dawes himself if he is available, please," said Biddy, in what she hoped was the careless tone of authority.

"Well—er—I'm afraid Mr. Dawes is very deeply engaged this morning," said the assistant doubtfully. "But I can give you any information you require, I assure you. You are interested in this table—a fine specimen."

"Yes, but I don't care greatly for the period," declared Biddy. "I must see Mr. Dawes himself."

"Well, madam, I am very much afraid... but if you will give me your name... ?"

"Kerlin—Miss Kerlin...."

"If you will take a seat, Miss Kerlin, I'll see what I can do."

The assistant went away. He was not very old, he had had to begin, and how had he managed it? Perhaps he had had money and influence, but they couldn't teach you about antiques. He had joined another man, older, in the next room, and now a third. They were murmuring in hushed tones, looking at her. Biddy's excitement mounted. One man brought a book and they consulted it ... were they looking her up to see if she were really a customer? ... But even customers have to begin sometimes! ... Not a woman assistant anywhere. ... There he was, going into another room, he was out of sight.

It seemed an interminable age before he was back again, walking towards her like an avenging fate, to tell her, she was sure of it, that unfortunately Mr. Dawes could not be found, that he was out, or engaged with a duke.

"If you will kindly come this way, Miss Kerlin," said the assistant with a courteous smile, "Mr. Dawes is now disengaged."

She had done it. They thought she was going to buy a table. Triumph and guilt, hope and alarm fought together within her as she followed him.

"Miss Kerlin, sir."

Joseph Dawes, rising to motion the visitor to a seat, looked sharply at Mrs. Devonshire's granddaughter. He had expected, from the old lady's description, something rather different from this tall, self-possessed and yet very youthful-looking child, something more dashing, more flamboyant.

"What may I have the pleasure of doing for you, Miss

—er—Kerlin?" inquired Mr. Dawes, glancing at a slip of paper as though to verify the name.

Biddy drew a deep breath.

"Mr. Dawes, I want to learn about antiques," she said.

"Ah, the study of a life-time," smiled the old gentleman indulgently. "Well, I have been learning about antiques for sixty years, and am at your service. You want a table, I understand, a period table."

"No, I haven't come to buy anything, Your assistant misunderstood me."

"Indeed?" Mr. Dawes looked positively thunderous. "My assistants are not employed to misunderstand. I shall look into this."

"Please don't... because it was my fault. I let him."

"Extraordinary!"

"I had to see you," offered Biddy in urgent extenuation.

"Young lady, I am a busy man, and since you seem to have obtained this interview under a misapprehension, I shall be obliged if you will come to the point," said Mr. Dawes, looking at his watch with a frown.

"I want to learn about antiques seriously, as a profession. I know a little, but of course you would think it a very little," offered Biddy. "I don't know how I am to learn unless I can be taken as a pupil by somebody who knows everything."

"Madam, I am sorry, but this is no school for young ladies."

Mr. Dawes seemed about to rise, and Biddy said quickly:

"Is it because I am a girl?"

The old man sat down again and looked at her over his glasses as though speechless at such effrontery.

"I didn't come to you first of all....I knew you were too important," admitted Biddy, "but nobody seems willing to tell me what to do. There must be some way to begin, or how do men do it?"

"Ah, you have consulted other members of my profession. And what did they tell you?"

"Nothing at all. That's just it. One or two were very polite; some I didn't even see; some were quite unpleasant, and three places I didn't like the look of and went away."

"Indeed? And may I inquire what displeased you?" asked Mr. Dawes with a touch of asperity.

"They were selling things that were not genuine and pretending they were."

"A rash statement from an amateur, Miss Kerlin."

Biddy smiled at him, a sudden smile, impersonal and eager, as of one collector to another.

"But there are places like that and you can't tell till you try. I merely got the names out of a directory."

Mr. Dawes threw up his hands and then sat back in his chair, looking fatherly.

"My dear Miss Kerlin, take the advice of an old man, and give up this idea. Believe me, it is a pretty hobby, but no work for a young and gently bred girl."

"It is the thing I want to do," said Biddy to that. "I mean to do it too, somehow."

"Well, of course, if you have unlimited capital and influential friends behind you...."

"No, I have neither. I am an orphan. I have just a little money—enough to live on with care while I learn."

"You are very inexperienced," said Mr. Dawes, with a

faint smile. "Do you seriously suppose that without recommendations and without fees you will find some one ready to teach you in a few months what it has taken the greatest experts a life-time to learn?"

Biddy flushed.

"I have £2,000," she said, "I was going to live on it, but I'll spend it if I can't get my training any other way."

"Come, come! There you betray the recklessness of youth, Miss Kerlin. I should feel very uneasy if I did not warn you to be more careful of your disclosures to a stranger. There are, even in my profession," said Mr. Dawes with a sigh, "people who might take advantage of this fancy of yours, and who would leave you penniless all too soon."

"I shouldn't give it up without making careful inquiries," said Biddy with dignity. "I haven't told any one but you."

Mr. Dawes bowed.

"Be wise," he said persuasively. "Take a business course that will fit you for a secretarial post, as many other young ladies of good family are doing nowadays."

"You must care for your work to succeed," argued Biddy eagerly. "I should be a bad secretary, and it is more than a fancy. The trouble is, you see, that until I get into a firm I am an outsider. And I know from watching sales that an outsider is terribly handicapped."

"Dear me, you surprise me. In what way?"

"If you want to buy anything ... the dealers bid against you immediately."

Mr. Dawes concealed a smile.

"Forgive me, but you seem very young to have had such

inconsiderate treatment at the hands of my colleagues," he said.

"Oh, I wasn't buying. I couldn't afford to. I went to watch and learn things. I have been going to every sale I could for three years."

"Hm!" The old man looked at the girl reflectively, remembering his promise to old Mrs. Devonshire, and aware of a certain quality in this member of her house, hardly a likeness, something more subtle than that.

"You have grown up among treasures?" he inquired suddenly.

"Oh no. My father was a scientist and we have always been poorish," said Biddy.

"Reserved," thought Mr. Dawes, "no flaunting of her family. Hm."

"Well, Miss Kerlin, I must send you away, but I will say this. There are still to be found here and there objects of vertu in unlikely places, even by outsiders. I do not advise you to go and look for them, far from it, but if you are determined that this is your trade, you might do worse. If you find anything, bring it to me, and you shall have a fair verdict and, if it is something I consider worth buying, a fair price."

Mr. Dawes stood up.

"Experience is your best teacher at present, but mind, it is a hard life, a life of many disappointments. You need a steady head, a will of iron and an inexhaustible patience, believe me."

"And yet you do need something else too, don't you think?" said Biddy slowly. "A sort of ... a well, a feeling? I can't explain it exactly."

"Ah, if you have that," admitted the old dealer, "I shall see you back, whatever I say."

"I'll be back," said Biddy, "if it takes me a year. You've been terribly good to me."

"Not at all." Mr. Dawes called a member of the staff. "Just take Miss Kerlin round, Williams, and let her see anything of particular interest before she goes."

"Yes, sir. Tables?"

Biddy and the old dealer exchanged a secret smile.

"Tables? certainly not. Anything, everything," commanded Mr. Dawes. "Good morning, Miss Kerlin."

A methodical man, he then drew out a sheet of notepaper and wrote to Mrs. Devonshire.

"My dear Madam:

"The young lady, Miss Kerlin, called upon me this morning. She has been seeking without success a post in a firm where she may learn the antique business. I believe I have dissuaded her from trying further which would probably be futile and might be dangerous if she fell into the wrong hands. I have vilified my profession in the hope of curing her of the fancy, but your granddaughter is not, I fear, a young lady to be lightly turned from her course. It is even possible she may succeed in spite of us. I shall make it my business to inform you of anything further I may learn of her activities.

"I should add that she gave me no information about her family or connections, though I made one or two opportunities. I felt this might relieve your anxiety somewhat, as showing she is not without dis-

cretion and has a desire to succeed on her own merits.
"Believe me to be, dear Madam,
　　　　"Your obedient servant,
　　　　　　　"JOSEPH DAWES."

CHAPTER SEVEN

BAIT

B IDDY'S IMMEDIATE response to that morning's
adventure exhibited her youth rather more than her
discretion. She decided to give a party. Frederika had not
yet seen the little flat, Sholto had not seen its green walls.
For more than a fortnight she had neglected them basely,
and now she decided she could draw breath for a moment.
She felt that her life had begun. True, she had obtained
no position, but she had won the interest of a man high
in her chosen trade, and that was something she had not
dared to hope.

Almost straight from this triumph, she sought a telephone-box, rang up Frederika, suggesting a country tramp
on Saturday afternoon, to include Sholto too, if he were
free, and a picnic supper afterwards in Wincey Street.

Freddy agreed with enthusiasm, and Sholto endorsed
the acceptance by letter quite unnecessarily the same night.
Early on Saturday afternoon a green 'bus was carrying the
three friends away through outer London to Buckingham-
shire, where they proposed to cut across country, returning
by train whenever, as Sholto put it, they met one that
looked tractable and sweet.

Sholto was in good feather after two weeks of anxious
despair, during which all his persuasion had not brought
him a sight of Biddy. Even the presence of a third person

could not damp his spirits, since the person was only
young Frederika, who never saw anything she was not
intended to see. For, after all, this was Biddy's party; she
had invited him of her own accord. Supper was to be a
housewarming, she said. Freddy and he were her very
first guests. This illuminating fact banished the picture
he had had of Biddy living an alien life which he was
not permitted to share. She had merely been busy, bless
her!

Berries were already scarlet in the hedges, the river, as
their chariot topped a rise, coiled away below them like a
silver snake, through fields and gardens and woods turning golden and red. Hoary with dignity and years the
castle looked over Windsor and Eton to Stoke Poges and
a poet's grave. In Burnham Beeches the leaves were already beginning to spread a crimson carpet under October's lovely feet.

They saw the autumn in its glory before them and, dis-
mounting, plunged into it joyfully, breasting the wind
with hearty zest. White ribbons of cloud were flung out
across the sky; rooks sat in the fields from which the har-
vest had been gathered as at an eternal feast, and a last
poppy lifted a saucy head at the edge of the road. The
sun, like a child's balloon, drifted down towards the west,
but slowly as from a day too good to leave.

They agreed with the sun, though not in so many
words, the traditional melancholy of the fall of the year
waking no response in their youthful blood.

Glowing and hungry, late in the afternoon they found
a deserted tea-garden on the outskirts of the Beeches, and
shared a vast meal of bread and jam with a robin just

about to get into his winter vest. He was a convivial bird
with a healthy appetite, and when Sholto addressed him
on the subject of his bulging front, he cocked his head and
gazed at the lecturer out of one eye.... Derisively, Biddy
declared, but Sholto said no, the bird was impressed and
would do slimming exercises in future.

Freddy threw the robin another crumb which he
promptly devoured.

"Of course," said Sholto, "if you are going to corrupt
my disciples, I shall have you ejected from the meeting."

At this moment the owner of the garden appeared and
said it would be two-and-three, darkly, as though she
resented it. They took this as a hint and said farewell to
the robin, making off in the direction of Beaconsfield in
search of a train.

"Because," said Biddy, "I want to look at all these little
towns. I might find something in one of them with luck.
You never know... or there might be a sale in one of
the houses coming off. You see them advertised on the
hoardings sometimes."

"How are you getting on?" inquired Sholto.

"All right. I haven't made any money yet, but I have a
sort of order. It is terribly exciting."

Sholto, thinking of Biddy rushing about the country in
all weathers to sales, was filled with disquiet, and yet she
looked so pleased about it.

"I wonder why you want to do this?" he said.

"Well, why do you want to do your job, and why does
Freddy want to play tennis?"

"Hanged if I know. Why do we? Why does anybody
want to do anything?"

"We can't just sit," said Biddy.

Frederika stopped for a word with an ancient cart-horse leaning over the fence. The other two tramped on, busy with their own private problems, off-handed about them in speech, because that is the way of youth, yet each seeing something, however vague, some light that seemed the one thing to pursue, secretly, eagerly.

Sholto wanted restlessly to get things done, vast things and many of them, politics, he supposed, would be the only way, but to let that out even to Biddy was impossible. A fine fool she'd think him.

"You see, I have to do something for a living, and I chose this years ago," remarked Biddy reasonably.

"If you hadn't to earn money, would you still be as keen, do you think?"

"Oh, rather."

"But look here, Biddy, won't you want to keep the things when you find them?"

"No...because I can't."

"That's no answer. That's just boasting of your stiength of mind."

She laughed.

"Then I don't think I shall....I can't explain. Of course I should like to have everything beautiful about me, but not too much...just a very little. It's finding them...."

"All hidden away and neglected," she thought, "and bringing them back to life, but that's ridiculous and sounds so sentimental. Sholto would laugh, any one would. And yet things are friendly or just horrid, they have a sort of life, and you couldn't make another person under-

stand if he didn't know it already. Mr. Dawes knows....
Grandmother didn't know, in spite of her lovely house;
she didn't even notice the old rose box."

"I don't like the thought of your having to go and bargain with a lot of men," said Sholto, frowning.

"Poor old Victorian papa," mocked Biddy with a burst
of laughter, which brought Frederika running.

"What's the joke?"

"Aha, you've missed it. If you will stop for a word with
all the local rustics what can any one do?" recited Sholto.

"I like horses, wish I had one," said Freddy.

"No, no, be kind to dumb animals. What you need is
an elephant, dear one."

"Funny!"

Frederika, hands in pockets, fell into step beside them,
grinning happily, her face lifted to the cold air and the
scent of turf and trees. Country-born, this was home to
her. She could outlast Sholto both in content and tireless-
ness on any expedition, as he knew well.

"Hard on her," he thought, "born to a place like Highways and then turned out by a fluke to make room for
that little rotter, James. Wonder what she thinks of it?
Life's a rum go.... Here we are, the three of us, all mixed
up, with the chances, any one would have thought a dozen
years ago, dead against it."

Sholto, remembering those distant days, said suddenly
to Freddy:

"If you want a horse, you young ass, murmur a word
in John's ear. He would let you hire one to ride in the
Row."

Freddy snorted.

"I wouldn't be seen dead in the Row!" she told him with scorn.

"No, perhaps the poor old horse would, though. Pity camels are so scarce. You'd look well on a camel, I must look out for one. Awkward to find a garage for it, unless we took the Albert Hall."

"You don't garage a camel, you stable it if anything," said Freddy.

"Not at all. My flock of camels are particular."

"Are you sure they are not really a herd of nightmares?" put in Biddy.

"Oh, of course, if I have to cope with two of you, I shall relapse into silence," said Sholto with great dignity. "That's right, laugh."

2

Biddy at home!

For that's what she had made of the green room—a home, thought Sholto, banished to smoke a cigarette while Freddy hovered in the slip of a kitchen and shouted news to him of the wonders being performed therein.

Darkness had come. Standing at the window, they had watched the old church tower at the end of the street, fading into the mist, and lights break out like so many friendly, watching eyes. Now the orange curtains were drawn, the gas fire glowing, the small round table set for supper, with fruit and cheese-straws, and coffee-cups on the mantelpiece for want of room. Biddy had made the cheese-straws this morning, and cooked a chicken to a lovely brown. But first there was to be an omelette, just to demonstrate what she could do to Sholto, who had doubted it, she said.

Sholto doubted nothing about her, except the one thing most important of all, that such a girl would ever waste a serious thought on him.

She had made this place with a mere twenty pounds; she had been rather extravagant, she said, for after all she had had blankets and linen, and knives and forks, stored away. You couldn't be sure of them in furnished rooms, and she and her father had bought them in an affluent moment. And the bookcase. It was a good one, but rather empty now, for she had given her father's books to his friends.

What had he been like? Sholto wondered. There was no photograph of him or any one else to be seen. Biddy's only two pictures yet were posters, rather well framed and colorful, bought secondhand for ten shillings each in a reckless moment to cheer the old brown walls.

Extravagant? Reckless? Sholto, who could remember how unhomelike some homes may be on forty times the sum, smiled at the terms she used, this girl who loved things that were beautiful and rare for their own sake, and yet who was able to get an effect like this for twenty pounds.

The sitting-room door-handle rattled suddenly.

"Seems to be some one there, Biddy. Shall I go?" called Sholto.

"Please!"

"Well, I'm dashed.... Hi, there, Miss Kerlin, a gentleman to see you."

Biddy's head appeared.

"Yes, that's the visiting cat. He often looks in...my only follower."

"Aha, that's all she knows," said Sholto privately to the visitor, who, however, brushed past him without a word and took up his place before the fire like the man of the house.

"I call him V.C. for short," explained Biddy, bringing in the omelette.

"Looks a military fellow," agreed Sholto. "Anglo-Indian, by his dark complexion. How do you like your mice, colonel, curried?"

V.C. ignored him and a little later, with an air of dignity and long-suffering, departed from the riotous company about the supper-table, the din being more than he could bear.

"Gone to his study, no doubt," said Sholto. "I rather think he has blood pressure, Biddy. The cat is quite flushed."

3

Somewhere about the same hour, Richard Dawnay was having an interview with his son, a stormy interview, for Herbert had urgent business, he said, elsewhere and was being detained at serious inconvenience to himself and others.

"I don't care anything about that, sir," cried his father. "You treat this house as a hotel and throw me a word as a favor when it pleases you. I'll have no more of it. It is high time you practiced your profession, and I tell you plainly your allowance will cease at Christmas. I will not pour money away on you and deprive your mother and sisters any longer."

"No one can make money at the Bar all in a moment," said Herbert sulkily.

"A moment? You've had three years. If it hadn't been for your grandmother you'd have had no profession. You know perfectly well my income could not have stood the strain of all your extravagant notions. How do you suppose I can provide for your mother and sisters on my pension in three years' time? I have had to cut out my golf, the only recreation I ever had, and deny myself in every possible way, and deny them, in order to save against my retirement, and you know it. Your grandmother has wasted her money, but I'll waste no more of mine."

"Well, Father, I'm the eldest grandson, and your only son. Hang it all! I have a right to expect something, surely? I am not the only one Granny has wasted her money on, as you put it," said Herbert injured. "The girls have had their bit, schools and coming-out and so forth, and God knows what Aunt Marion hasn't had for James. What else has the old lady to do with her cash?"

"Upon my word, have you no decency or sense of obligation, Herbert? I am ashamed of you. And don't you ask your grandmother for another penny, do you hear me? If you do, you will go out of this house and not return to it."

"Oh, all right." Herbert smiled a superior smile, knowing, he thought, one better than that. "And now, if you don't mind, I must be off. Can't afford to offend possible clients."

He left the room airily and on the way out, looked into the drawing-room in search of that good ally, his mother.

"The ancestor is acting the heavy parent," he confided. "Cutting off the old allowance at Christmas. Says if I ask Granny for help I am no longer his chee-ild. You'll have to see her for me, Mum, eh? You won't leave little Herbert to starve?"

"Oh, my darling boy, don't say such dreadful things! You know I'll do what I can, but poor Mother is so unreasonable, so sharp, and I get upset. If you would just earn a little, Herbert. I'm sure your father doesn't mean to be hard, but money is terribly scarce. Look, dear, there's actually a hole in the carpet now," cried Mrs. Dawnay, almost in tears.

"Never mind, Mum, something'll turn up. You can get round Granny, you know you can. And now I must fly."

Herbert went off whistling, hailed a cab and drove to the Embassy to meet his "client".

"Funny things, ancestors," he thought, "so fond of the high horse."

He believed in taking things lightly, and his father's admonitions did not weigh upon him. A touch of liver, no doubt, combined with a touch of fright at the state of the country. All the older generation were the same, dashed unfair too, considering how gay a time they'd had in that old pre-war world of theirs. After all, they made the war we hear so much about, but we have to suffer for it.

Herbert was not going to lose any sleep; his mother would see to it, as she had done in the past. And besides, there would be Granny's money coming along in the course of time. Bound to be. Come to that, he could probably raise a bit on his expectations if the worst came to the worst.

"When's the great play coming on, Herbert?" inquired his partner.

"Eh?...Oh, that's off, my dear. The fellow let me down, turned out a perfect fool and I had to drop the thing. If you'll believe me, he wanted music in the Debussy style. Well, I ask you, why not dear old Chopin at once?"

"I know—tum, tum, ti, tum, tum, tum," said the girl. "So Queen's-Hall-like...ghastly."

"However, I have another scheme that I think you'll agree is It. Not a word, however—anti-Talkie stuff, you might call it. No words, no music, just color, movement and light. I've met a decorator chap who is the last word. All the faces will be colored green, yellow, orange, blue and so on, hair gold and silver, background black, very subtle."

"But how thrilling!"

Herbert's partner thought pageants rather worse than the Queen's Hall, and what was this latest notion but a dear old pageant in disguise? Still, she liked to hear what was going on. It was her line to know things, so why damp the poor lad? Besides, he danced so well.

"Tell on," murmured Herbert's partner encouragingly.

4

Mrs. Devonshire sat at the Queen Anne desk, tearing up letters with an impatient hand. It was a task that must be done and it would take some hours each day, but she could not pretend that she liked it, and after every few letters she found it necessary to rest because her hand was shaking. The illness was gaining upon her, she was weak from pain and the long restless nights which she endured and denied to the doctor. When she could endure no longer she would give in and take his drugs, but no doctor in the world should coerce her before she was ready to permit that liberty.

Now that she was alone with none to see her, she sat inert for long moments, looking what she was, an old woman, grievously ill; but at a sound she was upright again, with some of the old fire in her quick glance.

"The letters, madam."

"What, more?" said Mrs. Devonshire, with a gesture towards the pile on her desk. "Upon my word, you would think the world had something better to do."

She took her post from the parlormaid and slit the envelopes briskly, but when the girl had gone she did not open them at once. They would tell her nothing she cared to know, ask her nothing she cared to give. She had an impulse to toss them into the fire, but remembered such an act might bring her visitors instead, even more unwelcome, two of them certainly. The third was from an old friend who spent her life in this curious fashion, covering sheets of notepaper with words in a beautiful fine hand, all about nothing.

"Nothing whatsoever," said Mrs. Devonshire, tearing the sheets neatly across unread with an air of satisfaction, because they at least could be ignored.

At the other two letters she frowned...Marion wanting something as usual, no doubt!

Marion had called but found darling Granny not at home. And on such a wet afternoon she had been certain of finding her in. Still, when one had a car, what did weather matter? A car must be such a comfort. Marion was so worried about dearest James and wanted Granny's advice. The boy had a wretched cough and the doctor had been quite alarming. He advised the South of France for the winter as a precaution, and said you could get down so comfortably by the Blue Train, but even if she were to let the house, which would be very inconvenient, Marion didn't see how they could possibly manage the expense. Mr. Crow was most unreasonable and would advance nothing, and surely as head of the family the boy's health should be considered....

On and on went Marion's letter, but darling Granny read no more of it. Head of the family ... words, words.... What family? ... Whose family? ... "and death duties so heavy," quoted Mrs. Devonshire with a gleam. She seized a sheet of notepaper and wrote:

"DEAR MARION:

"If your boy has a cough, see that he has plenty of fresh air and exercise and don't coddle him. I can give you no further advice, unless to suggest that to refer to him as the head of the family until he has acquired one is misleading and surely rather indelicate...."

"Comfort of a car indeed," said Mrs. Devonshire, finishing her letter with an indignant flourish. She had not been out in the comfort of a car on that wet day. She would take no more journeys till the last, but to all the world,

with a few exceptions—old friends, so old that they in
their own feebleness would not notice hers, and one or two
others who could tell her something she wished to know
—she was and would not be at home.

Wished to know...she repeated the phrase blankly.
What was it? She could not think, could not remember.
Her mind groped and for the second time of late found
only emptiness. Yet she had been thinking something...
something important.

Yes, yes, she had it, something she wished to know...
those who could tell her. Dawes and Edith. Relief swept
over her, leaving her shaken. This would not do. There
was still much to do. She must get on.

A few hours ago she had telephoned Edith, a thing she
had not done half-a-dozen times in her life. She had rung
ostensibly to ask the name of a book Edith had mentioned
on her birthday, and finding her not at home had left a
message with the servant. When Edith rang she must be
on hand to take the call in person, for she had a bait as an
excuse to summon her, here on her hand, should Edith
say nothing on the telephone which she desired to hear.
She twisted the loose ring round her old finger, then with
a sigh pulled the last letter from its envelope and found
the car confronting her again.

"DARLINGEST GRANNY,

"Mummy won't ask you and says I am impertinent,
but I know you will do something for your little May.
Gwyn and I are asked to a very special dance at a
simply huge house at Hampstead on Wednesday.
Mummy doesn't like our taxi-ing home so late. Would

you be a perfect angel and let us have the car if you are not using it that night, for a very special reason, precious? Now aren't you curious? Perhaps I'll come and tell you something if you're very good.

"Your loving
"MAY."

"The car, the car, the car," said darlingest Granny, tapping her foot. "They'll require the house for a wedding next, no doubt. Ah well, some one else can deal with that." She rang the bell and sent for Simpkins, who came with suspicious haste. Simpkins, on these afternoons, had taken to hovering downstairs on every kind of pretext, and whenever the drawing-room bell rang, appearing morose and anxious before the parlormaid's nose: "Giving me the creeps, that's what you do, I declare, Miss Simpkins. Can't I answer me own bell without being spied upon?" ...

"Telephone Mrs. Dawnay and say the young ladies may hire a Daimler for Wednesday night, and put it down to me," requested Mrs. Devonshire. "Say that is the best I can do. And then ring the company and tell them the car will be required. Wednesday night, mind. Not a month or a year."

"I can do no more," she repeated to herself as Simpkins departed.

If there was anything in this scatter-brain's hints, anything but a ruse to get the car, Gwen would be wanting to come as usual, to talk things over, to clamor for advice, for help, demanding as she had been all her life. Even in her own love affair—should she marry Richard? Did Mother think it was wise? How did it feel to be married?

Gwen was so frightened. And when her children were coming, frightened again, no reticence, no self-control. And always money, money, money to be poured out for this or that, as though it grew on the trees in Portman Square. Never standing on her own feet. ... Gwen would be wanting to come, but she must find her mother not at home, in bed with a cold, away for a change, anything. A dying woman would not have her house over-run by these people, fussing, frightened, demanding. She would have decency and peace. Gwen must not know, or Marion ... none of them.

Mrs. Devonshire tore up Marion's letter, tore up May's; they were finished and done with. She would have no more of them. From a drawer she drew out one more to her taste, of more account, and read it through again, the familiar phrases beating to the tune of her mood ... "not lightly to be turned from her course" ... "a desire to succeed on her own merits. ..."

Standing on her own feet, in short.

The parlormaid was at the door again.

"If you please, madam, Mrs. Fenwick has called with this book, but she says if you don't wish to be disturbed I was not to trouble you, she'd just leave the book; she had it in the house."

"No, no—show Mrs. Fenwick in ... but nobody else, please."

Mrs. Devonshire turned off the reading-lamp and closed the desk, moving to the dim center of the room lit only by the fading light and the glow of the fire. She twisted the ring on her finger as she moved and smiled again, triumphantly.

"I didn't mean to come in," said Edith, "unless you felt inclined for visitors. I ran round with the book you asked about, as I happened to have a spare copy."

"Good! You save me from a disagreeable duty...tearing up letters, which I detest. Letters either say nothing or ask too much. And you bring me the book? Thank you, Edith. You thought that it was amusing, as I remember."

"Very caustic," said Edith.

"Ah, like to like," flashed Mrs. Devonshire. "Well, curiously enough, Edith, I have a present for *you.*" She took off the loose ring, a fine hoop of sapphires and diamonds, and dropped it into Edith's hand.

"For *me?*"

"I came across it among my things a day or two ago. It has grown too large for me, and I thought of you," observed the old woman evenly. "Hugh was fond of it...but perhaps you have forgotten Hugh."

"No, I have not forgotten Hugh," said Edith gently, "or the ring and how he liked you to wear it. I...I wish you would go on wearing it."

"And lose it in the first hour?...Nonsense! You would have had it years ago I daresay if I had not been a jealous old woman."

"Oh, well, mothers are privileged to be jealous for their eldest sons."

"I doubt it....However, put it on. I am not afraid of your magnanimity."

"I am not in the least magnanimous," protested Edith.

"Exactly. Do you think you would have been offered it, if you were?"

Edith put on the ring, laughing a little, yet moved and seeking for words.

"I know how my second marriage must have hurt you, Mrs. Devonshire," she said, "but I will value it, more than I can say."

"Hurt me?" echoed her mother-in-law. "My dear Edith, it is quite evident to me that you have never been jealous. I was delighted."

She leant back in her chair, lifting her chin in the old triumphant fashion, and suddenly her heart was light.

"You were wise and right to marry, and Hugh would have thought so, for a more laudable reason than any of mine," she said. "You know that. And you are happy? I have no need to ask. You know, for some curious reason that is a consolation to me. I can't think why."

The ring shone in the firelight on Edith's finger. She looked at it and then at the old mocking face endeavoring to conceal all that the gift of it implied.

"Retributive justice, let us say," suggested Mrs. Devonshire, as one anxious to decide the point. "No? A deathbed repentance then, perhaps?"

"I am no good at this sort of thing," said Edith, shaking her head with a smile. "You need Sholto to cap your phrases."

"Ah, yes, a master mind. And what has he been doing this bright afternoon, I wonder?" Mrs. Devonshire's tone conveyed only the lightest and most casual interest, but almost as though some sixth sense might have been prompting her. Edith Fenwick looked towards the window and the gathering dusk, and once more she was seeking her words.

"They will be on the way back to town by now," she said; "they have been for a tramp in the country, the three of them, and are going back to supper at Biddy's little flat."

"So Biddy entertains, among her other activities, and owns a flat?"

"This is the first time, I believe. She has a bed-sitting-room, bathroom and kitchen."

"Indeed? Well, that sounds most adequate," remarked Mrs. Devonshire in a honeyed tone. Yet her heart sang within her and triumph was hers. Old and ill she might be, but she was not spent. Edith, even Edith had walked into her trap and told her what she wanted to know. The bait had been quite unnecessary, yet as it glowed on the hand of Hugh's wife she was not sorry to see it there, and knew that the old bitterness had gone. She had never doubted Edith's integrity, and now she could accept her kindness too, glad to know that both would be there for the child when she had gone.

"Out in the country, are they?" she remarked briskly after a moment. "But surely Biddy is tactlessly making a third? Sholto and Frederika—or am I wrong? It seemed to me there was an attachment in that quarter."

"Sholto and Freddy?" Edith looked amused. "Oh, dear, no. It is a purely fraternal one. They are great pals, fortunately, and as Sholto has many friends, Freddy has a very good time, but as for sentiment, she scorns it. Her sex instincts seem to be undeveloped....I believe that is the correct term."

"Certainly not. You should say, 'My darling is so innocent.'"

Edith laughed.

"My darling, as you call her, would let me hear of it, if I did. Innocence is the last thing to which they will admit."

"Yet she still vaguely imagines babies are found in cabbages?"

"Not she; but she thinks it would be a handy arrangement."

"Well, I can admit to sharing that view myself long ago," said Mrs. Devonshire, "and how indelicate we should have been thought to put it into so many words. Words, words, words, how seriously we took them, and how little they mean. We were muffled in words...."

She moved impatiently, then smiled as at a sudden thought.

"Can you wonder they have discarded them, these young people, and say nothing at all? This capacity for holding their tongues is positively instructive, Edith. Believe me, I've never had a more amusing year...."

"Let me send them all round to see you one evening," was Edith's impulsive response to that.

"No, no, my dear, I am old and crotchety, and should snap their heads off."

"They would get over it."

"But I might not, and think how humiliating that would be." Mrs. Devonshire dropped her mirthful tone. "The fact is, I am tired and not very well and I like to take my ease. The vigorous creatures are a little too much for me. When I feel equal to them I will let you know. I shall not forget."

"And here I sit, tiring you out," exclaimed Edith, jumping to her feet. "No, please don't ring or move. I can find my way quite well." Her cool hand held the old one for a moment; speech deserted them and was unneeded.

"You know I'll come any time you want me," said Edith from the door.

"Yes...good-by, my dear."

Mrs. Devonshire closed her eyes. The parlormaid came in to draw the blinds and turn on the lights, but she sent her away. It was restful in this old room with the chill of autumn outside the windows and the warmth of the fire within, and for the moment she wanted nothing more, not even memory, not even thought. Peace and the kindliness of familiar things enfolded her as she fell asleep.

CHAPTER EIGHT

GWYNNETH

MAY DAWNAY'S hint to her grandmother had been more than a ruse to get the car. Intelligent anticipation one might call it perhaps, which the dance at the simply huge house at Hampstead in due course converted into an accomplished fact.

The house was certainly immense and opulent to the last degree. A bronze St. George stood on the newel-post and slew the traditional dragon with one hand while he lighted the stairs with the other. Flocks of Mercurys sprang out of the walls on one toe to perform a like benevolent service for the ballroom; fountains, each illuminated (like the saintly, from within), threw up glittering spray behind a solid phalanx of hothouse blooms. All the furniture was modern, and the curtains, carpets and chair-covers were patterned in streaks of lightning, mountain ranges and the other spiky devices which have so intelligently replaced the fat roses, the swirls and twining leaves of the Victorian era.

May thought it was a lovely house, scrumptious, she told her young host, who had by sheer chance (which May knew all about) sauntered to the wide-open hall door just as the Daimler arrived, and then run down himself to lift her out, bodily, and give a brotherly hand to Gwynneth.

All that Gwynneth thought for the moment was that this was May's party; you couldn't doubt it, May was the

154

chief guest; for there was their hostess, Basil's very young-
looking mother, holding her by the hand and fussing over
her, and Basil himself hovering by, beaming all over his
good-tempered face.

May, in her pink net frock, all little frills, was the prettiest
thing, and Basil's mother said so to Gwynneth, as one
woman to another, and said, "We must be great friends,
you must call me Joy," and then squeezed her hand and
went to greet another guest.

Gwynneth stood, partners were brought, she danced, she
agreed that she was May's sister, that it was a good floor,
a posh show, a riot. She saw May's pink frock flowing
past, heard her happy laughter, knew that May was leaving her, but it was all right. It must be all right. Basil was
kind and he couldn't help his mother's looking like that,
and May would be happy. Perhaps it was as well they had
had the Daimler after all, though Gwynneth wished they
hadn't asked Granny for it. It was so hateful to be always
asking. Mummy would be pleased because of Daddy's retirement. It would be dreadfully quiet at home, but perhaps
May wouldn't live too far away, ... not that you could be
always going to May . . . even to look after her, you
couldn't. . . .

Basil and May swept down upon her, seized her from
her partner and, laughing, carried her off between them
into a corner.

"Gwyn, what about it? I want to send that chauffeur
fellow of yours home by Tube, and then when the show's
over I'll drive you both in the old 'bus out to a spot I
know where we can get bacon and eggs. Say yes. Be a
sport, girl."

"But he isn't our chauffeur; it isn't our car," said Gwynneth. "We can't."

"No, darling idiot, Granny's car," put in May. "Didn't I tell you? Oh, dear, it's such a perfect scheme, Gwynny. Couldn't we?"

"No. Not possibly."

"Oh, I say. I'd take care of the lot of you, 'bus and all, and the chauffeur will hold his tongue if I make it worth his while. Granny so strict, is she?"

"Oh, *you* know," gurgled May. "Portman Square. Can you fancy Portman Square going out at this hour for eggs and bacon?"

"We mustn't, Basil, we mustn't really," said Gwynneth. "Mummy would think we had been run over. She'd be worried to death."

"Oh, well, we'll have our own 'bus before long, shan't we, little one? We've done it, Gwyn. All fixed up, excepting the shouting and the jolly old tumult, as the song says."

Basil had given in and whirled May off again. She was pouting, suggesting a taxi for the bacon and eggs. Gwynneth would have to watch her; you always had to look after May. And she had let Basil think the Daimler belonged to Granny and talked grandly of Portman Square, impressing him. Gwynneth felt suddenly frightened and miserable. Was it as simple as that? All fixed up? He didn't seem to think there was any doubt. But what about Daddy?

Daddy would think all this display vulgar and terrible. Gwynneth knew that in her heart she thought so too. Mummy would shut her eyes to it, because she couldn't refuse May anything, because she was worried about money, because she was weak. She would ask Gwynneth's advice, and Granny's advice, and Aunt James's advice, and cry because she was going to lose May. The whole house would be made miserable, and May would have her own way and there would be an expensive wedding, and Mummy would think darling May had made a wonderful match, because she could always believe things if she tried. Gwynneth couldn't, and wished she could, and tried to shake herself into a sensible state, not minding about anything. May would be all right, perhaps Granny would help with the wedding without being asked. Perhaps Daddy would think Basil good enough, it was no use worrying. Being older than May made you old-maidish, even if you were only twenty-two. The egg-and-bacon ride would have been fun too, only you had to consider Mummy and look after May.

They wanted her to be a sport and go home in the Daimler alone, if she wouldn't come too in a taxi for the bacon and eggs, but Gwynneth said, no, no, no, not this time, not tonight. So Basil went with them in the Daimler to Lancaster Gate, and Gwynneth gazed out the window from the small seat, aware of May's head on Basil's shoulder, and finally ran up the steps and left them to their good night, with May's bag and slipper-case and evening coat on her arm.

Basil hadn't got out, except just to help May. He was telling the Daimler man to take him back to Hampstead, and May was letting him do it, but she oughtn't, they mustn't; it would be another hour at least on Granny's bill. There! he had gone, it was too late to say anything.

Gwynneth opened the door and went in, feeling herself a coward.

2

Mrs. Dawnay was worried, disappointed and upset. She felt she had too much to bear. As if the thought of losing sweet little May, the light of their home, was not enough, she had had Richard and all his puzzling questions to deal with. Who was this young Lorne? Where had the girls met him? With their brother, of course, quite properly, and a charming boy, as any one but Richard could see at a glance, and so well off. Did Richard think his own son's friends likely to be unsuitable acquaintances for his sisters then, and Herbert such a good boy? Surely his own mother should be the best judge of that. Suppose Basil *was* a stock-broker, young men had to have some profession; it was not as it used to be in our young days. And Richard had done nothing to give the darling girls the opportunities they should have had; he had left it all to her and now talked as though little May wanted to marry the butcher's boy. He had left the house saying he would look into the matter, and Mrs. Dawnay, directly she had given her household orders, had gone off to Portman Square to talk the matter over with poor mother and ask her advice.

Everything was going wrong, for early as it was, her mother was not at home, they said, and the parlormaid, who seemed a stupid creature, could not say when the mistress would be in—no, not even for luncheon, she thought.

All the afternoon Mrs. Dawnay had worried and rung up to Portman Square, and when at last she learned that her mother had come in, that woman Simpkins came to the telephone and said her mistress was resting and had given orders that she was not to be disturbed.

"Then, tell her when she wakes, Simpkins, that I will come round this evening."

But an hour later a call had come from Portman Square to say that Mrs. Devonshire had caught a chill and gone to bed, so would Mrs. Dawnay kindly postpone her visit.

Could anything be more vexatious? Poor mother never would have any one near her when she was in bed. It was one of her unreasonable whims, and this was so important, for really Gwen was counting on mother. There should be an engagement party in Portman Square (Richard would have to come round), and of course the wedding from there. So much more suitable than Lancaster Gate, and after all this was the first wedding of a grandchild, mother would surely be delighted. Darling little May, one of the youngest and only twenty, and marrying first.

At this point Mrs. Dawnay smiled with pride. She was not surprised. Not one of the child's cousins had her looks or her charm, and Jane, poor thing, must be twenty-six if a day. As for Frederika, the girl was a great hoyden, and Biddy, the naughty monkey, need not be considered. Not that she had what her Aunt Gwen called good looks, in any case. She hoped mother would not insist upon the cousins for bridesmaids; still Gwynneth would be first, that was her right, and one did not need to choose pretty bridesmaids after all, especially for such a lovely bride.

When Richard came home, she poured out all this vexatious news about poor mother, but he was quite short with her and said nothing was settled yet. He must see the

young man. Basil was coming this evening, she told him,
very properly, of course, though young men of the present
day did not expect that sort of thing, May had told her.
Still, he was coming, and Richard had better not say there
would be no money for May in case poor mother...

"You will kindly not ask your mother, Gwen. Do you
understand me?"

Richard had gone into his study and shut the door.
Talking to her like that...as if she hadn't enough to bear!
Gwen sat down in tears and wrote a letter to her mother
and had it posted off at once, saying she would be round to
consult her in the morning.

Richard Dawnay walked about the study doing nothing,
already a defeated man. He was sure it was no use and he
hated tears. Gwynneth opened the door and came quietly
in.

"What is he like, this boy?" asked her father.

"They seem very rich," said Gwynneth, and put her arms
round him. "Terribly new, Daddy, but we can't help it,
you'll have to give in. Basil's all right, I think, he's very
kind...."

"May must take her chance," said her father suddenly,
and held his favorite daughter close. Were they all blind,
these young men?

3

The next morning that woman Simpkins telephoned
again that her mistress was still laid up, and would try to
write to Mrs. Dawnay in a day or two.

Gwen was very much put out, and rather sharp with
Simpkins, asking if a doctor had been called and what was

being done for her mother. The doctor was with the mistress now, said Simpkins, and everything was being done, Mrs. Dawnay could rest assured. Perfect quiet was what was ordered for the mistress.

Gwynneth hovering at her mother's elbow, said:

"I didn't think Granny looking too well on her birthday, you know."

"Nonsense, my dear, your grandmother has never been really ill in her life and now, of course, a chill would alarm her. She has had no troubles, Gwynny, a very fortunate woman, not like your poor old mother, and all people who have everything they could wish for are a little unfeeling and selfish, though I am sure poor Granny does not mean to be."

Mrs. Dawnay, not being able to seek advice from her fortunate and selfish parent, decided to seek it from Marion instead.

Marion, however, proved too full of James's cough, though James was at home, and his Aunt Gwen could notice no sign of illness in the boy. Marion even went so far as to say that James's health was of more importance than a dozen weddings, and that the boy's Granny had written her a most curious letter, really she could only imagine the old lady was not quite right in her mind.

Gwen would not permit remarks of that kind about her mother, and the sisters-in-law parted with marked coolness, Mrs. Dawnay deciding that Marion was jealous, naturally perhaps, that little May should marry before the much older Jane.

It was Monday before the promised letter arrived from Portman Square, written in pencil and more upsetting than anything that had happened yet. Mrs. Devonshire was glad to hear her daughter's news and sent her congratulations and best wishes to May. She was unfortunately laid up and quite unable to see any one at present. The doctor had forbidden it and as soon as she was fit to be moved, she was to have a complete change. She must postpone the pleasure of meeting the young people until she was her old self again.

Mrs. Dawnay rang up her mother's doctor, who told her as much as doctors will, which was exactly nothing at all, emphasizing, however, that at Mrs. Devonshire's age perfect quiet and freedom from worry were essential.

Gwen, forced at last to stand on her own feet, prepared to meet Basil's mother, without the support of Portman Square, but with this unfortunate parental illness as an excellent reason why any formal rejoicings should be postponed for the present. May's grandmother was so devoted to her, said Mrs. Dawnay with much motherly meaning to Mrs. Lorne, who said it was so delicious to meet this sweet, old-fashioned atmosphere, and went away to make fun of it in her own circle, while not forgetting to mention Portman Square.

The announcement was sent to *The Times* and *Morning Post,* and May, with Gwynneth in attendance as usual, spent every spare moment away from her Basil in and out of the shops and changing her mind about the trousseau. On one of these excursions the two girls, returning from Whiteley's, saw their outcast cousin, Biddy Kerlin, in circumstances which the whole family at Lancaster Gate agreed to be truly shocking.

CHAPTER NINE

MISS SARAH VERSCHOYLE'S STOOL

BIDDY, with Mr. Dawes's offer to spur her, had taken his advice and given up seeking a post. She spent her days instead hunting for treasure in out-of-the-way corners of London, in little, secondhand shops in mean streets and at sales unlikely to attract the more important dealers and experts.

She felt that she had been given both a challenge and an opportunity, and her spirits rose to both. If there was an object of vertu to be picked up in London she would get it somehow, though it should take her months to find, and if London proved unfruitful she must go further afield, into the country towns. Lack of capital was her most serious difficulty, but she carried her check-book with her daily, ready to sacrifice her forty-one pounds. The great thing was to show Mr. Dawes that she had something in her—that inexplicable something which he understood—and to do it before he forgot her existence too. For the latter reason time was important, she must not waste an hour.

Biddy had worn out two pairs of shoes, however, and yet gained nothing but experience. The calculations in the back of her notebook were becoming complicated, and at night she cut down housekeeping expenses ruthlessly in imagination, only to find that a young and healthy appetite ran them up again by day.

From time to time she came across bargains that tempted her, antiques of a kind, but remembering that she must have an iron will, she let them go. To begin it was important to make no mistake. She learned too a useful lesson at one of the first sales she attended, when a good-natured Cockney woman offered to bid for her if she fancied anything.

"If you open your mouth, dearie, the dealers'll think you want it bad and up the prices'll go. Now me, I might be in the secondhand line myself."

Biddy, realizing that she was too well dressed, took the hint and arrayed herself thereafter in a hat made shapeless by the rain and a mackintosh which, with a good deal of enjoyment, she plastered with mud.

"I am in disguise," she explained, meeting Sholto by accident in the Tube one evening, and gleefully exhibiting her thick, serviceable and very dusty shoes. "You are not required to recognize me."

"Just try to stop me."

Sholto, in spite of all protests, got out at Queen's Road, and walked with her to Wincey Street. It was nearly seven o'clock, a dark and stormy evening. Sholto himself was late and she had been grubbing all day, she said, among funny little shops south of the river, and let the time slip by.

He hated to think of her in such surroundings and then coming home to cook a lonely meal, probably inadequate. He tried to persuade her to run in and change and come out to dinner with him, but she was tired and dirty and meant to have a bath and tumble into bed, she said.

For almost the first time in their knowledge of each

other Sholto was glum and out of spirits, and Biddy irritated by his unreasonable arguments against her work.

At last she lost her temper altogether and told him to
mind his own business, and then was all the more indignant because he looked so much abashed. Leaving him at
the door with hardly a word, she rushed upstairs and into
the flat.

She flung off her things, filled the bath and tumbled into
it, feeling guilty and utterly miserable. The hot water re-
freshed her body but could not soothe her mind. She was
a brute and now she had lost Sholto, her best friend...
lost him?

Biddy found that she was shaking and said to herself in
a frightened way quite new to her that she was tired and
probably hungry, that was all it was; but though there was
a dreadful emptiness within her, she could not face the
thought of food and, after walking about the room aim-
lessly for some time, she locked up and crept into bed.

Discouragement, as the wakeful night wore on, added its
quota to all the rest. Here all these weeks had gone on and
she had done nothing at all, nothing. Mr. Dawes had forgotten her existence by this time. Perhaps he had never intended to remember it, but was just being polite, or finding
a way to get rid of a troublesome visitor.

She went over the interview with Mr. Dawes, and saw
it now all in a different light. He had been inwardly mocking her, thinking her cocksure and absurd, and probably
even dishonest, getting in by pretending to be a customer.
He would never give her the chance again.

Biddy tossed on her pillow and hated the thought of herself. Even her grandmother had not been able to put up

with her and had sent her away. That was a nice disgrace, for she must have done something, even though she did not know what; seemed ungrateful or casual or crude. She had not meant to be; she admired her grandmother enormously, and yet in the end she had lost her temper and said hateful things. Well, that couldn't be helped; she had done it and her grandmother naturally would never speak to her again.

And now Sholto. Back at the heart of the trouble, Biddy knew this was the worst of all. Her grandmother's favor had been like a fantastic and lovely dream which could not be expected to last; Mr. Dawes's interest had been a miracle where she had expected none, but Sholto belonged to the world of actual things; his friendship and Freddy's and the whole jolly background at Buckingham Gate were real and her own.

Biddy, for all the responsible years behind her, was very young at this moment, and yet in one sense older than she had ever been, young enough, ignorant enough in the ways of her own generation to believe Sholto would never speak to her again; old enough to discover in a flash at last why this should seem too much to bear.

She sat up in the darkness on the edge of her bed, and suddenly out in the night with a slow, hoarse chuckle, the old church clock struck three.

"All's well, all's well, all's well."

"That's all you know," said Biddy, with a shaky attempt at humor, but the realization of the hour at least had its effect, and she turned on the light and went into the kitchen to heat a cup of milk. This was good for sleeplessness, she had given it to her father on many a night. The thought of him at that moment somehow steadied her, for

he had not found her hard to bear and because he had died,
having done the thing he set out to do, she had decided
that it would be mean to grieve for him. Self-pitying and
contemptible, that was what it would be, because she was
alone.

And here she was on the verge of it, sorry for herself
and moaning.

She drank her warm milk and ate six plain biscuits,
finding herself unexpectedly hungry. And then she felt
rather better, re-made her tumbled bed and turned off the
light again. Drawing the curtain aside, she looked out and
saw a clear sky, frosted with stars and a rim of light on the
horizon which was probably the moon.

"I hope it's a blue one," she said to herself with a sudden
laugh and turned in, thinking of Sholto. She would write
to him in the morning and say she had been a beast.

"Because," said Biddy hopefully, "I do believe he likes
me a bit."

2

She awoke so late that she did not even hear the postman pushing a letter through the door. It lay on the rug,
face upwards before her waking eyes, and she knew the
writing at once.

Jumping up, she tore it open with a shaking hand, then
collapsed with laughter and relief on her bed.

"PROTECTION OF ANCIENT BUILDINGS."

"The historic, residential flats known as Villiers Mansions, Buckingham Gate, are in serious danger of an-
nihilation, owing to the hump of one of the residents,

which threatens to remove the roof. If you are interested in the preservation of this architectural treasure, please be at Piccadilly Circus at one sharp.

"By Order,

"SHOLTO FENWICK, *Camel-ier.*"

Biddy wasted that morning singing about the little flat, to the evident astonishment of V.C., who retreated before her song with an air of offended majesty. Nor did she go to Piccadilly Circus "in disguise," but wearing her favorite suit and a flower in her buttonhole.

Sholto, waiting mournfully between hope and despair, could hardly believe his luck when he saw her glowing cheeks. The two young fools, in the happy embarrassment of being together, talked nonsense throughout the meal and, before they knew it, Big Ben was striking three.

"Sholto, this is awful, you will be sacked," cried Biddy. "You must go at once."

"Ah, but I'm up on business," invented Sholto. "Every Wednesday. I say, let's make this a fixture. It's a mug's game, lunching alone."

"No, you are not going to provide me with weekly lunches."

"Ah, but the firm pays when I lunch a possible customer. And after all, though you may have no consideration for me," said Sholto, "you wouldn't like the roof to fall in on Freddy and Edith and poor old John."

It was the first reference to their disagreement and Biddy laughed.

"All right...sometimes anyway. When my temper is too bad, I'll send you a postcard."

"That'll be once in ten years." They left the restaurant, and he added calmly, "But there won't be any need for a postcard in the years if I have any luck."

"Thought transmission?" suggested Biddy.

"Well, I wasn't exactly thinking of that."

He looked at her out of the corner of his eye, making ready for flight.

"Why not the good old family pincushion?" was what he intended to say, but his courage failed him. He left the explanation in mid-air instead, and Biddy, as she said good-by and walked up Regent Street, smiled to herself, making guesses at it happily, and not too wide of the mark.

Having wasted the greater part of the day, she decided to go home through some of the small streets leading to Paddington and beyond, which she had not yet explored. She did not hope to find anything here, but it was just as well to make sure. Biddy had a map of London, which she was marking off, determined to do the thing thoroughly while she was about it.

As she had expected, she drew blank, but the afternoon was to be momentous, none the less. In a small cross street full of tall houses, most of which seemed to be let out in apartments, she caught sight of a notice of sale and stopped to read it.

"EXECUTORS' SALE"

"In the estate of Miss Sarah Verschoyle, deceased, the contents of No. 17, Crecy Street will be sold by auction at this address on Thursday, October 16th, at 10 A.M. On view, Wednesday, October 15th....

"The household effects comprise ..."

Biddy did not wait to read the list, which would tell her
nothing, but after looking up at the house, almost with a
sense of trespass, she went in.

Miss Sarah Verschoyle might have lived there for a long
time; somehow she sounded like it; perhaps she had stayed
on and on from Crecy Street's better days and seen it come
down in the world and take in boarders, unable to move
away since this was her house, and she too had grown poor.
Perhaps she had kept some treasure because it had been in
the family and she could not bear to part with it.

Biddy, standing in the hall with its unsightly Victorian
wallpaper, felt like a thief, and then told herself not to be
a fool. If there were any treasures here, they would be sold
tomorrow to somebody, and very likely there were not.
Miss Sarah Verschoyle might have kept lodgers like the
rest of the street, and moved in only a year or two ago,
having bought the house with her savings.

The rooms told her nothing, except that genteel poverty
had lived here. The furniture was heavy, ugly and com-
monplace, the carpets worn into holes, and the ornaments,
china and glass quite worthless. The basement had been
let off and a kitchen made on the ground floor. Biddy,
coming down from upstairs, pushed open the door of this
room and glanced in, expecting nothing.

The next moment, holding her breath, she was kneeling
on the kitchen floor.

3

"Into a *pawn*-shop, carrying a thingummy," cried May
Dawnay the next afternoon, dancing round the tea-table
and seizing a toasted scone.

"Sounds all right," said her cousin Jane. It was not Jane's habit to visit her aunt at Lancaster Gate, but May's engagement had given her an opportunity. She was anxious to find out something about Herbert's movements. He had been evading her of late.

"My darlings, how very queer! But you didn't, I hope, speak to the naughty girl?"

"Not much," gurgled May. "If you had seen her, Mummy! A dirty old mackintosh, though it is such a fine day, and a frightful hat. She didn't see us, luckily."

"But what was she carrying into the pawnshop?" asked Jane.

"Oh, you know...old fire-irons, poker and tongs, they looked like, and one of those things they used to blow fires with. What do you call them?"

"Bellows," explained Gwynneth, taking her tea and sitting down in a corner, wondering whether it hadn't been rather mean after all not to speak to Biddy.

"Shocking!" said Mrs. Dawnay in a horrified tone; "but that is what comes of misbehavior."

Jane Devonshire laughed shortly.

"You are quaint, Aunt Gwen, misbehavior is more likely to keep her out of the pawnshop than send her into it."

"Really, Jane!"

Mrs. Dawnay looked round at her innocent darlings protectively, but Jane, who had been listening, exasperated, for half an hour to a tale of the vast wealth into which sweet little May was marrying, was in no mood to be silenced. Smugness about pawnshops from Aunt Gwen, who had a husband and home and daughters marrying money, was a little too much.

"Well, pawnshops are not dens of iniquity, you know," said Jane, "and poverty is not necessarily a sign of vice. If Biddy has to pawn her fire-irons and wear shabby clothes, she can hardly be finding life a riot, believe *me*."

"Ah, my dear, I suppose the wretched man has left her," murmured Aunt Gwen who, like so many virtuous people, lowered her voice when she had anything particularly scandalous to say, under the vague impression that this sanctified the remark.

"Man? What man?" exclaimed Jane, bewildered and yet with an uneasy sense of having heard something of this before.

"Married man," chuckled May over her fourth toasted scone. "Biddy went off with him and they were thrown out of a night club."

"Oh, rot!" retorted Jane, who had heard so much of May's innocence this afternoon that she was ready to contradict her about anything or anybody. Biddy hardly came into the question; Jane was merely concerned with the fact that May was a little toad.

"Hush, hush, May, you know nothing whatever about such things!" exclaimed Mrs. Dawnay. "You don't understand what you are saying.... At the same time, Jane, my authority for the story is your own mother, and I don't consider rot is a nice word for a drawing-room conversation, I don't indeed."

"It is a pretty bad conversation, I'll admit, but, if you'll forgive my saying so, Aunt Gwen, you began it," said Jane, who now recognized the Biddy legend with uneasy fury. "If Mother said anything of the kind, you ought to know her too well to believe it. She is always getting things mixed. What do you suppose she knows of night-clubs or Biddy either, except that she is jolly relieved, like the rest of the family, that Granny turned her out?"

"Jane! I don't know what you mean. You must be out of your senses."

"Very likely I am," said Jane, "but you know it's true, all the same. Oh! I am sporting no halo, I am as bad as the rest of you, but if the poor kid is so hard up she has to pawn her fire-irons I'm sorry for her, and I wouldn't be such a snob as to cut her in the street either. Now I'll go. Thanks for tea and so on."

Gwynneth left her corner to see her cousin to the door.

"Look here, we didn't exactly cut her," pleaded Gwynneth. "Biddy didn't see us."

"Oh, shut up," said Jane. She hesitated on the steps and threw back: "You might give Herbert my address, will you? He seems to have lost it.... Probably just as well you didn't speak to her anyway. She'd have hated it, if I'm any judge."

"Yes... I didn't know she was a friend of yours, Jane," said Gwynneth.

"Friend?... Of course she's no friend. Don't talk such dam' rot. I hardly know the girl."

Jane stalked off, using her lipstick fiercely as she went.

4

Biddy meanwhile, unconscious of the fiery discussion raging about her in Lancaster Gate, sat on her sitting-room floor and looked with joy and triumph at Miss Sarah Verschoyle's stool. Worn, scratched, dirty, it had stood for how long, she wondered, in that little back kitchen in Crecy Street? And before that, where? There must have been many wheres in its life, she thought, unless she was utterly wrong. And was this an object of vertu?

Biddy did not know. But she was sure that it was very old and its shapely legs had been fashioned by no careless hand. For an hour since bringing it home she had cleaned and polished them and now they stood before her, shining faintly as though their lost beauty might at last return. The cover, stained and grimy with coal-dust and all its pattern worn away, was of hideous tapestry, badly put on. Turning the stool about, Biddy discovered that this had merely been sewn on to another below, and in a moment she had cut the threads and lifted it away. The result was cleaner, certainly, but that was all that you could say. A fearful pattern of black and violet stamped velvet confronted her, the pile worn white in the center. This was tacked on with purple gimp, and very carefully, so as not to harm the frame, she began to ease the tacks one by one, until the end was loose and she could look inside.

It was an anxious moment, for suppose she found nothing more? Yesterday, sitting on Miss Sarah Verschoyle's kitchen floor, she had felt and prodded the stool, trying to decide how many disguises it might be wearing, if any at all. Well, she had found two, and now what? She put in an exploring finger and felt a rough surface ... wool-work. Oh, she was getting on. Once more the stool was undressed and stood before her, a worsted Victorian object in scarlet and green.

Biddy sat back on her heels and laughed.

"My poor dear, what a life they've led you," she said to

it feelingly. "Of course you may have been born to that, but somehow I don't think so."

Once more she set to work, but this time the task was more difficult. The afternoon was fading, and she got up to turn on the light, conscious for the first time that she was stiff and aching. She lifted the stool to the table and stood above it anxiously, and then she discovered that the worsted work was worn into a hole. Peering in, she could see yet another cover inside.

Half an hour later she was cooking her supper with a joyful heart, peering round the kitchen door at intervals to look at her treasure again. It was no longer a kitchen, drawing-room or parlor stool. It was an object of vertu, in Biddy's eyes, at least. Fine, very old silk embroidery in delicate shades covered it now, soiled here and there, it was true, but surely it could be cleaned with care, and the lovely rounded legs polished again. She herself was afraid to do anything more to it. Just as it was, she must carry it in the morning to Mr. Dawes.

It was a Cinderella of a stool and she had rescued it. No more coal baskets should bear it down, no more serviceable Victorian boots. It had been made, she thought, for the little satin slippers of some beauty in rich brocade and powdered hair. She could not tell what its value might be; her pleasure was not concerned with pounds, shillings and pence, hardly more with the fact of having seen beauty in disguise while others passed it by. She could not have explained it to herself, though the exaltation sang her to sleep and awoke her to new wonder in the morning.

5

In Dover Street next day, waiting among objects of
vertu so much more imposing, Biddy had her first mis-
giving about the stool. It was so small and shabby a trophy
among these Sheraton, Jacobean tables, old walnut-wood,
Boule and lacquer and the rest, stretching away through
room after room. Even the reproductions were worth large
sums, she knew. Looking round she could see no footstool
anywhere, and became sadly convinced that Mr. Dawes
would scorn to deal with such a trifle.

Ignorant that Mr. Dawes's offer to advise her had been
prompted by anything but the enthusiasm of a connois-
seur, Biddy presently followed an assistant to his office in a
state of almost apologetic trepidation.

"Ah, Miss Kerlin, you have not yet given up your idea
of becoming my most serious rival then?" said Mr. Dawes,
offering her a chair.

Biddy smiled.

"I think I've found something," she said.

"What, already? ... In a few days?"

"No, it is weeks. I was beginning to be afraid you would
forget all about me....Even now, you may think very
little of it."

This suddenly seemed to her the wrong thing to have
said, so she added: "But I think it is quite jolly of its kind,
myself, and old."

She unwrapped the little stool, and set it down before
Mr. Dawes, with what she hoped was a careless and confident air.

The old expert took it in his hands and looked it over with an inscrutable face.

"Ah, now that would take a young lady's eye. A very pretty bit of needlework," said Mr. Dawes.

"But look at the legs," said Biddy in a scandalized tone.

Mr. Dawes obediently looked at the legs.

"Yes," he said, "quite a pretty little piece. Where did you pick it up, Miss Kerlin, if I may ask?"

"I bought it at the late Miss Sarah Verschoyle's sale," returned Biddy, having carefully rehearsed this speech.

"Miss...Verschoyle?...Some acquaintance or friend of yours?"

"No. I had never heard of her till I saw about the sale. I have been watching for sales," said Biddy. "I must have been to nearly ten since I saw you, but this is the first thing I have cared to buy."

"Indeed? And what did you have to pay for the little stool?"

"Oh, I didn't pay very much for it," said Biddy carelessly.

The old expert's eyes twinkled.

"Well, I suppose I must not press you about the price," he observed. "And what were you expecting me to do with it, make your fortune?"

The girl smiled faintly.

"No...only begin it, perhaps. It might not be important enough for you to trouble about but I couldn't be sure. I know it is worth something. That cover is a good age, and I thought it might be the original one."

"How did you arrive at that conclusion, I wonder?" enquired Mr. Dawes. "Because of your knowledge of old needlework?"

Biddy, after a moment's hesitation, opened the small parcel she carried.

"No. I took these three covers off, and you see how worn they are. I don't know how that could have happened to a footstool, except after many years of use, and there may have been others still. And then there are the legs and frame. They felt very old to me. I know they can be faked to look old now, but they would hardly have been doing that sixty or eighty years ago, would they? I reckoned the wool-work to be at least mid-Victorian."

She fitted the old covers loosely into place.

"That is how it looked when I bought it, and of course the legs were very dirty. It was being used in the kitchen and was sold with a set of fire-irons and a bellows. I think I am quite justified in telling you all the facts as you are so kindly advising me," said Biddy. "I paid five shillings for the lot."

"I see.... Having examined it and found the various covers and drawn your conclusions," nodded Mr. Dawes.

Biddy said rather wistfully: "I'm afraid I gambled on the covers and only came to the conclusions when I found them. I had no chance to do anything but poke it, and it felt thickish. It was the shape of the legs and a feeling that it must have come a long way down in the world to be in a kitchen looking like that. The name Sarah Verschoyle sounded goodish, though the house was shabby. I looked up books of reference at the Free Library—Burke and so on—and there were various Verschoyles, but I didn't find a Sarah. I suppose you would think, if the stool is worth anything at all, it is more luck than good judgment?"

"Luck is not to be despised, my dear Miss Kerlin," said Mr. Dawes, "though in this calling, as in any other, it would be disastrous to depend upon it. You seem to me, for an inexperienced beginner, to have gone about the thing very well—used your reason and your powers of observation as well as your instinct, that feeling you speak about. Be careful, however, and remember the road to knowledge is a long and hard one. Now about your find. There is no very great value in footstools, but the little piece may found your fortune yet, if your determination and patience hold out. It was quite worth rescuing at—five shillings, did you say?"

"Four-and-six really," said Biddy smiling, "because I pawned the fire-irons and bellows for sixpence, so that I wouldn't have to carry them home, and they were very worn and battered, and there was no shop handy to sell them to. The stool *is* genuine as far as it goes, isn't it?"

"Quite, and worth a few pounds, if we can find a buyer."

Mr. Dawes considered the little stool, or so it seemed. Actually he was thinking of a house in Portman Square, with which he wished to keep in touch.

"I am willing to give you three pounds for it, Miss Kerlin. I may some day sell it for rather more, or sacrifice it for less. You see, I propose to gamble on the possibility of your finding me something no collector could resist. Well, what do you say?"

"I suppose you would think me indiscreet if I offered to take less," said Biddy. "But it is not worth that, I don't want you to do it out of kindness."

"It is worth that to me, and I am willing to pay some-thing to establish friendly relations. I won't promise you such a handsome profit on the next deal, however," said Mr. Dawes, smiling.

"No, of course it is an enormous profit if you look at it in percentage."

"But not so great when you remember wear and tear, eh? How many hours' work have you put in, for in-stance?"

She gave him a brief history of her days since their last meeting, and he listened with interest. He knew little of young people, but he believed that old Mrs. Devonshire was mistaken about this one. There was a quality about her that pleased him, an impersonal, quiet keenness and a re-sourceful and enquiring mind.

As they concluded the deal for the stool and he wrote her a check, he added a few words of further advice, and these were given to an aspiring colleague rather than to the granddaughter of Mrs. Devonshire of Portman Square.

"Remember that modest beginnings are not to be de-spised, Miss Kerlin, particularly at the moment, when comparatively few people have a great deal of money to spare. Old china, enamel and glass are worth your atten-tion, for instance. And when the weather is too inclement don't risk your health, go to museums and live among treasures for a few hours instead...."

He took her to the door himself on this occasion, and Biddy went away feeling that she had left her object of vertu in the hands of a friend.

CHAPTER TEN

ROYALTY

"INTO A *pawn*-shop, Richard," said Mrs. Dawnay in a hushed tone, telling him all about it.

She had a new grievance now, a new worry. It was so unpleasant at this time of all others that there should be all this talk of Biddy (first cousin to the bride). And suppose something worse happened and it got into the newspapers? The poor woman's imagination recoiled from the possibilities that suggested themselves. The girl might be driven to do something desperate...gas-oven...one read such things almost every day...."A granddaughter of Mrs. Devonshire of Portman Square...." Gwen could see it in the headlines.

"You have told your mother, I suppose?" said Richard, not that newspapers or gas-ovens had occurred to his mind, but because if the girl were in such straits something should be done for her, he thought.

That was so like Richard. Tell poor Mother, who was ill already, too ill even to see little May and dear Basil? Worry her further about naughty Biddy? Impossible.

"Well, in that case, my dear, you had better see the child and find out if she is in serious need," said Richard Dawnay.

"Really, Richard, how can you be so mad? Mix myself up in this dreadful affair? I have my innocent girls to think of, and surely we have enough expense as it is. Besides," said Mrs. Dawnay triumphantly, "I don't know where she is living.... It was sheer chance that the children saw her."

Richard said no more. Women were beyond him, hard and callous to a degree where any but their own were concerned. Certainly Gwen's responsibility was less than her mother's. The old lady had turned the girl out of doors and, whatever her reason, should have seen that she was at least provided for.

He had seen little of Gwen's niece, but he had girls of his own, and he could not dismiss the subject from his mind with comfort. Remembering the Kerlin Fund, he lunched at his club for some days until he ran across Sir Neville Willesden. His mother-in-law's strictures notwithstanding, he spoke of the Fund and asked if anything was to be done for the girl. The family had lost touch with her, he explained, and he and his wife had been greatly disturbed to hear that she had been seen pawning her household goods.

Biddy's adventure with the fire-irons therefore brought her an invitation to lunch with her father's old friend. Sir Neville, remembering his interview with old Mrs. Devonshire, was non-committal to Richard Dawnay on the subject of Biddy and the Kerlin Fund; it occurred to him that the girl's maternal relatives were a queer lot altogether, but he was sufficiently concerned to feel that it was high time for him to get in touch with her. He wrote to her at her bank, having no other address, and in due course was reassured by the sight of a glowing Biddy, evidently in excellent health and spirits.

"You've been neglecting me, young lady," said the old man fiercely. "Now, what do you mean by it?"

She explained that she had been busy, getting to work.

"You evidently knew I had left my grandmother, as you sent the letter to the bank."

"Yes, so I discovered. How is the money lasting out?"

"Splendidly. I saved so much while I was at Portman Square, I have still about forty pounds as well as the income," said Biddy, beaming.

"Hm! Then if that is the case why were you pawning your fire-irons, I should like to know?" demanded the old man, fiercely knitting his brows.

"You don't mean to say you caught me?" exclaimed the girl in high delight.

"Er—no, the matter was reported to me. Come now, out with it."

She told him the story of her first deal, and the old man nodded and smiled, remembering the fight he had put up to prevent that mad journey to meet her father, and how he had given in and, later, been glad of it. You could not judge Kerlin's daughter by ordinary standards, he thought. She had inherited that quiet doggedness. It was in the blood.

"Who saw me, Sir Neville? Do tell me," begged Biddy.

"Never mind...some one who put it to me that if you were in such straits, this Fund should do something for you."

She looked at him with horrified eyes.

"Oh no! You mustn't. I wouldn't touch a penny of it," she cried, rather white. "Why, I am richer than I have ever

been, and I am so proud of the Fund. You can come and
see for yourself.

"You can even burn the mantelpiece, if you like," she
added with a forlorn attempt at humor, "because it's my
own...there aren't any landladies...."

"Ha, ha! you'd poke fun at an old man, would you? If
I come will you make me an omelette?"

"Rather! Let's fix it up now."

The engagement was made, Sir Neville glad to have
turned the conversation successfully. She had been upset,
poor child, for all her light tone, and he had been clumsy
and blunt, as usual.

"It was only my little joke about the Fund; a nice treasurer I should be, playing fast and loose with it to please
every fool who made a suggestion. All the same, my dear,"
said Sir Neville, "if the time should come when it seems
necessary to touch your capital, I hope you will consult me
first. These temporary difficulties can sometimes be tided
over by cunning old men like me."

"I should come to you as a matter of course," Biddy
assured him. "You are my oldest friend."

"Well, well, and with all these new friends you haven't
forgotten an old man. I breathe again. And now let us
drink to the omelette, many omelettes."

2

Thinking the matter over when Biddy had left him, Sir
Neville could only conclude that her maternal relatives, all
being people of substance presumably, wished to see the
girl provided for without trouble to themselves. That was

the way of relatives, but it exhibited little knowledge of Kerlin's daughter.

The old lady in Portman Square had shown some concern for the Fund, however, and hadn't she made him a sort of promise to contribute to it? Sir Neville, recalling the interview of some weeks ago, rather thought so, and decided that it would do no harm to let her know the position, just to keep the Fund before her mind.

He wrote to her therefore:

"MY DEAR MRS. DEVONSHIRE,

"You may like to know that your suspicion that I should be approached about the Kerlin Fund on behalf of your granddaughter was not without foundation. Acting on your advice, I refused to countenance the suggestion, very fortunately, since I find the girl herself would not accept money from the Fund in any circumstances; and is in no need.

"You will, I know, be glad to learn that our figures have crept up a little since I saw you, and now stand at £2,853, still less, alas, than we shall require for the endowment of an adequate scholarship, but none the less in these bad times a considerable tribute to the memory of your son-in-law and my valued friend.

"I am, dear Mrs. Devonshire,
"Yours to command,
"NEVILLE WILLESDEN."

In due course he received a reply written in the third person to say that Mrs. Devonshire thanked Sir Neville Willesden for his courtesy, and begged him to excuse a personal letter as she was for the moment indisposed. She congratulated him on the growth of the Fund, which she was bearing in mind, and about which he would receive a communication a little later.

This was vague but promising, for a contribution from that quarter might well be considerable.

Sir Neville felt pleased with his own diplomacy and a little surprised at it, having no idea that Mrs. Devonshire was not the lady to be taken in by any diplomat. She was merely proposing to pay him for benefits received.

3

The form of payment, coming to her in a malicious flash, had amused Mrs. Devonshire mightily; it would so neatly pay some other people also for their impertinent interference. And there was a pretty irony in giving money to the memory of a man whom in life she had refused to receive. Besides, it would perhaps please the child.

"Ask Mr. Crow to be good enough to bring my will and see me tomorrow, Simpkins, during the nurse's absence," she had commanded.

For it had come to that at last; nurses in the house, two of them. Mrs. Devonshire would never leave her room again, and Simpkins, an old woman herself, must be considered, must be made to feel that there was a more important trust for her—to guard her mistress's privacy, order the house and answer the telephone.

Simpkins, hating the competent, professional women, loving to circumvent them on every occasion, had summoned Mr. Crow forthwith. A pretty thing if the mistress

could not have her way in her own house because of a
pack of nurses, dying or not dying, thought Simpkins.
Wild horses wouldn't make Patty Simpkins give in to the
hussies.

During the hours they were off duty she took up her
post in the sick-room, watching fiercely for some need,
some order, some recognition from her old friend.

After every visit she confronted the doctor, defying him
to keep from her the condition of the patient. Hadn't she
heard with her own good ears the mistress order this, and
in her presence, meaning her to hear.

"Tell Simpkins quite frankly, nobody else. She has been
with me for forty-five years. She can keep a still tongue—
even to me."

That's what she had said. And the fancies she had, she
that was never a one for fancies either. Would have a footstool she'd bought, ill as she was, from Dawes, set up on
the top of the tallboy where she could look at it.

Now why a footstool? But there, you couldn't argue
with the sick. If she had wanted the kitchen stove removed
to the tallboy, wild horses wouldn't have stopped Simpkins
from bringing it somehow, though the whole household
starved in consequence.

Sometimes when Simpkins believed her asleep or dozing
she would suddenly find her gazing at the stool as though
pleased with herself, for she was still capable of that, and
of having her laugh too, sharp as of old.... Such as when
Mrs. James rang up, very imperative to know whether the
mistress was gone away for her change yet or why not?

"Aha! a little surprise for some people my change is
likely to be," the mistress had remarked, quite brisk and

sarcastic. And then: "Simpkins, fetch up my Waterford glass and pack it very carefully in the bottom drawer of the tallboy."

After that from day to day she would ask for some other article to be put away; clear as day her mind was, knowing exactly where each was to be found. She seemed set on having these things under her eyes, queer things, Simpkins thought them privately, but said no word to that effect. Since the mistress wanted them there, then there they should be, and no concern of any one's.

The tallboy was nearly full at last, and suddenly Mrs. Devonshire said:

"There, I have done. Lock it and take the key. Give it to Mr. Crow when the time comes. He will know."

When the time comes.

Simpkins, creeping back to the chair beside the bed, saw that her eyes were closed as though in sleep, and knew that the time would come relentlessly and she would be left alone. The iron strength which had nerved her through these dreadful months fell away at the desolation of that thought, and she sat shaking all over, her old face distraught.

"Now, no taking some little cottage in the country, my good girl," said the patient suddenly, and the wild horses were needed then to pull poor Simpkins together. "You have been used to space and comfort here as well as work. You have earned your rest and the other things can be bought."

The words died away. Mrs. Devonshire turned on her pillow, and after a while began again:

"I won't have you going to the country, do you hear?

In London there are houses...as large as this, which have become, they tell me, quiet hotels. Go to one and take your ease. There will be money enough in a modest way ...that is my wish...see to it."

Peremptory to the last, quite angry about it, you would have said, but Simpkins knew better, Simpkins, ousted by the starchy nurse and crouching, old and broken, outside the door of her friend.

"And how are we now?" said the nurse in the cheerful tone that is considered fitting from the hale and healthy to the infirm.

Mrs. Devonshire made no answer. She disregarded the playful conversation of her hired attendants. How was she? That was for them to say. Let them stand on their own feet. But for Simpkins she would not have had them in the house, now she could no longer stand on her own.

The lucid hours, when she was free both from the pain and the drugs, were few and she would not have them filled with the vexatious chatter of strange, silly women. Resolutely she turned a deaf ear to the nurse and looked at the footstool on the tallboy, and saw Biddy in a primrose gown, waiting beside her with a serious face.

Mice and black beetles....Something about mice and black beetles....Never mind what it was, she could not remember, but it had been amusing at the time....One of her triumphant moments for some reason...yes, yes, it was coming back...laughter flashing between them for the first time....Ha, ha, Miss Independence, so aloof and courteous, but no match for an old, determined woman in the end....Mrs. Devonshire smiled, and the nurse said brightly:

"There, dear, we are feeling nice and drowsy, aren't we?"

A silly woman, like Marion, who had married poor handsome James, a mere boy, ten years younger if a day ...at Oxford.... He never should have gone to the place ...and the fees were so high now, the money would be wasted. Poured away. No brains in that family, but what could you expect with a mother like Gwen?... Herbert, a name she had always disliked...and there was that silly creature telephoning, pestering poor Simpkins.

She turned over wearily. Marion, James, Gwen, Herbert, threading her mind in confusion, the passage of the years forgotten, nothing very clear except a sense of anger and frustration.

The rose glass box glowed on the table under the shaded light. A pretty thing...and old...she had thought so at the time...some one had given it to her...was it Hugh? ...It was high time the boy was coming in.... He was so fond of fussing about the place, so fond of it...the great fellow...well, that was the way to live and the only way, standing on your own feet.... Hugh would be late for dinner, and she must dress.... What was Simpkins thinking about sitting there in that outrageous uniform ... like a housemaid...she must have lost her senses...and the room so hot.

"Throw up the window, girl," commanded Mrs. Devonshire impatiently. "Do you wish to stifle me on this hot summer night? Air, air—let us have air."

"Yes, dear," said the nurse, bringing a fresh pillow and slipping it under her head.

4

"It is a conspiracy, I'm certain of it," thought Marion. "I write, I call at the house, I spend money on telephone boxes; I am not one of the lucky people who can afford such a luxury myself, and what happens? Nothing, except lies. No answers to my letters; that woman Simpkins answers the telephone and pretends Granny is unwell or going away for a change. I go to the house and she is resting and cannot be seen, and yet there's an elaborate car at the door, and voices in the drawing-room.

"I am not blind *or* deaf. There has been mischief-making and they are determined I shall not see Granny and tell her about James's cough. Of course it would suit some people very well if my boy were to die," said Marion tearfully to herself. "The head of the family, and then Herbert would get Highways.... I can see it all. Gwen is very sweet to your face but I never trust such people myself, and of course she wants Granny's attention because of this wedding we hear so much about. The poor woman is quite foolish over the match, though a Devonshire might have looked a little higher, I should have thought.

"As for Granny being ill, I don't believe a word of it. ...She is never ill, a robust woman like that.... Perhaps if she had suffered as I have she would have a little more thought for others.... I am sure my poor head... I shall go down to the Stores and look round and see if a little fresh air will do me good. I am so worried, what with Granny and now this preposterous letter about James. Will not get into Oxford if he doesn't study, indeed? What need has my boy to study and ruin his health? Of course he will get into Oxford, he is a Devonshire. I always felt that tutor was no good, in spite of Mr. Crow, a most annoying man as I have said from the first. I have told Granny over and over again that I was convinced he was keeping our money back, but she does nothing. Crow is probably in league with the Dawnays, if he isn't spending the money himself."

Marion dressed, called the housemaid to get her a taxi, and drove to the Army and Navy Stores. The Tube made her head worse and besides she needed fresh air. (Nevertheless, she ordered the driver to close all the windows. The cold was more than she could endure.)

She would look at those grand pianos again. It was disgraceful that she had no piano, really she felt quite ashamed. Marion did not care for music but considered a grand piano was one of her rights, and besides it would be so useful to put things on, James's new photograph and the bowl of goldfish lit with electric light, which she had bought last week, any number of things.

She had estimates and offers and descriptions of grand pianos from nearly every firm in London, but not the Stores. She spent an hour hearing different makes, comparing them, objecting to them, being half-convinced, and finally leaving the department, saying she would think the matter over and let them know.

Marion was an expert at this kind of shopping. She had almost chosen complete new furnishing for Highways in the same manner, explaining to patient assistants that "my son, you know, will shortly be coming into his estate, and I shall be needing a quantity of things, as the place has been let during his minority."

In the course of time she had even convinced herself that this was fact and not fiction. When the boy was twenty-one and Mr. Crow could no longer control the finances, the present tenants must be sent packing, and the heir should come of age with speeches to the tenantry and his photograph in all the newspapers.

It was a great grievance to her, the father of all her grievances, that she had never been allowed to take her rightful place as mistress of Highways. At the time of Hugh's death in France, by which the property passed to his younger brother and her husband, Highways had been turned into a Convalescent Hospital for officers, with Hugh's wife Edith in charge. This had been very clever and calculating of Edith, Marion considered, enabling her to stay on when she had no longer any right to the place, though any one less hard than Edith would have been prostrated with grief at the death of poor Hugh and only too anxious to get away. The arrangement had been made with the Government, they argued, and could not be up-set, and even James, the heir, had weakly sided with this view. And then two years later he had gone, of influenza in a base hospital, leaving Marion and the boy James with this scandalous burden of double death duties, and Crow, of all people, as the child's trustee. The Devonshire family was obsessed with Crow, and what was he but a solicitor after all? Most unsuitable!

Marion, having finished with the pianos, felt faint and retired to the restaurant for a cup of tea, after which she decided to look round at the new fabrics and obtain some patterns.

On the way she encountered Edith Fenwick, who had

been giving her household orders, and though she disliked and distrusted the woman with good reason, she felt it was just as well to be civil. Edith might know something.

"Why, dear, how surprising to run in to you," said Marion. "We so seldom meet, but then nowadays, I suppose, we are in different worlds, and I am such a busy woman. And what is your news? You haven't, I suppose, seen poor Granny lately? You are not so much in touch as the rest of us, naturally, these days."

"I saw Mrs. Devonshire for a few moments some weeks ago," said Edith, endeavoring to hasten away without impoliteness, but frustrated by Marion who stood fussily before her.

"Ah, then you haven't heard the story that she has caught a chill? I don't believe a word of it, Edith, and I am most uneasy, I assure you. I can get no reply to letters, and that woman Simpkins, who has far too much influence over Granny, answers the telephone and will give no information whatever. It is all very peculiar."

"I am sorry, but the weather *is* treacherous, isn't it?" said Edith. "And now I must run, I am afraid. I have an appointment with the hairdresser. I hope you will soon have better news of Mrs. Devonshire."

"Ah, you are evidently in it too. I might have known it," said Marion to Edith's retreating back. "I shall call upon Mr. Crow and tell him what I think of the whole family. I shall call at the very first opportunity. People need not imagine they can plot and mischief-make and hoodwink me."

5

Edith Fenwick broke her appointment with the hair-dresser and went home, feeling uneasy. Marion's exaggerations might mean little, but Edith remembered that her mother-in-law had admitted to not feeling very well, which was unlike her, on that brief visit weeks ago, when for the first time also Hugh's name had been mentioned between them.

Edith, though not herself a possessive woman, had understood that bitter silence, knowing the peculiarly strong tie between the mother and son. And though she had been touched and surprised by the gift of the ring, she had supposed that softening to her was merely the result of Ferderika's frequent presence in her grandmother's house as Biddy's friend. The girl was so like Hugh, grew more like him every day.

Now Edith wondered whether after all she had been mistaken, and it had been instead the gesture of a woman old and ailing and in her own grim fashion trying to make amends. But then she had suggested as much mockingly, which was against it, and talked of a death-bed repentance!

No, whatever else Edith might believe she could not see old Mrs. Devonshire indulging in anything as incredible as that. She was no sentimental weakling. She had borne her troubles like a stoic, and she had had her disappointments too, no doubt. Those two grandsons, for instance. . . .

"Poor old thing, if Freddy had been a boy she might have been some comfort to her," said Edith to herself with a faint smile. "Perhaps she gave me the ring because I did my best."

As soon as she reached home she telephoned to Portman Square and asked for Simpkins.

"I was so sorry to hear Mrs. Devonshire is laid up with a chill," she said. "How is she this morning, Simpkins?"

"Well, 'm, she hasn't had too restful a night," returned Simpkins cautiously.

"How wretched for her. Is there anything that I could send her that she might fancy, do you think? Has she anything to read?"

"The mistress is not partial to reading in bed at any time."

"Oh, she's in bed? Then I mustn't keep you from her, Simpkins. I know she is in good hands, but if you think there is anything she would like or anything I could do, I wish you would tell one of the maids to ring me. I am quite at liberty, and I realize how tied down you must be."

"Thank you, 'm. You are very kind. She does depend upon me and that's a fact."

"Of course she does, she thinks the world of you, naturally. And you are wise to persuade her to stay in bed in this treacherous weather. You won't forget to send me word if I can be of any use. Good-by, Simpkins."

Simpkins, who could be short and non-committal to the peremptory enquiries of Mrs. Dawnay and the suspicions of Mrs. James Devonshire, had lost her nerve a little under Edith's kind and considerate tone. There had been a forlornness in her old voice in spite of all her care, and Edith could tell that she was anxious.

This might mean little, however. The poor soul would have worry enough with Marion's enquiries and the responsibility of the sick room. It was probably nothing more.

When Simpkins telephoned her later in the afternoon she became sure of it.

"The mistress sent her love and thanks to Mrs. Fenwick and was feeling more comfortable. There was nothing she fancied at present, but would Mrs. Fenwick kindly give the theatre tickets she was asking the agency to send round to Miss Freddy. The mistress was unable to use them to-morrow night, and thought it might amuse the young lady and gentleman to go."

"Then if she had intended to go to a theatre," decided Edith with relief, "there can't be anything very serious the matter."

The tickets arrived shortly afterwards, three of them, for a new play.

Edith smiled to herself. "I believe she ordered them on purpose," she thought, "and I can guess who the third was intended for, as she knew I would."

"Freddy, come here. Your grandmother has sent you some theatre tickets for tomorrow night. Hadn't you better send Biddy a line, as there are three, and say you and Sholto will call for her at eight. You can have a taxi. Tell her you have the tickets, and John and I are going out to bridge. I should not mention where you got them till you are in the theatre, or she may refuse."

"Oh, cheers, what a lark."

"And don't forget to acknowledge the tickets. Do it at the same time."

"I can't very well tell her we're taking Biddy, I suppose," said Freddy, "but I'd jolly well like to."

"Then tell her, as long as you do it nicely."

"I can't think why Granny turned on her like that, you know," remarked Freddy.

"Oh, people have these little disagreements. They'll get over it if they're left alone," said Edith.

"Well, personally I wish they would and Biddy could go back, but Sholto doesn't, for some reason."

"Really?" Edith, aware that she was being given information, looked quickly at her daughter's face, but Freddy was engaged with the tickets.

"I say, Edith, front stalls at seventeen shillings. Granny does do you well, doesn't she? What a thrill!"

She was off, whistling joyfully, to write her letters, and Edith knew that she was blissfully unconscious of what she had suggested. That was Freddy all over, absurdly child-like in some things, blind as a young bat, like her father . . . just as Hugh had been until his moment came. Dearest, funny old Hugh, with his blunt speech and his solid, transparent, everyday virtues.

Edith looked at the diamond and sapphire ring which Hugh had liked, and thought of her own young love, and then of Sholto . . . Sholto and Biddy. So it was like that? Once or twice she had fancied so, but it was so difficult to be sure what that young man was thinking. She was fond of him and hoped it would be all right, and in this new preoccupation worried no more about Mrs. Devonshire, beyond saying to Freddy:

"Be nice to your grandmother now, and don't fling Biddy at her head."

"I've been terribly polite," protested Freddy, "and tactful too. I've even called you Mother. I've said 'Dear Granny, you were a sport to send me those perfectly priceless seats. As Mother is going out with John I've asked Biddy. I hope you don't mind. Love from Freddy.' "

6

"What grandeur and what scandalous extravagance," exclaimed Biddy reproachfully to her host and hostess as they settled into their stalls the next evening. "You know, you are a dreadful family. I can't cope with you."

"Ah, but this grandeur is assumed," explained Sholto. "Normally, Freddy and I sneak into the pit with the rest of the proletariat, but tonight we are the guests of the mighty."

"I suppose you mean Edith and John," said Biddy to that.

"You wrong them, lady, Edith and John may shell out for birthdays and Christmas, but they don't believe in promiscuous charity. Guess again."

"Granny sent me the tickets," blurted Freddy, now that Biddy was safely wedged between them and could not escape.

She showed no intention of flight, however, and said eagerly:

"I say, how decent of her. She always does things in the grand style, doesn't she? When she took me to anything I used to feel as though I belonged to a Royal House.... All the same I am sure she didn't intend you to invite me."

"The gift was unconditional," Sholto assured her, "absolutely without any fee or surcharge, carriage paid and F.O.B."

"I told her anyway," added Freddy with glee.

"Oh, Freddy, you shouldn't."

"Of course she should," Sholto defended. "Truth before everything. We teach our little Freddy to be frank and open. That is why her manners seem so bad. Besides, these things get about.... 'Dear Mrs. Devonshire (or Mother or Granny as the case may be), I hardly like to say so, but I actually saw your granddaughter, Biddy Kerlin, out with that notorious jam-maker, Sholto Fenwick—at a *theatre!*' Mrs. Devonshire sweetly: 'Ah, really? Well, perhaps it may interest you to know that I provided the tickets for this orgy which you find so singular.'"

Sholto's mimicry was good and Biddy laughed.

"Well, perhaps you are right. There certainly does seem to be a good deal of interest in my movements.... The curtain is going up—I'll tell you in the interval."

Later, she gave them the history of the fire-irons, and Sir Neville's anxious summons to luncheon.

"You see, I am always caught," she added cheerfully. "You would think there was a detective dogging my footsteps, wouldn't you?"

"Oh, I say, rot!" exclaimed Sholto, scowling. "If I thought Mrs. Devonshire would dare I'd go and beard the old dragon and ask her what she meant."

"My poor lamb, don't be absurd. She had nothing to do with it, she barely knows Sir Neville, and he would have told me."

Sholto opened his mouth to argue, then closed it and

grinned instead. Biddy, recognizing the source of that sudden meekness, smiled too, feeling a happy glow within her.

'I love to think I am so important that my movements are chronicled," she said. "Don't go and rob me of these simple joys."

"Jealous, that's what I am," declared Sholto. "I wouldn't rob you, I merely want to share 'em. Come on, let's hoot the next act in chorus and we'll all get our movements chronicled ... to Bow Street."

"All the same," said Freddy solemnly, "I think Granny must be ill."

"Why?" Biddy looked startled.

"Well, she's so funny. First Edith and then me. She gave Edith a ring the other day, not for anything either. Just sort of pushed it at her. Sapphires and diamonds. Lovely."

"You silly rabbit, that's a sign of intelligence, not illness," cried Sholto. "Who wouldn't give Edith a ring? All the same I rather wish I had nipped in the day she was chucking rings about."

He gazed around him.

"I could do with a ring," he finished sadly to the air.

"You would look a mug in it," said Freddy to that.

The curtain went up again and Freddy's eyes to the stage. Sholto's were less intent upon it, and every now and then the tall girl on his right knew that they had turned her way. She did not hear much but the music herself, she was excited and happy, and yet a little apprehensive lest her grandmother should be vexed about the ticket, and not give Freddy any more.

And then there was Sholto, that was another thing.

Biddy's heart missed a beat, for she had forgotten how this might involve Edith and Freddy, who had been good to her, in trouble with old Mrs. Devonshire. Families were so complicated and she was unused to them and liable to forget. People and their relations to each other made life difficult, you had to be careful, she thought sadly.

The music rose, colors whirled before her eyes, she heard laughter and applause, and joined them with an anxious heart.

She loved the theatre, and this had promised to be such a splendid evening, but now she felt that she had no right here, an intruder in her grandmother's seats, as she was an outcast from her house.

"If only I knew what I had done, I shouldn't mind so much," she said wistfully to herself, and felt Sholto gently touch her hand as though half afraid.

"Liking it?" he asked.

"Perfect," said Biddy with a little gasp.

There, she was spoiling his evening, and somehow that seemed so base a treachery that she turned her head and smiled into his anxious face. After that for the rest of the evening nothing mattered any more. They were together and happy, the future and its problems far away. The most foolish jokes from behind the footlights became pearls of wit and set them laughing, the music was a celestial harmony carrying them to the stars.

The show was over at last and they came out into the cold night air, lifting their faces to it joyfully. Sholto shot off and captured a taxi, much to Freddy's indignation. She was hungry, she said, what about supper? A nice host he was. She clutched him by the arm, nudging violently.

"Oh, lord." Sholto looked round at Biddy, contrite. "Come along then. In you get and we'll sup."

"You'll do any supping there is in my flat," declared Biddy firmly. "It will be going from the sublime to the ridiculous, but let us scrounge."

They scrounged accordingly, and sitting round the gas fire in Wincey Street ate sardines and bread and cheese with the gusto of youth, and drank lemon squash, Biddy having mislaid the key of the wine-cellar, she said, but found two lemons and a half.

"Well, here's to the giver of the feast," cried Sholto, raising his glass.

"To the giver of the tickets," said Biddy suddenly. "Royalty first."

"Ladies and gentlemen," said Sholto grandly, "we stand ...for both these toasts."

"Royalty" at that moment, unconscious of the title just bestowed upon her, was lying awake in her room, watching the firelight playing on the old tallboy and the graceful legs of Miss Sarah Verschoyle's stool.

It was a pretty thing, she thought, going over the tale Mr. Dawes had told her, and smiling to remember that he had almost made it a plea for Biddy, who was in no need of pleas. The need perhaps had been her own and now it was filled and she was satisfied.

Tonight Mrs. Devonshire felt better than she had done for many weeks and her mind was clear. Lying here quietly she thought of the little party at the theatre of which Biddy was one, her guest (whether she knew it or not) for the last time. Amusing that, but the girl had always amused her, which was curious since she had never cared for girls. But the world had changed and that was fair enough. She did not grudge the world its changes, and perhaps she had gone with it a little way.

"After all, there is no denying I was a girl myself once," she ruminated with a flash of her old humor.

She looked back at that girl for a moment, but saw instead two bright blue eyes and a quiet face breaking suddenly into a smile.

CHAPTER ELEVEN

MR. CROW

Devonshire: On October 26 at her residence 49, Portman Square, Mary Octavia Brigid, widow of the late Frederick Devonshire of Highways, Sussex, in her 76th year.

ALL OVER England people of the pre-war generation, reading that notice, remembered and spoke of her, for whatever else she might have been she had not been a woman to forget. *The Times,* in the obituary column, recalled her as a great hostess and a great personality —of late living in retirement, who had known intimately the most brilliant society of her day. The deceased lady, who had been a widow for twenty-five years, said *The Times,* had lost both sons in the War, Colonel Hugh Devonshire, D.S.O. having fallen with great gallantry at Ypres in 1916. She was survived by one daughter, Mrs. Dawnay, the wife of Mr. Richard Dawnay, C.B.E.

No mention was made of the errant Brigid who had married David Kerlin, which was considered perfectly right in certain quarters, or of the present heir to Highways, which was denounced as scandalous and a conspiracy at least in one.

These notices, however, did not appear in *The Times* until Monday morning, and Mrs. Devonshire had died on

Friday night, quietly and smiling a little in her sleep, as though some private joke amused her.

It was left to poor Mr. Crow to inform the family, and, as he looked for the last time at his old client and friend, he thought it was very probable she had been smiling at that. It would be like her.

His firm had served her family for generations, and he had known her as perhaps no other creature had done, high-handed, obstinate, impatient, sardonic and yet with it all, he thought, a great lady for whom it was a little thing to perform this last service, highly disagreeable as it would undoubtedly be.

Mr. Crow knew well what he was in for, but he knew also too much of the history of the last fifteen years for the comfort of those who might assail her memory. Now she was gone to her rest he would have no compunction either. Having suffered much at the hands of some of Mrs. Devonshire's descendants, Mr. Crow felt a certain very human satisfaction at the prospect of having occasion to speak his mind.

He had taken the precaution, before leaving for Portman Square on Saturday morning, to telephone Richard Dawnay and ask him to break the news to his wife, saying he would call upon Mrs. Dawnay later in the day. He had emphasized the fact that there was no need for her to come to the house as it would only distress her, and her mother had particularly requested that she should be spared as much as possible. Mrs. Devonshire had charged him to make all the arrangements and to remain at Portman Square until after the funeral. She had also stipulated that there was to be no mourning.

It was no great surprise to Mr. Crow that these requests should be disregarded, and he had barely finished his interview with the doctor, when Taylor informed him that Mr. and Mrs. Dawnay were downstairs.

Gwen was in black and closely veiled, her tears flowing, hysterical, as he had expected her to be, one moment lamenting her loss, the next heaping reproaches and making accusations.

Richard Dawnay endeavored to soothe her.

"Hush, hush, Gwen, let Mr. Crow speak. This has naturally been a great shock, Crow. Was my mother-in-law's death so sudden that we were given no warning of any kind?"

"Mrs. Devonshire has been suffering from an incurable disease which, however, only became acute within the last few months. She would neither give in to it nor have any one informed, sir. You know her indomitable courage and her strength of will, I have no doubt," said the lawyer gravely.

"Why wasn't I told?" sobbed Gwen. "Why was I kept in the dark?...her only child...it is an outrage."

"My dear Mrs. Dawnay, your mother did not desire you to be distressed. There was nothing to be done. She had every care and I can assure you the greatest specialists were called in consultation. I myself knew nothing definite, though it was clear to me she was in failing health."

"Was there no doctor in attendance then?" enquired Richard Dawnay, frowning.

"Certainly, and nurses also. I understand they were forbidden by your mother to mention her condition."

"Nonsense, nonsense, Crow, this is all very irregular. A

doctor has no business to regard the fancies of an old sick woman."

"Then he would have been turned out of the house. Your mother-in-law was in no condition to be thwarted, but entirely capable of dealing with any one who disregarded her wish, I can assure you. She was not, if I may say so, at any time in her life a woman of fancies."

"That Simpkins must have known," exclaimed Gwen, "telling me lies day after day that poor mother had a chill and was going away for a change. There is one thing I am determined upon, she shall go, now, this very day."

"My dear Mrs. Dawnay, pardon me, I am in temporary charge of the household and have my late client's instructions with regard to these things."

"I never heard of such a thing," cried Mrs. Dawnay indignantly. "If I am not the mistress of the house now my poor mother has gone, I should like to know who is. You forget yourself, Mr. Crow."

"Hush, Gwen!"

"I am Mrs. Devonshire's executor, madam. If you have any doubt of this, her will, when it comes to be read, will confirm all I have told you. And I may say that the same clause occurred word for word in an older will made many years ago," said Mr. Crow with what patience he could.

"So there was a new will?" exclaimed Mrs. Dawnay eagerly. A question trembled on her lips, but it did not need a slight cough from her Richard to drive it away. There were after all certain things she could not do, foolish though she might be. She had the conventional belief that she had loved her mother deeply and was plunged in grief at her loss; she was too shallow to admit to herself that all

this fuss which she was making was sheer hypocrisy, and
that it would have irked and terrified her far more to see
her mother ill and dying; but at least she could not bring
herself to speak of the will, though the worry of having
kept silence was to give her no rest till she knew.

"I feel faint," said Mrs. Dawnay, instead.

Mr. Crow, rather glad of it, sent for a glass of whisky
and soda and the nurse, and drew Richard Dawnay into
another room to discuss the arrangements for the funeral.
He was, after all, the only man of the family and a gentleman, no need to affront him, thought the old lawyer, better
let him suppose he was being consulted. As for the good
lady, she had always been a silly creature, not a touch of
her mother in her. Curious how often you come across
that dissimilarity in families...a throw-back, wasn't that
the term?

"Have—er—the other relatives been informed, Crow?"
enquired Richard Dawnay later as they prepared to go.

"No, sir. I have that unenviable task still before me.
Naturally, as Mrs. Dawnay was my client's only surviving
child, she was notified before any one else," said Mr. Crow
with a bow.

"Quite right, very thoughtful of you. This is a heavy
task for you, I am afraid, and if I can be of any use please
call upon me without hesitation. Now, Gwen, my dear, I
must get you home. I don't think you had better—er—
venture upstairs—eh, Crow?"

"Far wiser not, my dear lady. You are over-wrought and
have your young people to think of," said Mr. Crow tactfully. "Let me give you my arm to the car."

He had disposed of them at last and with less of a scene

than he might have expected, thanks to the presence of poor Dawnay, who would have his hands full enough, if Mr. Crow knew anything.

It was already eleven o'clock by this time and, with many things to see to, it was nearly two before the lawyer was at liberty to think of the other members of the family. He would not try the telephone again, he decided, or there would be another invasion. Better call in person on Mrs. James Devonshire and Mrs. Fenwick.

He had not seen the latter for many years, the former he had seen far too often, and if he decided that as the widow of the eldest son, Mrs. Fenwick should have preference, it was not without a sly humor at his own expense in choosing the unknown before the known evil.

2

The Fenwicks were at luncheon when he sent in his card, and Edith hurried out to him, looking surprised.

"Mr. Crow, I hope nothing is wrong?" she said, and then very gently pushed him into a chair, seeing how exhausted he looked. "Won't you let me get you something? I am afraid you are not well."

"No, no, thank you." He remembered her now. A woman of courage . . . a girl of courage she had been years ago. It was the concern of her tone that had suddenly shaken him, concern for his old friend, he could not doubt.

"I am the bearer of bad news, I am sorry to say," he said. "Mrs. Devonshire died last night."

"Oh, *no.*"

Edith sat down abruptly. He told her what he had to

tell without interruption to the end, grateful for her quiet, yet feeling his years now. He had been armed only against stupidity and cupidity, and here were neither, he was convinced.

"But how like her," said Edith when he had done. "She hated intrusion always, didn't she? I can't help being glad she had her way. I—I admired her tremendously. I hope she didn't suffer, she had had so much to bear in other ways."

"Very little pain on the whole, I think, considering; none at the last. She had had, as you say, many troubles, some inevitable, Mrs. Fenwick, how many of us escape them?" said Mr. Crow sententiously. "Others, a little forethought on the part of her family might have averted. I may tell you in confidence that there has been a constant drain upon her resources for years. I say this because she spoke to me of how difficult it was to deal equitably with her estate. She wanted you to know that if she had done nothing all these years for your young daughter and much for some of her other grandchildren, it was from stress of circumstances only. In fact, she wished to say as much in her will, but I dissuaded her, feeling it perhaps better left unsaid."

"But of course Freddy is in no need, and we should not have dreamt of letting her worry for a moment if we had known," exclaimed Edith. "Poor dear, why, she sent the child seats for the theater only two nights ago, Mr. Crow, ill as she was. She was always giving her little pleasures."

"Ah, well, there will be something more than that," nodded Mr. Crow. "There are some jewels for Miss Freddy,

I think, and your stepson is to choose a memento—Mr. Sholto Fenwick, am I right?"

"How good of her," said Edith. "They *will* be pleased. Mr. Crow, does...have you had an opportunity to tell Biddy Kerlin?"

"Ah! there you remind me. Can you by any chance give me that lady's address?"

"Yes, of course. She is going to be upset, I am afraid, poor child," said Edith, worried. "I almost think, if you don't mind, it would be better to let us tell her."

"I should be infinitely obliged, I should indeed," declared the lawyer with relief. "And now, Mrs. Fenwick, I must not keep you. You will remember what Mrs. Devonshire desired, I am sure—no mourning, none of the ladies of the family to attend the funeral. The memorial service, yes, if they so wish, and all who can possibly do so, to be at Portman Square on Wednesday at three o'clock for the reading of the will."

"Won't you let me give you some lunch before you go?"

"No, no, thank you. I have had luncheon, and if you will take this charge of Miss Kerlin off my hands, I must get on. You will perhaps be good enough to bring the young lady on Wednesday and of course Miss Freddy and your stepson. Thank you, Mrs. Fenwick. It has been a pleasure to meet you again, and I only wish the occasion had been a happier one. Good-by."

"One moment, Mr. Crow," said Edith. "My mother-in-law's poor old maid, Simpkins, I am afraid she must be terribly upset."

"Oh, alas, yes, quite broken up, poor soul, but I have the

nurse there still and we've got her to bed under doctor's orders."

"I would take her gladly and look after her," said Edith doubtfully, "if she'd come."

"That is kind, but unless I'm mistaken, she will want to be there...one of the old devoted servants...the breed is dying out, I am afraid," said Mr. Crow.

"You will let me know if I can do anything for her?"

"Indeed yes, and again good-by, Mrs. Fenwick."

Edith went with him to the lift, and then slowly returned to the dining-room, where the family were lingering over their coffee and making frivolous bets about her visitor.

"Now then," cried Sholto, "out with it, Edith. I suppose John is seeking a divorce and the old Crow came to inform you. Or have you been breaking the gaming laws?...I say, what's up?"

"It's Mrs. Devonshire," said Edith to John.

"Oh, lor'! is she up the pole because I took Biddy?" exclaimed Frederika.

"Don't be ridiculous, Freddy, she meant you to take her," said Edith, almost roughly. "Your grandmother died last night...it seems she has been dying for weeks."

There was a sudden silence round the luncheon-table.

Sholto thought, "Poor old dragon! She was such a sport in her way...I always had a sneaking affection for her."

Freddy, round-eyed, was saying to herself: "I won't ever see her again now. How funny! I won't be able to tell her what a good show it was the other night, and how Biddy said she was Royalty. I thought she'd have liked that and it might have made her ask Biddy to go back. Now she can't. Death's so beastly. I wish she wasn't dead."

"I was uneasy the other day when I heard she had a chill," Edith was saying to John, "but when the theater tickets came for the children I thought I must have been dreaming. She wouldn't have any one told.... Poor Mrs. Devonshire, I wish there was something I could have done, but there wasn't, of course.... I've promised Mr. Crow to tell Biddy.... I'm afraid she will be upset."

Sholto suddenly shot up from his seat.

"Look here, I'd better.... She may see it in some dam' paper and get a horrible shock."

He was out of the room in a moment, getting his hat. Edith went after him, and said to his back:

"Bring her here, my dear. Say I insist upon it or that Freddy is upset and needs her, anything to make her come. She can't be allowed to stay in that flat alone, worrying."

Sholto nodded glumly.

"If necessary, telephone to me, and I'll come and add my persuasions, but bring her if you have to carry her," urged Edith.

Sholto for the first time in his life put an awkward arm around her and, much to his surprise, she kissed him.

"Good luck," she said.

3

"It's a conspiracy," declared Marion. "I knew it. I've said so over and again. I've been kept deliberately from poor Granny. Why wasn't my boy informed? He is the head of the family and should have been with her at the last. It is Gwen Dawnay we have to thank for this, and well I know it."

"Mrs. Dawnay knew nothing whatever, madam, and has not seen her mother. No member of the family was informed of Mrs. Devonshire's illness by her own express command," recited Mr. Crow sharply.

"I don't believe it," said Marion, more from habit than anything else. She nursed a long-standing feud with the lawyer, who for many years had had the thankless task of making her keep within the income which only great sacrifices on the part of her husband's mother had secured for her and her children. An inherently stupid woman, she was incapable of understanding money, and was firmly convinced that there were vast stores of it in the family which rightly belonged to her son.

The news that no one had seen her mother-in-law revived her spirits and stimulated her greed.

"And what has she left?" she enquired eagerly.

"That you will learn in due course," retorted Mr. Crow in a scandalized tone.

"But you can give me a rough idea of the figures surely? In fact, it is most important for me to know. My boy's position requires it and it is my right. I demand to be told," said Marion haughtily.

"Good afternoon."

"You think you can do as you like, do you? We'll see about that," she called after him. "I can tell you this: the moment my son comes of age the business and Highways will be taken out of *your* hands, and very quickly."

"Very good, madam. But I shall not trouble to wait for that distant event. Now that my old friend can no longer be served, I shall apply to the Courts to be relieved of the trustee-ship to your son. His Majesty's judges will perhaps be able to make you see reason, which is and always has been entirely beyond my poor capacity."

Mr. Crow, with a bow, departed, and Marion sat down among her knick-knacks feeling distinctly alarmed. Courts, judges, what did the man mean? He was her enemy, she had always known it. As if she hadn't had trouble enough!

James had gone out in spite of the cough which she fondly supposed him to possess, and would not be in till late. There was no one upon whom to pour her grievances at this hour on a Saturday afternoon. She could not even go and tell the Stores she would take the best grand piano in the shop, for the Stores would be closed.

Marion thought she would go and see poor Gwen...a visit of condolence....Gwen must know the size of her mother's fortune. And then about the mourning. This idea of no mourning seemed to Marion's common little soul hardly quite nice, so economical, as though they could not afford it. Certainly there were many little things about which she wanted to consult Gwen, and seeing that there was a death in the family, she would take a taxi. It would not do to be seen in public, for what would people think?

Gwynneth came to her aunt in the drawing-room and said her mother was asleep and she didn't want to wake her as she was so upset about Granny. She wished privately that Aunt James had stayed away, for if mummy heard her and came down she would begin to cry all over again. May had gone off with Basil saying, what was the odds, staying at home wouldn't do Granny any good, which was quite true, Gwynneth agreed, but even May's support would have been something. Gwynneth wondered if Granny would leave them much money, and then whether it wasn't rather beastly to be thinking of that, only it would be such a relief and besides Mummy would be upset if she didn't. All the same, they had been a pretty big expense to Granny, she remembered unhappily, not only school fees and Herbert's fees, but that time he got into such a scrape and owed all that money. Gwynneth, though she was only fifteen at the time, had been told because Mummy had to tell some one, but May didn't know to this day.... Herbert had refused to stay at home this morning, saying he was too busy; that was the best of being a man, you could make excuses and get away.

Gwynneth, pouring out the tea, vaguely heard her aunt's voice going on and on, and answered mechanically.

"...So wonderful I should have given poor Granny that nice cozy bed-wrap for her birthday, it must have been such a comfort to her," said Aunt James. "It almost looks as though I was prompted to do it, for I was at my wit's end and then something said to me, 'a bed-wrap.' I've often been told I'm very psychic...."

Mrs. Dawnay, from her bedroom above, heard the murmur of voices in the drawing-room and rang her bell to ask who was there.

"I must go down," she decided, learning that it was her sister-in-law. "She will expect it and a cup of tea will do my head good. Perhaps Marion will know something ... not, of course, that I shall ask...."

4

"That you, Janey?"

"Well, I must say, Herbert, it is something new to hear

your voice. About time you did give me a ring," said Jane
at the other end of the telephone.

"I know, I know, old thing. I've been rushed to the
uttermost. So the ancestor's gone—had you heard the sad
tidings?"

"What?"

"Yes, passed out last night. Well, R.I.P. and all that.
Mean to say you hadn't heard?"

"Heard, of course I hadn't heard! I never hear a dam'
thing."

"I say, you do seem peeved."

"Oh, shut up," said Jane.

"All right, all right. The old girl must have left a tidy
sum, so here's hoping some of it comes our way. Any idea
what she was worth?"

"No, I haven't, and if you're only ringing me because
you want information you can go to the devil," snapped
Jane, banging down the receiver.

She stood in the middle of the untidy studio and shivered
suddenly. Why on earth had she done that? With a little
stringing on Herbert would have asked her out or come
over here. She was alone. She couldn't stick it, she would
be thinking of Granny, lying there in Portman Square,
and get the jim-jams. But Herbert made her sick ... all
these weeks not a word from him, and now wanting to
make use of her merely, pump her about Granny's money.
As if she knew, as if she had a hope of anything with
James and Mother always cadging.

Jane seized a cigarette and smoked it fiercely, then put
it down on the edge of the mantelpiece and rouged her
lips. No, she couldn't stay here alone; she couldn't go home

either, her mother's complaints and guesses would make
life hideous.

She pulled on her hat, found her handbag and keys,
puffed at the cigarette again uncertainly, then flung it in
the empty fireplace and ran out of the studio, banging the
door. Whether they liked it or not, some one would have
to put her up for the week-end. She couldn't stay here
alone.

CHAPTER TWELVE

DARK STEEDS

S HOLTO RUSHING tempestuously to Wincey Street, cursed the traffic signs which seemed always to be turned against the taxi and wished he had gone by the Tube instead. Edith's suggestion that Biddy would be upset at her grandmother's death had sent his doubts and hesitations flying, and all he knew was that he must get to her as fast as possible. He might have been going to ward off some deadly peril rather than to convey bad news, and it was not until he was actually on the stairs that he realized how much he was taking for granted and how poor a consolation his presence might easily be.

If she was going to be hurt by this news he saw suddenly that all his love for her could not prevent it, or the countless other griefs which life and death might deal her, unless she cared for him, perhaps not even then. In that moment he had a sharp sense of the loneliness of every human creature, and he was appalled.

Biddy had resisted their persuasions to go out on this Saturday in order to devote herself to shampooing the flat, as she called it. Having completed this operation, she had taken up some mending, when she heard a man's step on the stairs.

Supposing it to be the grocer, she flung open the door to take in her order, and found Sholto instead.

"You didn't read the notice on the gate," she said in a tone of reproof. "No hawkers, no circulars.... Sholto—is anything the matter?"

Sholto came in awkwardly and closed the door, not looking at her. He put his hat down, and she exclaimed again: "Sholto!"

"I've come—there's a bit of bad news in the family, as a matter of fact," stumbled Sholto. "Edith promised we'd let you know. Old Mrs. Devonshire...she died last night."

Biddy stood quite still and Sholto, looking at her at last, saw that she had turned slowly white. It was more than he could bear and he caught her in his arms.

"Biddy, darling, don't mind, please don't mind. The poor old girl has been ill for months and wouldn't let on. Sweetheart, it's all right, isn't it? Just the shock has knocked you over a bit."

She clung to him, shaking, her face buried in his coat.

"I'm a clumsy brute, bursting it out at you like that," said Sholto miserably, "and I wouldn't hurt a hair of your darling head. I love you so, Biddy, and like a selfish ass I wouldn't let Edith come. She'd have done it so much better...eh?"

"No," said Biddy.

Her voice was quite steady, but sounded vague and far away. Sholto held her close, afraid to believe she realized what she was saying...what he was talking about. Her stillness troubled him, for after all why should she mind like this, unless because she had been too much alone and worrying about the quarrel with her grandmother secretly. The old girl had turned her out and it was no fault of Biddy's, she had done nothing to deserve it.

"We had no business to let you live alone like this," he said. "I've always hated it and you shan't be alone another minute." (That was the way, divert her mind, make her argue.) "You'll marry me at the first church we can catch."

Sholto looked hopefully at her brown head. Even a fierce denial would almost have relieved him at the moment, but none came.

"You can't catch one at this hour in the afternoon," said Biddy, "and I am used to being alone."

"Oh, Biddy!"

At the pain in his voice she lifted her head quickly and said with a protective smile:

"It's all right...I'm muddled, don't look so worried.... You're terribly good to me...."

She drew herself out of his arms but he caught her hand and she let that stay, gazing uncertainly round the room and saying: "I was just going to mend my stockings."

"Never mind the stockings. You are going to put a few things in a suitcase and come home with me. Edith insists. She said if I came back without you, there would be murder," said Sholto eagerly.

Biddy looked frightened.

I think I'd better not," she pleaded.

"I've been told to carry you if necessary," he declared, trying to bring a smile. "And then Freddy has the pip a bit and wants you. The whole family wants you. More than my life's worth to tell 'em you won't, Biddy. Come on, now, might as well come quietly. I'm a nasty fellow when roused."

"I should be a rotten guest," said Biddy in a low voice.

"Oh, but we like our guests on the ripe side."

She laughed suddenly, then caught her breath, her hand clutching his as though that steadied her, her eyes dark with distress.

"Oh, I *wish* I'd gone back, Sholto...but it isn't any good wishing, is it?"

She broke from him and ran into the bathroom, banging the door. He heard her moving things noisily and called to her, his heart in his mouth.

"You can come in, if you like," she said. She was throwing her pyjamas and toothbrush into a small case.

"Just for tonight," she thought. "I can't let him worry, or any of them. I know it's just their kindness, only Freddy might want me. Grandmother may have wanted me and I didn't go. I must put in a frock for dinner, and satin shoes...."

She hardly noticed Sholto, standing in the doorway till he took the case gently out of her hands. He was so grateful to her for giving in that he was afraid to speak, afraid almost to touch her, lest he should find her gone again.

"I think I'd better wear a coat, it seems cold," said Biddy, vaguely looking round her and then going back to the corner cupboard in the bathroom for it. He took that from her too and held it ready and as she slipped her arms into it, she leant back against him and looked up.

"I do love you," she said earnestly.

"Oh, my dear!" cried Sholto, gathering her close.

They had locked up at last, and a taxi was carrying them to Buckingham Gate through the windy afternoon. Leaves and scraps of paper were fluttering along the footpaths and whirling in the air as though lovely autumn had become desolate and down-at-heel, and cared no more for anything.

"Edith will have a fire, I'll bet," said Sholto. "She has a splendid weather eye, springs fires on you all the year round, if necessary. Biddy, darling, you know I won't try to stop your antique-ing if you've set your heart on it, only it can be a sort of hobby when we are married, can't it? I couldn't bear you to be working all day long."

Biddy smiled at him wistfully. She remembered with a strange feeling of unreality that everything was changed. There was no reason now why she should not love Sholto ... perhaps there never had been, but she was so uncertain and confused. She had come with him now because he was in need of her, but the present was too heavy for her to think about the future yet. She longed to get away by herself into the dark and fight her misery alone.

She could not tell him that, and it did not even enter her head that he knew it in his own fashion, and was trying to help her by talking of other things. Standing alone had become a habit with her, because all her life it had been a necessity, and she had the awkward shyness of the solitary. Though she loved him she could not yet give herself up to the comfort of his presence.

Biddy had known greater grief before. She had lost her father, but that had been a different matter, her own private loss and therefore to be borne. Her grandmother was like a stranger who had been good to her, and whom somehow she had basely failed. She had seen her father die, but her grandmother had died old and alone, and perhaps wanting her, at the very least believing her ungrateful and a disappointment.

That Mrs. Devonshire could have sent for her was too facile a consolation. Biddy did not even think of it. The old, still figure, lying in Portman Square, would have been amazed could she have known how magnificent she had always seemed to this apparently aloof young member of her house.

She ought to have gone back, although that had seemed impossible, as though it would be begging for favors which she had never asked for, certainly, but had accepted and then somehow lost.

How had she lost them, what had she done? Of course she had lost her temper and talked of paying off back duty, for one thing. The phrase which had pleased her for weeks afterwards seemed dreadful to her now, and dishonest, too. In her heart she had never believed that a sense of duty had had anything to do with her grandmother's kindness to her. That there was no other visible explanation had merely accorded with the whole delicious unreality of that incredible year in Portman Square.

"Sleepy?" asked Sholto gently to her bent head, and she opened her eyes and forced a smile. Buildings raced past the taxi windows, and she saw that they must be nearly at Buckingham Gate.

Biddy sat up resolutely and pulled herself together.

2

The elder Fenwicks usually played golf on Saturday afternoon, but Edith had persuaded Freddy to take her place and get a few lessons in the game from John, on the plea that she wanted to prepare for Biddy.

From what she had seen in Sholto's face she hoped there might be some cheering news for them when they re-

turned, but she gave them no hint of this. Her real reason
for packing them off was to have the girl for a little while
to herself, always supposing Sholto succeeded in persuad-
ing her to come.

In the general upset she had had no opportunity to tell
Sholto that Mrs. Devonshire had left him a memento in
her will, and now she reproached herself that in her confusion of mind she had not asked Mr. Crow whether Biddy
also had been remembered. She felt convinced that the girl
would not be left out, but certainty would be more use
than a thousand surmises, if Biddy proved in need of consolation and reassurance. True, Mr. Crow had asked her
to take Biddy to the house on Wednesday, but presumably
the entire family were being invited to hear the will, so
that might be merely a matter of form and mean nothing.
A natural delicacy forbade Edith to ring up the lawyer
and ask him point-blank. She could not put such a question to him in Mrs. Devonshire's house where she lay
dead, even if it had been possible to explain the reason
for her curiosity. Here in her own drawing-room his
mention of the legacies to her children would have made
it simpler.

Edith's knowledge of the quarrel between Biddy and
her grandmother was of the scantiest, but she suspected
that the girl had just the kind of sensitive reserve that
would make her self-reproachful now, and probably without reason, which is the way of the young. Certainly there
had been no bitterness on Mrs. Devonshire's side. Edith
knew well that the mention of any one under the ban of
her mother-in-law's serious displeasure would have evoked
merely an impatient silence, and never the half-sardonic

amusement with which her occasional references to Biddy had been received.

Her own name had been heard in that ominous silence often enough in all probability, she thought with a faint smile, but in spite of that she could still believe Mrs. Devonshire to have been an essentially just woman. Dislike or displeasure notwithstanding, her mother-in-law had more than once upheld her in difficult moments long ago, and whether her new kindness of late had been to her as Hugh's wife or Frederika's mother, Edith, who would never have sought it, was glad it had come about.

No, whichever way she looked at it, the absence of Biddy's name from the will seemed incredible, but certainly she could not venture to say so, lest after all she should prove wrong.

Edith, putting flowers in the girl's room, and making it look as cozy and home-like as possible, wondered why she was thus crossing her bridge before she came to it. Biddy might be in no need of consolation or—a much more likely possibility—would perhaps not seek it from her.

"Should I at her age?" she asked herself. "Of course not. I don't know what has come over me, unless it was the look on Sholto's face. I wish they'd come or I could know how he is getting on. This waiting is intolerable."

She went to one of the drawing-room windows and looked out. Grey blankets of cloud were piled up in the sky, the buildings had that curiously blind look that belongs to a London week-end, and down in the street the few pedestrians visible were either struggling against the wind or being swept along with it. It was a day for dismal thoughts and early as it was Edith turned on one or two lights and poked the fire into a blaze. At the same moment she heard the lift come up, and after it the sound of a latchkey in the door.

3

"Got her," said Sholto. "It very nearly came to carrying though."

He had his arm round Biddy, possibly to usher her in, but from his expression Edith fancied not.

"Good for you," she said. "It was nice of you to come, Biddy. It is such a dismal day, we wanted you with us. Ring for tea, will you, Sholto, while Biddy takes off her things."

She took the girl to her room and helped her off with her coat, explaining Freddy's absence.

"John was going to be done out of his golf, and I persuaded her to take him on. Men mooning about a flat on Saturday afternoon are a distressing sight, Biddy."

"I do think you were sensible to make them go," said Biddy, "but I hope you didn't stay at home just for me? I'm always here. I'm becoming a regular parasite."

"Parasite indeed! I hope it is something far more exciting than that you are going to be in this household," said Edith.

Biddy, who was bending over her suitcase, looked up quickly.

"Has he told you?" she asked.

"Not a word; but he doesn't usually walk into the flat with his arm round a girl under my very nose."

"Did we?...Did we really? As a matter of fact, we are both a bit mixed and absent-minded."

"One of the most certain symptoms, I believe," said Edith smiling. "Biddy, dear, I am more pleased than I can say. It is the very nicest thing that could possibly have happened."

"He's such a darling, nobody could help it," offered Biddy obscurely.

She felt awkward and inexperienced and wished she could be like Edith, so gracious and composed, but Edith, desperately seeking the right word, was just as conscious of her own shortcomings.

She thought, "She's hardly older than Freddy, poor child, and I ought to be able to reach her better than this. She's had too much responsibility...."

"Yes, he is a darling," she agreed. "He rushed off to you in such a state that I guessed, Biddy...Sholto is usually so calm. That is really why I sent the others out. I wanted you for a little while to myself if he brought you back... both of you," she added hastily, to a sudden apprehensive look in the girl's face.

The gong rang for tea, a tattoo that spoke of Sholto's hand.

"He is getting impatient, the rascal," said Edith. "Just hang up your frock and come along, my dear. You can put your other things away later."

Biddy did not want to talk...could not, perhaps, she decided. It would be easier round the fire, with Sholto's light touch to help them both.

Sholto was waiting for them at the drawing-room door.

"What did I tell you?" he cried to Biddy gayly. "A fire! Isn't she the perfect housekeeper?"

"That's a nice way to begin," said Edith, "throwing the

poor child's mother-in-law-elect's virtues in her face already."

"*What?*" shouted Sholto. "You old lynx! And here I was, preparing to break it gently."

"Good news doesn't need to be broken gently, darling."

Sholto, beaming at this unexpected title of endearment, said to Biddy in assumed indignation:

"Just listen to that! She's glad to be getting rid of me at last. The wicked stepmother, that's what she is."

Biddy, put forcibly into an easy chair, with cushions heaped behind her head, leaned back and watched them both, warmed by the kindness that always enfolded her in this household, loving their affection for each other. The wind whistled mournfully outside the windows and she thought of her own little flat, where she had wanted to stay alone, and then incredulously that she would have been far more miserable if Sholto had allowed her to do it.

"I don't think I am really so fond of being alone," she thought. "I'm just used to it, it's a habit...I never imagined I should be marrying any one...how queer it sounds, and what a good thing I can housekeep a bit. It will be much more fun to do it for Sholto than just for myself.... I wouldn't ever have met him if it hadn't been for grandmother....Oh, I *wish* I'd gone back!"

It had returned upon her again, she could not keep it away, and Sholto's voice and Edith's hardly reached her consciousness any more as the old puzzle began revolving in her mind, coming back always to the desolate picture of her grandmother dying alone.

"Even if I couldn't have done anything, I'd at least have been somebody to laugh with," she thought, and remembered the majestic figure sitting at the dining-table in Portman Square, making witty comments on the world she lived in, as though the girl opposite were some guest of importance to be entertained.

She had unrolled the pageant of the years before Biddy's dazzled eyes, playing for her laughter and finding infinite entertainment in this exercise of an old power, but even more than that in the swift response to it from so unlikely a source. The girl was too inexperienced to realize this, or to know how much bitter disappointment with her grandmother's own stock she had all unwittingly assuaged.

Sholto brought her tea and sat on the hearthrug beside her with his own.

"Hear that? She says her rejoicings have nothing to do with me and I'm a conceited ass. That's the way she speaks to me, Biddy. Such language from a lady! She says she's only so pleased at getting you into the family ... under her thumb, is what she's thinking of. Be warned."

"If I have never been able to get you there, I am hardly likely to succeed with Biddy," said Edith.

"I'm not sure it mightn't be rather nice," remarked Biddy wistfully. "Do you think I'm so tough, Edith?"

"No, toughness wouldn't daunt me," returned Edith, shaking her head with a smile.

Biddy smiled back suddenly out of her troubled eyes, and to the older woman there seemed to be at once gratitude and pleading in her glance.

"It is your youth and my antiquity that are against me," said Edith lightly, yet still aware that she was feeling her way. "Thirty-eight is much further from twenty-one than forty-eight from thirty-one, or fifty-eight from forty-one, in spite of the mathematicians."

"Lady Methusaleh, what rot you talk," remarked Sholto. "You grow younger every day, and you know it. Biddy and I will pass you at a run before you know where you are. Don't listen to her wily tongue, old thing. She's trying to make you burst into tears of pity for her decrepit state. It's a dodge ... working on your sympathy."

That was true with a difference, thought his stepmother, watching the pair of them, Sholto hooking his arm in hers and expecting her to drink her tea at the perilous angle produced; Biddy for the moment diverted from graver matters, her young face alight.

"I must finish my tea and leave them to it," she decided. "I'll invent some letters to write, though I daresay they will see through it and offer me a newer device."

She was not far wrong.

"But how tactful," said Sholto gleefully to her departing back five minutes later.

Edith paused in the doorway.

"I thought you seemed to need a little practice before John and Freddy came in," she retorted with friendly malice, and was rewarded by a shout of laughter.

She realized that Biddy had not mentioned her grandmother's death, that she herself had not been able to mention it either, and that this artificial silence was certainly all wrong. Perhaps, however, the girl had said all she needed to say to Sholto, and almost certainly Freddy would bring the subject up. They understood each other, these young people, shared the same point of view.

Edith heard her family come in, but decided to let

them make their own discoveries, and presently Freddy dashed along the hall and put her head in the study door.

"Of all the dark steeds," she said.

"Surprised?" enquired her mother.

"I should think so. Jolly good notion too. My word! what a day! Well, I'm off to have a bath if any one enquires."

"They won't, my dear, your little nose is out of joint at present," said Edith, experimentally.

Freddy felt her nose.

"Seems all right.... Besides, I've ordered the kind of room I want in their flat or whatever they have. It's all fixed."

Freddy stamped off to her bath, whistling, then stopped the whistle in mid-stream, as it were, politely remembering her grandmother.

"I must tell her about her trinkets," thought Edith, "or perhaps better not as we don't know for certain whether there is anything for Biddy. No, I'll tell none of them. Let it come as a surprise."

She fell to thinking of Mrs. Devonshire's questions about Sholto and Freddy a few weeks ago, sorry she had not been sure then of the real state of affairs. It might have pleased her mother-in-law, possibly even brought her round, persuaded her to send for them.

"I have a horrid feeling I have been clumsy about this somehow," she thought in distress. "But how absurd! There was nothing I could do."

As she was changing for dinner Sholto knocked at her door and came strolling in. He was already dressed which was in itself unusual. Such exemplary punctuality was not one of his virtues.

"I am inclined to like you, Edith," he remarked.

"Flatterer, to what am I indebted for this sudden change of front? Out with it."

"She's pretty blue, I'm afraid. I thought perhaps you could talk to her...I blunder about," said Sholto. "She won't say anything, but I know she liked the old girl.... Oh, damn!"

"Don't worry, my dear, we should not like her not to care. After all, her relations with her grandmother were unusual, but she will get over it in time. Perhaps no one can really help her. I will try, though," said Edith, seeing his anxious face.

"What children men are," she thought helplessly. "He can't expect to take possession of a girl like Biddy all in a moment. If she were as shallow as that he would not be happy with her for a month."

Yet now that she was committed to broaching the subject to Biddy, Edith felt at least the relief of resolution. She had no opportunity during the evening, but as goodnights were being said, she remarked to the girl:

"I am going to have some hot milk, Biddy, and I will bring you some presently if you can take it. Strange beds are always inclined to make one restless, and it may send you off to sleep."

"I should love it," Biddy admitted.

She was already in bed when Edith knocked at the door, and she said gratefully:

"The way I am spoiled in this house...."

"We haven't really got our hands in at spoiling you yet

...I suggest an aspirin. You look a little tired, which is not to be wondered at," said Edith, sitting on the edge of the bed. "I wish your grandmother could have known this news, Biddy."

Biddy, holding the glass of milk in both hands, looked at it dumbly.

"She might have quarreled with you all then...for liking me," she said at last.

"Not she. She knew we were very good friends, and I think she was pleased.... She even chaffed me about being a capable aunt."

"She was like that...she wouldn't give me away, but I must have done something...and she had been so good to me."

The girl put the half-empty glass on the tray beside her bed, and pulled the eiderdown a little higher as though to conceal her face.

Edith looked past her and said as casually as she knew how:

"I suppose we all of us have some reason for self-reproach in that way, Biddy. I have certainly, and I daresay she had, and yet if she could see us sitting here worrying about it, don't you think she would laugh?... and want to knock our heads together?"

"I know it's futile," admitted the girl in a difficult voice. "I've got to get over it...it's all right."

"I knew her, not in the charming, intimate way you did, but for twenty years and at one time very well," Edith went on. "Believe me, Biddy, if she had been seriously angry with you, she would not have spoken your name, much less joked about our being friends."

"No." Biddy sounded suddenly hopeful. She finished her milk and smiled at Edith. "I have been feeling so beastly because I didn't go back, but even now I don't see how I could have done, without its seeming as though it were cupboard love. It is all so difficult.... But you are right about that and I'm glad ... I shall be more sensible in the morning ... I am sort of topsy-turvyish."

"Of course you are. Try to get off to sleep and not think about it any more. I'll go away and let the warm milk do its work. Dream about Sholto, Biddy darling. In fact, I think that is almost a duty."

Edith put out the light and went away on this note, and Biddy sank down in her comfortable bed, hearing the wind outside, and engaging her mind with the luxury of being sheltered in this friendly household, with Sholto near and perhaps at this very moment thinking of her.

"I'm getting drowsy ... I'll dream of you," she said to him in imagination. "You're much nicer than any one in the world, and I haven't told you that yet, have I? I'll certainly dream of you."

She did her best, almost but not quite falling asleep, and presently beginning to turn in that semi-wakefulness which is the forerunner of an endless night.

"But I could have written," she said, quite definitely sleepless at last, and staring into the darkness, "even if I couldn't go back, I could have written and thanked her for having me all that time at Portman Square. If she wasn't really furious with me, it makes it worse, because perhaps she wanted me, and she was all alone."

She could not shut out the thought of that lonely death and her responsibility. Neither reason nor fortitude could do it. Perhaps it was because her grandmother bore no comparison with any one she had ever known and had been set apart in a kind of splendor in her eyes, that an end so desolate for her seemed beyond common bearing.

For all her poise Biddy was very young, and the news had not merely shocked her, it had caught her with complete surprise, as something she had never even remotely contemplated. That vigor, that unquenchable spirit, that upright carriage had seemed far removed from sickness and death, or any mortal weakness. She had supposed her grandmother would live for years.

A sleepless night will magnify distress for maturer minds than Biddy Kerlin's; misery had its way with her, she could no longer fight it, but lay staring into the darkness, until one by one the forms of things became visible dimly in the unfamiliar room. It would have been a comfort to get up and walk, but she was afraid her movements would be heard and some one come to her. Through the curtained window she could see the glow of London which never quite goes out. It always seemed friendly when she awoke at night in her little flat, but it had no comfort for her now. She wished she were at home in her own much harder bed, which had grown used to her and kind, knowing her ways. There she could hide her misery, but here it stood revealed in an alien world and must be conquered before the morning.

Over the voice of the wind Big Ben chimed the quarters, steadily, interminably, and then the hours in a tone of thunder and reproach. He seemed to be booming over her head and before long she was waiting for him, her mind

defenseless. He had joined the host of her enemies to send
sleep away.

Biddy sat up and buried her head in her hands; she
crept out of bed and walked round the room on tiptoe,
touching things blindly, turned back the curtains and
looked out at the sky with roofs and spires like shadows
laid upon it. It was no good. Nothing had any word for
her, she might have been walking in her sleep. Shivering
she crept back to bed again, pulled the bed-clothes over
her ears, tried to close her eyes which stood open pain-
fully as though propped up by some invisible instrument.

"I must sleep," she said, "I must sleep. I shall be so dead
tomorrow Sholto will notice and worry, and they won't
let me go home. I must go home."

Relief came at last; towards dawn she slept, fitfully at
first, but soon the deep sleep of exhaustion. She heard no
movement of the waking household, and knew nothing
until suddenly Freddy was standing beside her with a
breakfast tray in her hands.

"Rain's coming down like a ton of bricks," announced
Freddy. "Jolly, isn't it, because we none of us have to go
out? Edith wouldn't let you be wakened. You're not to
move either, because you can't have a bath on top of
breakfast. They are all coming to call in a minute."

Freddy put down the tray and lit the fire, then, perched
on the bed, poured out coffee, buttered toast and saw that
the guest had a hearty meal. Edith and John looked in to
greet her; Sholto appeared, lifted Freddy coolly to the
floor and took her place, and Biddy's hand when he could
get it.

It was morning and, with all this care enfolding her,

easy to smile and say she had had a splendid night, though her body felt bruised and aching all over, as though from some physical ill.

The rain beat against the window in a steady stream; Sholto casually announced that he had had a rise in his salary for virtuous behavior, another hundred a year, and that Edith had offered a little car for a wedding present, so that Biddy could learn to drive him to work and then go off treasure hunting in it when she felt inclined. Freddy said the color of a car was important, and Biddy had better choose it as she would have to live with it. Sholto enquired whether this was their wedding or hers, she was making so free with.

Biddy, lying back on her pillows, felt warmed all over and comforted. They were doing and saying all this to cheer her, and she would be cheered.

She watched Sholto's dark head, and loved it, and felt his strong fingers in her hand. And she thought:

"She gave me this too really. She gave me everything. Oh! I wish she knew."

<h2 style="text-align:center">4</h2>

After all, she did not return to Wincey Street that day. Such an outcry from Sholto greeted the suggestion that she could not press it, and having concealed her sleepless night, there was no visible reason why she should go. Later in the day she learned from Edith that they hoped to keep her with them at least until after her grandmother's funeral, and then it was discovered that in the general confusion no one had told her about the reading of the will.

"But I shan't have to go, Edith, shall I?" exclaimed
Biddy hastily. "I should feel so awful going into her house
now she isn't there, when she turned me out. She mightn't
like it."

"She particularly wished that all her family should be
there, you see, Biddy, and as far as that goes, she mightn't
like it if you didn't," said Edith cleverly. "Mr. Crow
asked me to take you, and Sholto is invited too. I hardly
think you ought to stay away."

"No..." said Biddy, "I suppose not. If Sholto is going
it does make a difference, and of course you and Freddy,
but I never quite feel I'm a member of the family. I don't
get used to the idea."

"Then I shall certainly keep you by force until Wednesday so that you can get used to being a member of this
one, while I have the chance," declared Edith.

"That's different."

"I'm glad to hear it, because I'm fond of Sholto myself,
and I don't want to lose him entirely."

"Oh, Edith, you're laughing. I thought for a moment
you were serious," cried Biddy. "Why, he thinks there's
nobody like you in the world...and so do I."

"Why, you little duffer, of course I was laughing." Edith
put an arm round the girl. "You are not used to people,
I know, but please get used to them and be young and
irresponsible. You have some one else to take responsibility
now, so you had better practice letting him. He'll love it."

"He's been having a good shot at it for some time," said
Biddy smiling. "We very nearly came to blows." She
paused and then added awkwardly: "I feel absolutely at
home here though...I always have from the first."

"And it is your home now as well as Sholto's," said Edith. "So no more references to parasites, or I shall think you are just being polite to your mother-in-law elect."

"You are not old enough for the job."

Edith laughed; that was better, she felt. Her reference to her years had not, after all, passed unnoticed. In time she might even persuade this inarticulate young creature to trust her and talk to her.

CHAPTER THIRTEEN

BENEFITS TO COME

THE HOUSE in Portman Square from which old
Mrs. Devonshire had gone out for the last time, was
awaiting the arrival of her family.

The blinds had been drawn up, and in the sunny afternoon the long drawing-room glowed as usual with the
serene elegance of a room from which the presiding personality has but momentarily gone. A fire burned in the
grate and there were chrysanthemums in a crystal jar on
the marquetry table under the window. Simpkins had
seen to that, quickly vigilant after her first collapse, that
while the house remained, all should be as the mistress
would have wished it to be.

Fiercely, Simpkins was determined that there should be
no criticism from the family of matters that had been left
in her hands. Old and grief-stricken, she had yet rallied
iealously to this last trust.

Mr. Crow was amazed at the dexterous and unflagging
service which surrounded him with comfort as though he
had been a guest in the house, and shook his head over a
world from which such excellencies were all too quickly
passing. As soon as the family had departed this afternoon,
he would see the staff in a body and convey to them the
gratifying manner in which their late mistress had remembered them, make them a little speech in short. It would

be a pleasant duty, and he only wished he could look forward with equal satisfaction to the task immediately ahead.

Mr. Crow was afraid that he knew better. He had had the library prepared for the ceremony in order to keep it as strictly business-like as possible, and had set the hour for three o'clock, in the hope that the visitors would have the grace to go home immediately afterwards. There were some among them if he knew anything who would like to sit gossiping around his old friend's fireside, drinking her tea and discoursing on her failings, and he did not propose to give them an opportunity if he could help it. The next thing they would be over-running the house.

"I think it would not be advisable to make any preparation for refreshments, other than perhaps wine and biscuits in the library, Mrs. Simpkins," he remarked confidentially. "If the ladies should desire tea perhaps you would have something quite simple conveyed to us as we sit. This is—er—not quite an occasion for a ladies' tea-party, and I am anxious to get my business done."

"They'll ask," said old Simpkins bluntly.

"You think so? Then perhaps we had better be prepared. In the library, if you will be so good, shall we say at four o'clock? Thank you, Mrs. Simpkins."

Simpkins was pleased at her title, though "Mrs." she was not and never would be. A pack of men indeed! ... Wild horses would not have made her Mrs. Any One, but it showed a very nice feeling in the gentleman, who could not be expected to know one way or another. Very kind indeed he had been to her too, seeing how badly she was taking the loss of the mistress, telling her with his own

lips that he had it all set down in black and white about
the money for "P. Simpkins, my maid and faithful friend
for nearly fifty years." In due course she should have a
copy of the document to keep, he had promised her.

"Faithful friend for nearly fifty years," and in fact it
was only forty-five. Ah, you would think she had known
that fifty was what Simpkins had always hoped for, and
perhaps she did, she that always saw through you so easily.

So Simpkins had her consolations to keep her up while
there were still matters needing her attention, though the
Memorial Service yesterday morning had nearly brought
her again to the point of collapse.

Very beautiful it had been, said the staff, conveyed
there in a car by Mr. Crow's arrangement, and given seats
at the back of the church. Such flowers and such a congre-
gation! The staff had felt a reflected glory from that last
tribute to their mistress, but poor old Simpkins had only
known that it was indeed the last, the last of her friend.

"And you that grand, Miss Simpkins, sitting with the
family," said the staff, for so it had actually occurred. As
she went in, bewildered, some one had taken her hand and
led her up to the front of the church.... Miss Biddy it
was, and next thing she was sitting with Mrs. Fenwick
on one side and Miss Biddy on the other, and all the
family indeed close by. Simpkins had been too far gone
in grief for pride, she had wept on the young lady's
shoulder, seeing nothing, hearing nothing, and even forgetting that Miss Biddy had neglected her grandma's
birthday and never sent her a word.

More than that, Mrs. Fenwick had driven her back to
Portman Square herself and been most kind, even offer-

ing to help her find a comfortable home, when she learnt
what the mistress had desired Simpkins to do, and saying
she would telephone later in the week and come in a taxi
to fetch her.

Simpkins, wandering about the lonely house, knew that
her trust was nearly done, but she could not even imagine
the life ahead of her when, according to orders, she was
to take her rest and her reward. What were rest and re-
wards to her? She had all the newspapers, from which to
cut out the pieces about the mistress, and she would have
the document in due course, Mr. Crow had promised her.
She would buy a book and paste these treasures in, and
that was all she knew.

That she would in times to come enlarge upon them to
an interested circle and be pointed out as that "funny old
Miss Simpkins, who is so well connected, you know, she
used to live in Portman Square," Simpkins could not fore-
see, for she was still Mrs. Devonshire's maid and not yet
an old lady of private means, taking her ease in some
quiet hotel.

2

A ring at the bell and only a quarter to three! Mr.
Crow looked at his watch and decided that some people
were always in an unseemly hurry on these occasions. No
doubt of it, money was a debasing influence, showed you
human nature at its worst. All his old client's sense of
equity would not satisfy some members of her family.
Nor all the Archangel Gabriel's, as she had drily remarked, when he had ventured to suggest as much.

Mr. Crow, retreating from the library in order to escape

sly questions from the first-comers, whoever they might be, thought of the many times this will had been under discussion, and how vigorous a mind and how caustic a tongue she had brought to it even at the last. That codicil, for instance:—

"The Kerlin Fund, in memory of my late son-in-law ...

"Put in the son-in-law, mind. Just as well to remind them of the man's claim, and it will be a little surprise for them, among many. Upon my word, I wish I might be there."

Well, well, who could say? An unseen witness, perhaps, thought Mr. Crow, or better still, released from all such vexations. She had had too many, poor lady, with one and another of them, and some people, unless he were much mistaken, would find themselves reaping the whirlwind this afternoon.

There was another ring at the door and the sound of footsteps in the hall. Taylor came to announce that Mr. and Mrs. Dawnay and family had joined Mrs. James Devonshire and Mr. James in the library. Mrs. Dawnay had enquired why they could not go into the drawing-room and be comfortable.

"Let me know when every one has arrived, my girl, but see that they go to the library and nowhere else," ordered the lawyer.

"Why, Marion, you are an early bird," Gwen was saying, rather offended that any one should have had the bad taste to arrive before her in her poor mother's own house.

"Well, dear, I have to depend on a public conveyance and they are so uncertain. I have no indulgent husband to bring me by car, though darling James did want me to have a taxi for once," said Marion fretfully. She had been peering under the blotting-paper on the writing-desk, looking into pigeon-holes and even opening drawers in the hope of catching a glimpse of the will, and was vexed that Gwen had arrived in time to interrupt these investigations. She also suspected, quite unjustly, that Gwen had come early for the same purpose, and now took a seat with an air of general hostility.

James was wandering about the room, gazing at the books, the pictures and the furniture. Herbert joined him condescendingly.

"Well, old lad, what figure do you put the grand stakes at—fifty thousand or over?" inquired Herbert.

"Must be a sight more than that," muttered James. "From the way the money flies to keep up that hovel of ours, a great shop like this must cost about £10,000 a year, and a nice slice the Government will take. A swindle, I call it."

"Oh, I don't grudge the jolly old Government their whack as long as I get mine," said Herbert generously. "Let's hope you are right, my boy."

He rejoined his sisters, feeling cheered, and whispered young James's estimate to them, taking care that his father should not hear.

The old boy had a quaint idea that there was something rather shocking about making a guess at Granny's fortune. So dam' silly.... Herbert wondered whether James would take a bet on it, but decided this would be risky. That young fellow might have gleaned something from old Crow. Ten thousand a year would mean what? ... A cool hundred thousand or pretty nearly, and the grandsons should come pretty well out of that, bound to get more than the girls... stood to reason. Why, a thousand or so would be riches to the lassies. Herbert had spent the last two days looking at cars, and there was a flat in the Temple he had his eye on. He began to contemplate a few other little trifles in the way of expenditure, feeling himself already a man of means.

"Really, I think Mr. Crow should have been here to receive us," said Mrs. Dawnay restlessly. "As my mother's only surviving child I feel I have the right to that courtesy and also to say where the will shall be read. I dislike this gloomy room. I never did like it as a girl."

"Well, my dear, I warned you that we should get here before the appointed time," said Richard.

"There, I knew it," thought Marion triumphantly.

The door opened, but only to admit the Fenwicks and Biddy, with Jane Devonshire, who had strolled up as their taxi reached the house.

"How do you do, Edith, this is a very sad occasion. Poor, poor mother," sighed Gwen, wiping her eyes. She kissed Frederika (who hastily retreated), and looked past that naughty Biddy, thinking it most brazen of the girl to come here. And what right had that young Fenwick to be present, she would like to know? Most peculiar of Edith to bring him, but she always had been a peculiar woman. If Mr. Crow asked the young man to leave, Gwen thought it would be quite within his rights. In fact, if she had an opportunity she would suggest it.

May had seized Jane and pulled her down beside them, whispering. Jane, with an eye on Herbert, endeavored to respond. He was looking very pleased with himself, she thought. If he came in for a pile from Granny there would be no holding him. Getting spoiled already. Men had all the luck. Jane herself was expecting no pile, she had given up expecting anything in this world, and poor old Granny had never had much time for her. Other people had seen to that.... Creepy it was sitting in her house and knowing you would never see her any more. Pretty beastly...all perching round like a lot of hawks, waiting to snatch her money.

Gwynneth had smiled kindly at Biddy, who had not noticed, she was afraid. She had gone away with the Fenwicks and was sitting there, saying nothing. Biddy looked white and thoroughly miserable, Gwynneth thought, and wondered if she had had to pawn anything else, and if Aunt Edith knew and would help her. Biddy had been in church yesterday, and had taken charge of Simpkins and put her down in the front with the family, and Mummy had said it was great impudence. Biddy should know better, and who was she to arrange where the servants were to sit?...But then Biddy had lived in the house after all, and Daddy hadn't seemed to think it mattered. Neither did Gwynneth. If only Mummy wouldn't get so upset about things...she would be crying again in a minute, she was on the verge of it now.

Biddy was thinking: "I always loved this room. It is so dignified. I'll try to count the books to occupy my mind, directly they begin. I wish I hadn't had to come. I used to come in here and read about antiques. I'll begin from the shelf where the books about them are, and go to the right. If only I didn't feel so hollow inside. I hope it was all right for me to come and she wouldn't mind. I suppose this house and everything will belong to Aunt Gwen now, but I can't imagine any one else in it but Grandmother. I can't believe it.... I wish they'd begin...."

Mr. Crow had come in at last. He bowed to the company punctiliously, first to Mrs. Dawnay, who was suddenly so much overcome by the gravity of his manner that she forgot the complaints she had proposed to make, and put her handkerchief to her eyes instead. Having bowed in turn to the Fenwick party, and Mrs. James Devonshire, Mr. Crow took his seat at the desk. There was a flutter of movement in the room, but he ignored it, polishing his spectacles with care and perching them on his high-bridged nose, then taking a key from his pocket and inserting it in the lock of his bag.

Mr. Crow was not to be hurried, there was a proper decency to be observed, and his severe expression was an intimation that he proposed to maintain it.

As he took out the papers and set them neatly before him, Mrs. Dawnay gasped as a prelude to hysterical tears. He looked at her over his glasses, then took these off and laid them significantly on the desk.

The lady having been persuaded to control herself, Mr. Crow cleared his throat.

"Ladies and gentlemen, I need not say that this is a very distressing occasion. I feel sure you do not wish to be detained from the business in hand to listen to anything I have to say on the loss of my old friend and esteemed client, a loss that is naturally to all present too deep for mere words. With your permission I will therefore read the will, only asking each of you, if you will be so good, to refrain from interruptions, and to keep any necessary questions until later."

"Certainly, certainly, very proper, sir," answered Richard Dawnay.

Mr. Crow cleared his throat and began:

"This is the last will and testament of me, Mary Octavia Brigid Devonshire, widow, of 49, Portman Square, London. I direct that my remains shall be interred simply and privately, and request that there shall be no mourning and that none of the women of my family shall attend the funeral. I appoint William Crow, Solicitor, of Parkinson, Crow & Dorset, Lincoln's Inn, the sole executor of this my will, and direct that he shall take complete charge of my household until such time as it shall be convenient for it to be dispersed.

"I further direct that all my just debts, funeral and testamentary expenses, and the mortgage on my house in Portman Square shall be paid and satisfied by my executor as soon as may be after my decease—"

"Mortgage?" exclaimed Marion at this point in a hoarse whisper to Gwen.

Mr. Crow looked at her sharply, however, and she subsided.

"As a first charge upon my estate I bequeath to my executor the sum of £3,000 to be converted into an annuity for P. Simpkins, my faithful maid and friend for nearly fifty years. . . ."

"Very handsome," murmured Richard Dawnay, "very handsome indeed."

"I bequeath also to the said P. Simpkins all the wearing apparel of which I may die possessed.

"I direct my executor to pay to each of the servants in my employ at the date of my death three months' wages, and the further sum of ten pounds for every year of service in my house.

"I bequeath to my young friend, Sholto Fenwick, step-son of my daughter-in-law, Mrs. John Fenwick, the sum of £100 and any twelve books from my library which he may choose, in recognition of the benefit and amusement I have derived from his conversation."

Raised eyebrows and several smiles greeted this item; Mr. Crow permitted himself a benevolent glance in the direction of Mr. Sholto Fenwick, and then cleared his throat ... perhaps as sailors clear a deck for action.

"I direct that all my personal furniture and effects with the exception of such articles as may be mentioned elsewhere in this my will, shall be removed and sold, and that my freehold residence known as 49, Portman Square shall also be sold, the moneys from both such sales free of legacy duty to be divided equally among my five grand-daughters or such as may survive me. I make this be-quest after due consideration of the conditions prevailing in the world today and the fact that my two grandsons have received monetary gifts from me during my life-time...."

An electric shock seemed to go round the company. Gwen beamed at her darlings and then began to whisper frantically to Richard.

Marion exclaimed: "What does it mean? I don't under-stand this...."

"Madam!" said Mr. Crow, in a tone of reproof.

"If you would kindly read that through again, Crow,

perhaps Mrs. Devonshire did not quite catch the drift," suggested Richard Dawnay, tactfully.

Frederika, her eyes nearly starting out of her head, gazed across at Biddy triumphantly, but Biddy had her face hidden by Sholto who, with his arm round the back of her chair, was leaning over her. Edith motioned to her daughter to attend to Mr. Crow.

The lawyer, reading the paragraph through again, went firmly on to the next, determined not to be interrupted this time:

"In making the following specific legacies to members of my family, I wish it to be clearly understood that I desire no article to be kept for sentimental reasons, or in memory of me, but to be converted into ready money if occasion should require.

"I bequeath to my daughter-in-law, Edith Fenwick, widow of my elder son, Hugh Devonshire, my Crown Derby dinner and tea-services; and to her daughter, Frederika Devonshire, any jewelry of which I may die possessed, and the portrait by Sargent of her father, the said Hugh Devonshire.

"I bequeath to my daughter, Mrs. Richard Dawnay, my drawing-room carpet or any other carpet she may prefer in my house, and my Georgian silver tea and coffee service; and to my son-in-law, Richard Dawnay, the contents of my wine-cellar, if any.

"I bequeath to my daughter-in-law, Mrs. James Devonshire, the portrait by Sargent of her late husband, and such photographs of her son as she may have given me from time to time.

"I bequeath to my orphaned granddaughter, Brigid Kerlin, the following articles: The walnut writing-desk, the two round tables, the cabinet and contents, and any six chairs she may prefer in the drawing-room, the mahogany cabinet at the foot of the staircase in the hall, the tallboy and contents, the rose glass sweet box and the small stool from my bedroom; the wooden chair and refectory table which stand on the first landing, and the mirror and secretaire from my boudoir. And since I have had no opportunity of consulting her tastes in this matter, I desire that she may be permitted to exchange any one of the articles above mentioned for another after consultation with my executor ..."

"Well!" gasped Gwen, in a whisper to her husband. "What an extraordinary conglomeration."

"Hush!"

"I revoke all former wills and declare this to be my last. In witness whereof, etc., ... one moment," said Mr. Crow, "there is a codicil ... yes, yes ... here we are. ...

"I bequeath £100 or such other sum as may remain from my estate when all debts, legacies and dues above-mentioned have been settled, to Sir Neville Willesden, to be devoted to the Kerlin Fund in memory of my late son-in-law, David Kerlin."

"Oh! how good of her," cried Biddy, the color suddenly rushing to her face, and then as quickly draining away. The revelation contained in her own legacy had bewildered and shaken her, and this seemed to put the final touch to her distress. She looked about her wildly, and Edith, after one glance at her face, said a word to Sholto, and helped him lead her from the room.

"Take her home," she whispered, closing the door on

them, and with an apologetic glance to the lawyer, returned quietly to her place, ignoring the significant whispers of the family.

"The young lady is upset?" suggested Mr. Crow. "Is there anything I can do, Mrs. Fenwick?"

"No, thank you, Mr. Crow. I have sent her home with my stepson. He will look after her."

"Other people are also upset," exclaimed Gwen indignantly, feeling that her rights were being infringed, and beginning to cry again.

"Of course, of course, Mrs. Dawnay, but I shall not have to keep you any longer. In short—that, ladies and gentlemen, completes the bequests of my late client," finished Mr. Crow, and with a sigh waited for the tempest to burst.

Marion began it stridently.

"But where does the money go? Who gets the fortune? ...It belongs to my boy as the head of the family.... What is the sum? I have a right to know."

"Your boy, Marion, has no more claim than mine," retorted Mrs. Dawnay indignantly to this. "Herbert is the eldest grandchild."

"Herbert indeed? He is not even a Devonshire! It's a conspiracy.... I knew it!"

"Ladies, ladies!" Mr. Crow rapped the table sharply. "This is most unseemly. Must I remind you that we are in a house of death? If you have any questions to ask me, I must request you to do so quietly and with suitable respect for my client's memory."

"I insist upon knowing the extent of my son's fortune!" said Marion haughtily.

"I think, Crow—er—no residue was mentioned—an oversight, no doubt," suggested Richard Dawnay, with some hesitation.

"The residue, sir, is contained in the last item. I may say that your mother-in-law went into the matter of her property with me very carefully only a week before the end, in her anxiety to deal equitably with her heirs," explained Mr. Crow. "As far as we can see, when all other matters are disposed of, there will probably be a trifle of £100 or a little more or less, which she desired to go to this—er—Fund."

"What is it, Richard? I don't understand," said Gwen, beginning to weep afresh. "Who gets poor Mother's money?"

"Exactly! Who gets it?" echoed her son. "Something jolly fishy here, if you ask me."

"Herbert, will you be silent, or leave the room?" thundered his father. "Then you mean us to understand that my mother-in-law died a comparatively poor woman?"

The lawyer bowed.

"That is so, sir."

"Oh, rot!" burst out the boy James.

Mr. Crow looked him up and down.

"You think, young man, that money flows from some invisible spring under the foundations of this house, apparently. Mr. Herbert Dawnay seems to have the same impression. Well, young gentlemen," said Mr. Crow, "you had better realize that this spring—a spring of kindness from which you have both benefited in the past—has dried up."

"It's a swindle," began James, but was silenced by his uncle.

"Will you hold your tongue, sir," said Richard Dawnay, "and permit Mr. Crow to continue."

"You know as well as I do, Mr. Dawnay," proceeded the lawyer, "that every private fortune in the country has dwindled during the past fifteen years or more. Mrs. Devonshire, like the rest of us, has had to face enormous taxation, depreciation of dividends, mounting expenses, as well as perpetual calls upon her which she was too generous to withstand. You are no doubt aware that she twice paid the death duties on Highways out of her own pocket, to save the already burdened estate, first for her son, the late Mr. James Devonshire, and secondly for her grandson. I believe I am also right in saying that with the exception of Miss Kerlin and Miss Frederika Devonshire, she has educated her grandchildren. You will correct me if I am wrong."

"No, no, not at all. Mrs. Devonshire was most generous," admitted Richard uncomfortably.

"There have been other matters, I need not remind . you," went on Mr. Crow drily; "all of which have entailed heavy sacrifices upon my late client."

"Yes, indeed—er—no doubt. Then at what figure would you put her—er—estate, roughly?"

"That we shall know only when this property has been disposed of. Her liquefiable assets, apart from house and furniture, are in the neighborhood of £12,000."

"Then why did she keep up this great house?" said Marion. "I call it disgraceful. She must have been out of her senses."

"Madam!" expostulated the lawyer, for the moment shocked beyond speech.

"I don't know what you mean, Marion," exclaimed Mrs. Dawnay, indignantly. "Poor Mother's house was her own affair and her money too, though no one would think so, I'm sure, by the way some people have sponged upon her."

"It's a conspiracy," retorted Marion. "And you are at the head of it. Don't think I'm blind! . . ."

For a few moments pandemonium reigned, the sisters-in-law losing sight of the main issue, and exchanging home-truths with an icy courtesy.

"And what became of Granny's car, I should like to know?" said Marion suddenly, producing a calm.

The family had completely forgotten this envied possession, and looked inquiringly at the lawyer.

"Mrs. Devonshire owned no car," he replied. "That also she sacrificed six or seven years ago."

"Oh, but she did have a car, excuse me, Mr. Crow," said Gwen with dignity.

"You are mistaken, Mrs. Dawnay. Your mother hired a car from time to time when she required one."

"Ring for tea, Gwynneth, I must have some tea or I shall faint."

Edith Fenwick, who had been uncomfortably trying to catch the lawyer's eye, stood up and came to him.

"Perhaps we might slip away, Mr. Crow . . . do you mind?" she said in a low voice.

"Certainly, Mrs. Fenwick . . . most unpleasant for you. Let me see you out . . . no, no, please, I insist."

He accompanied them to the hall door, as though glad of a respite, and mopping his forehead.

"Very painful all this, very, and I must thank you for your consideration, Mrs. Fenwick," he said. "I hope the little girl will be none the worse."

"She is feeling Mrs. Devonshire's death very much," admitted Edith.

"Poor child! I wish I could see so much sensibility in some other quarters, I do indeed. And this is the young lady who gets her Granny's jewels, isn't it?"

"Nice of her, wasn't it?" said Freddy. "I *was* surprised."

"Well, well, I shouldn't wonder, between you and me, my dear, if she wasn't hoping to surprise you," beamed Mr. Crow. "Oh, by the way, Mrs. Fenwick...."

He felt in his pockets and produced a sealed envelope.

"I wonder if I might trouble you to put that into Miss Kerlin's hands? The keys, I understand, of the cabinet and tallboy which, with their contents, form part of her legacy. Mrs. Devonshire had them locked and gave me instructions to hand her granddaughter this envelope.... Let me see, though.... No, no, I shall need to ask Miss Kerlin to go through the contents with me before the valuation of the furniture for probate, and make a list. We must not be irregular.... Perhaps I had better keep this and meet her here—in a few days if she is equal to the task. Can I get into touch with her, or may I communicate with you?"

"With me, Mr. Crow, if you will. She is staying with me," said Edith.

"Excellent; then I will say good-by and thank you again. Good-by."

The lawyer turned back with a sigh, and at the same moment the library door opened and Jane Devonshire stalked out, shutting it behind her.

"Make you sick, don't they?" she said. "Well, I'll be pushing off."

She walked out into Portman Square, paused to use her lipstick and then went on again, trying to realize what had befallen her. Against all reason and expectation, she had been remembered, and for the life of her Jane could not see why. And the lordly Herbert and that insufferable young brother of hers cut off without a cent!

For the first time since her father's death when she was twelve years old Mrs. Devonshire's eldest granddaughter looked at the world and pronounced it not so dusty after all.

CHAPTER FOURTEEN

A LAST LAUGH TOGETHER

EDITH, DRIVING home, resolutely put the scene she
had just left out of her mind as something altogether beneath contempt, only thankful that Biddy had not seen the
worst of it. Frederika's popping eyes had been eloquent
enough, and she had had to keep a firm hand on that blunt
young woman to prevent her from an open fight with
James, who had taken a chair near Freddy, and muttered
insolent comments from time to time. Had Biddy remained, Edith knew that she could not with justice have
tried to silence her defense of her grandmother, though it
would certainly have brought abuse and probably accusations upon the girl's own head. As it was, the Dawnays
and James Devonshires had been fortunately too much intent upon their own grievances to remember yet that Biddy,
in spite of the quarrel with her grandmother, had been
more generously remembered than their own children.

"Pigs, weren't they?" said Freddy. "Jolly nice Biddy
getting all that furniture for their house. She will be
bucked."

Edith nodded with a faint smile at this naïve mention
of the furniture, about which she had certain suspicions
of her own.

"She seemed more pleased about the money in memory
of her father. I suppose she couldn't take it all in at first."

"Funny we never knew him. You did, though, didn't you, a little?"

"Yes, when he and your aunt were first married, but then the War came and we were at Highways and they were in London, and every one either busy or fighting, and we lost touch....I suppose we ought some of us to have looked out for Biddy if we hadn't been selfish, but her father was a difficult man to know and wrapped up in his work....However, she is all right now, and I think this legacy will cheer her up."

"She had been looking a bit pipped," admitted Freddy. "You know...when nobody was watching...in between times...."

"Of course, after living in the house...quarrel or no quarrel, I believe Biddy was nearer to your grandmother in the end than any of you...." Edith thought of the drawing-room in Portman Square and her mother-in-law looking round it on her birthday morning and saying:

"Dear me, what an opportunity the girl has missed. She might have asked me to set her up in business."

It had been a triumphant look, thought Edith, for all her pretense at malice, and if these articles left to Biddy were antiques, as she strongly suspected, she who had dropped a hint of the girl's ambitions, would know that she had done at least one thing to give comfort to the old woman whose kindness after years of hostility had so touched her in the end.

2

Biddy had broken down at last, crying her heart out in Sholto's arms, and because tears were not easy to her, they had given her a severe headache and perhaps, though she did not know it yet, a measure of relief.

The specious comfort of the legacies could not help her, for now she saw without any shadow of doubt that she should have gone back. Her grandmother had not been really angry with her, whatever she had or had not done, and that phrase, "I have had no opportunity of consulting her," had cut Biddy to the heart. She did not recognize its real intention—to silence any suspicion on the part of the family that the girl, while staying in the house, had feathered her own nest. Biddy saw in it a reproach and one that she felt, alas, was well-deserved.

She had not said anything much of this to Sholto; even he could not help her, no one could help her, and it would be selfish and beneath contempt, she felt, to let them try. It was no good to worry either, it was too late. Biddy faced that desolate phrase with the incredulity that wiser heads have brought to it.

The sight of Sholto's anxious face gazing down at her brought back her self-control at last, and by the time Edith and Freddy came in she was calm, though somewhat weary-eyed and ready to hear with composure the end of the will.

Edith, having given it briefly, rang for tea, and sat down on the arm of the girl's chair.

"Feeling all right?"

Biddy nodded and forced a smile.

"Lucky about that furniture, just when you are going to be married," remarked Freddy. "Won't you and Sholto be smart?"

"It isn't furniture," said Biddy, looking up quickly at Edith. "Don't you know...didn't any of you notice? They are—objects of vertu.... I get more than anybody really, except perhaps Freddy's jewels, they are the most valuable things in the house."

Her voice broke in spite of herself: "Even the little red box I gave her... and I didn't think she knew."

"She knew a great many things no one suspected," remarked Edith. "I thought they were antiques, but I couldn't be sure.... And did you notice how cunningly they were set down in the will, as though they were nothing in particular?... That was where she was so clever and far-seeing. She meant you to be protected from jealousy and abuse, my dear, from other members of the family...."

"I never thought of that," admitted Biddy. "I am in such a maze I don't remember really what they were, except the William-and-Mary cabinet, and the Jacobean table, and the Queen Anne desk...."

"And the tallboy," supplemented Freddy.

"And contents," added Edith, reminded of Mr. Crow's message.

"I don't know why she should have chosen those things ... it seems so strange. She didn't even know I cared for them."

"Perhaps she cared for them herself," suggested Edith, with a faint smile for her own duplicity.

"Come on," said Freddy, "we'll write down what we can remember. Where will you put them? Will you sell them or what?"

"You concern yourself with those Crown jewels," advised Sholto, "and leave my property-in-law alone."

Biddy let them argue and recall her legacies and dispose of them, happiness fighting with the sadness within her.

She had not dreamt that her grandmother might have been moved by affection to leave her these things, and to do it so carefully that she could not be envied or abused, and she was amazed and touched. But again this made her own guilt all the worse. The will must have been made, she supposed, when she was in the house and for all her anger and disappointment her grandmother had not changed it or cut her out.

And then there was the legacy to her father's memory ... and Biddy remembered that she had never mentioned him! Had it been just a sense of duty after all then? ... a kind of reparation for not being too kind to her daughter Brigid? ... paying off back duty, in fact, said the inventor of this phrase guiltily to herself.

Biddy decided despondently that she would never know, drank her tea and sat up to pay attention to Sholto, remembering at the same moment that she had been here for days and it was high time for her to go.

There was no possibility of that, however, she found, for Edith presently delivered the lawyer's message about the keys and the necessity for her to go to Portman Square again in a few days, adding that she had promised that Biddy would await a telephone call at Buckingham Gate.

Biddy looked at her suspiciously, and then at Sholto, but found no evidence of a conspiracy between them. His delight was altogether too plain. And she thought in surprise: "I'm taking him away from them before long, and when I do go home he'll always be coming over to me. And they don't even hate me!"

Gratitude and tenderness filled her; she felt at that moment, if they had asked her to stay forever, she could not have refused.

Freddy's gruff voice, an excellent antidote to any emotional state, suddenly broke into her consciousness:

"You have a right to change anything you like. Are you going to?"

"I wouldn't for the world!"

"Well, you can pick out my twelve books for me, darling, at the same time," invited Sholto.

"I wouldn't do that for the world either.... She wouldn't like it.... I never heard of such a thing!" Biddy looked scandalized, and Sholto leant over the back of the chair and kissed her eyes.

"Perhaps you are right ... you are always right," he said. "All the same, you are marrying a very useful fellow, remember. It isn't every one who can get a prize for conversation."

3

On Saturday afternoon Sholto and Biddy walked along Portman Square to keep the appointment with Mr. Crow. The fine weather which had followed Sunday's storm still held; the day was mellow and tranquil, and in the old square garden the sunlight lay in golden patches on the grass.

Biddy, who had looked out on this square every day for a year, felt that each tree was a friend to which in an hour or two she would bid good-by. Very soon the house would be dismantled and sold, and she would never want to come this way again. The only grandeur she had ever known had been here, and now it was gone.

She looked at the house incredulously because it showed still the same serene face to the world as when it had been the residence of Mrs. Devonshire of Portman Square, and then she was rather proud of it for standing up to its changing destinies as though some greatness still remained from the mistress who had ruled it for fifty years. She too had stood up to change, and Biddy, dimly recognizing this and paying tribute to it in her heart, did not know that in capturing the imagination of her own inconspicuous self, that old magnificent figure had done what would have seemed to her, could she have known it, something more incredible still.

Biddy thought of her "objects of vertu"; the phrase of old Mr. Dawes had always pleased her, and it had a peculiar justness in her eyes for these treasures which miraculously had become her own. They too would have to be moved from the house, but tenderly, and she must be there to see it done. She would ask Mr. Dawes to give her his advice, and she hoped he would perhaps agree to take them in for the time being if she paid him well. After all, she had forty pounds....

He might care to buy some of them...he would at least be able to advise her whether they should go to Christie's. ...Perhaps Mr. Crow would let her have the valuation figures....

Biddy's mind went over these matters mechanically and she thought: "I shall get a lot of useful experience, but the first thing is to find them a home. I could never let them go just anywhere. I'm glad they are mine because the others might not have understood.... They have always known them...and perhaps they just think them old and dull.

Aunt Gwen said they were a conglomeration, and that shows you."

She was piling up a defense of busy thoughts against the pain of going into the empty house and meeting her legacy face to face, of walking through the familiar rooms guiltily wondering whether her grandmother would mind, in spite of her will, which perhaps she had been too desperately ill to change.

Sholto, talking now and then, and watching her out of the corner of his eye, thanked his stars the lawyer had so obligingly chosen Saturday afternoon. He couldn't have known a moment's peace of mind, thinking of her going to this job without him, even with Edith or young Freddy for company. She kept so quiet, this girl of his, but in a way he understood that, and knew that in her blacker moments he could raise a smile. Sholto was both a rallying force and a defense force in one, in fact.

His own legacy had amused him mightily, and touched him none the less. He could see the good old dragon dictating it with a gleam in her eye, having the last word, as was her due. And he had met Biddy in her house, under her stately wing. At the door he remembered this debt to her, and acknowledged it with a quickening of all his senses towards the silent figure at his side.

Taylor admitted them. Only the two oldest servants still remained, and Simpkins, for whom Edith had called an hour ago, to take her to look for a home.

Biddy said: "I'm glad you are still here, Taylor....I hope you are going to be all right."

"Oh, yes, miss, we were all most kindly remembered, thank you," said Taylor severely. "I am going home next week for a rest as you might say....I wanted to ask you, Miss Biddy, if I decide to take service again, might I use your name as a reference ... as one of the mistress's heiresses —like, and you having lived with her?"

"Why, of course, if it would be any use to you, if I'm important enough," said Biddy, startled. She scribbled her address for Taylor and then followed Sholto into the drawing-room, trying to believe this was all an incredible dream. Taylor asking her for a reference! ... Taylor snapping up the blinds and bringing her morning tea ... old Simpkins mending her torn frock and saying austerely: "Somebody has to do it." Biddy herself suddenly set down in the middle of all this splendor, and desperately trying to hide her fear and her delight. Memories came thronging.

"Found out, that's what I am!" said Sholto. "Marrying an heiress. Fortune-hunter."

"Oh, darling," said Biddy, "I'm glad I have a little bit. I've been so worried to think of making you poor. You've not been used to it."

Sholto, speechless, caught her in his arms and only released her at the sound of the opening door. Even then he firmly retained her hand, and to the old lawyer coming in they presented a rather pleasing picture, though possibly he had that view already in his mind from chance references in this very room.

So this was the young man whose conversation had amused her? ... A rascal, she had called him, with quite a gift for impudence.... "Plays cricket," she had said, "and makes jam, if you can think of anything more ridiculous. He informed me it was the best jam, and then watched to see if I knew my 'Alice in Wonderland,' but I did not—to disoblige him—or tell him I had known his jam when he was in the cradle.... This new world, my friend, will still have excellent jam. Let us take comfort from that."

Well, the boy had pleased her, and that was in his favor, thought Mr. Crow, shaking hands benevolently with his visitors, and leading Biddy to a seat.

And this child too! He remembered his first meeting with her, it must be ten months ago. "I have a granddaughter staying in the house...you would not know her, my daughter Brigid's girl," Mrs. Devonshire had said. "The chit who ran off to the Arctic to meet her father—Kerlin, the explorer. You shall observe her at tea and tell me your impression." He had waited with misgivings, which was of course what she had intended; he had caught her mocking eyes upon him as the girl came in with her fresh, serious face and sudden smile and her young air of dignity. And when they were alone again she had remarked triumphantly, "Aha! you are surprised...I am even occasionally surprised myself. Twenty years old, no mother, no chances, living, I suppose, from hand to mouth, and you see her.... What becomes of environment, my friend, and all our fine theories? Don't tell me at this stage of our acquaintance that she gets that quality from my blood...and I doubt her father's. The man was a boor. Did she fetch it in from the Arctic Seas? Upon my word, the problem amuses me...."

"From my blood...."

The lawyer had known better than most people the source of that bitter phrase, had seen her, after the loss of her sons, slowly give up her own place in the world, her car, her menservants, jewels, capital, one thing after another, against all his persuasions and advice, for her grandchildren, only to find it had been fruitless in the end. His perception, however, took him no further than that. A conservative, conventional, elderly man, he blamed the times, thought it was all very sad, a pity, but alas, inevitable, and now he rejoiced that at least she had had amusement and an outlet for her affections in this girl who, no doubt, had been devoted to her grandmother and a comfort in the declining days of her life. It did not enter Mr. Crow's head that this pretty picture was entirely a work of his own imagination. Mrs. Devonshire had not taken him—or any one else—into her complete confidence; it was not her habit, and well as he thought he had known her, he did not realize that all the amusement, affection and devotion in the world would have been nothing to that restless spirit, without something more...that something which had brought her a sense of fulfillment at the last, transcending disappointment and vexation, and left her, dying, a happy woman.

Mr. Crow delivered the keys to Biddy, and watched her with approval as they began their business, listing the articles of her legacy, the cabinet filled with delicate old Chelsea and other china, the two marquetry tables, the Queen Anne bureau and the six chairs. The girl was grave and quiet and touched the things gently. When she came to choosing the chairs she did not hesitate.

"These would be the six my grandmother meant," she said. "They are Sheraton....You see, all the things she left me are objects of vertu, that's why I feel sure, but I'm afraid they are the best chairs in the room."

She looked at him uncertainly, and as though in apology.

"Well, my dear young lady, there were no conditions,

and it is for you to choose. The six Sheraton chairs, then," said Mr. Crow. "And now I think we will ask Mr. Fenwick to look round the library and choose his books, and Taylor will bring us a cup of tea in there before we go upstairs."

Much better, he thought, to leave the tallboy until the last, for that visit to his old friend's room was bound to be a little upsetting. He, for one, would be glad enough to get it over, for the girl looked heavy-eyed.

The books were chosen and tea came in. They talked of old London, which Mr. Crow remembered, and this square in the days before shops had begun to encroach upon it, when ladies went out in broughams, and cars were unknown, prehistoric days, said the old lawyer prosily. He was precise, he took his time, nothing could hurry him, and Biddy, pouring out tea, wished it were finished and they could go home, and then reproached herself because in his heavy way he was trying to be kind.

Sholto wondered whether the old boy would allow him to go upstairs and look after Biddy, or in his Victorian respectability, expect him to stay here cooling his heels. Finally he managed to put the question.

"Dear me," said Mr. Crow, "no, I don't think there can be any objection, unless Miss Kerlin . . ."

"I would like him to come," said Biddy. "We're engaged. I don't know whether my aunt told you."

"Now that is delightful. I congratulate you both. Excellent!"

This was better. The lad would be a help if the moment proved too painful.

They finished their tea and went upstairs, pausing on

the way to look at the inlaid cabinet in the angle of the stairs, Biddy opening it to show them the multitude of drawers within.

"Very fine, very fine, my dear, and you will take care of it, I am sure," murmured Mr. Crow.

Biddy, following him, was conscious of a new idea, a new dismay. Had her grandmother meant her to keep these things then? Was that the explanation... in spite of the note in the will that nothing was to be kept? She would keep them gladly if she only knew, but she was so confused and how could any home of hers and Sholto's do them justice? Perhaps Mr. Crow would know if she could only manage to ask him without being a fool and bursting into tears.

The pity of this poor lost house tore at her heart, and the dreadful feeling that her grandmother, having so much, had yet had nothing she desired.... All the family quarreling about her will, caring only for that, and she herself so undeserving, given these things, and not understanding why!

They came to the wooden chair, centuries old, she suspected, and the Jacobean table, and then to the boudoir looking on the square. They had had tea here sometimes when they were alone, the room was full of memories, but her grandmother's room she had never seen, except for a glimpse of old rose hangings when the door happened to be ajar.

As Mr. Crow went in she saw the rose coverlet on the bed and then, with dim eyes, the old glass box on the table beside it. She walked in blindly and touched it, fighting for her self-control.

"Ah, yes, the tallboy, here we are," remarked the lawyer cheerfully.

The girl turned slowly and gave a cry. On top of the tallboy, shining and familiar, stood Miss Sarah Verschoyle's stool.

Biddy, shaking from head to foot, thought she must have lost her mind. Sholto had gone to her, and she clutched him, trying to explain.

"It's mine...the one I found and sold. I can't understand it....I must be dreaming!"

"Perhaps it is a pair, or something," suggested Sholto, but she broke free and lifted it down and sat on the floor with it, recognizing every familiar mark.

"No, no, it is the same. I *can't* understand it."

Biddy, putting a distracted hand to her forehead, looked up at the lawyer.

"I found this at a sale and sold it to a dealer....I can't think how it could have come here," she said. "Do you know?...it is all so queer."

"Well, no, I can't say that I recall the stool," admitted the old man.

"Did she tell you...do you know why she left me all these lovely things?...I can't make it out, Mr. Crow."

"Ah, there can be no doubt about that, my dear," smiled the lawyer comfortably. "She left them to you as a token of her affection, we may be sure. Now suppose we open the tallboy and see if there is something more to be added to our list."

Biddy unlocked the drawers and put a careful hand in the lowest one, still kneeling on the floor. Sholto bent above her, Mr. Crow stood by with his list open, ready to write.

"It's her Waterford glass," said the girl in a trembling voice.

In the next were six crystal goblets and a number of small articles of value in porcelain and china. Each drawer in turn produced its treasures, but Biddy was speechless now, and merely took them out of their wrappings for the lawyer to see, then put them tenderly back again.

"She gave me everything," she thought brokenly, "and I didn't come back."

She was standing up now and there was only one small drawer left. Sholto pulled it open for her, then chuckled at what he saw inside.

"I say, Biddy, the locked diary I gave her to write her Memoirs in. And she has left it to you.... Good God, you'd think she must have known...."

Biddy took the diary from him and smiled. The key was in the lock and she turned it curiously and opened the first page. The next moment she had clasped it to her and run from him to the window, turning her back on the two men, forgetting them.

Thus comfort came to her at last.

"Aha, Miss Independence, that was a fine trick I played you, wasn't it, picking a quarrel, to get you out of the house of an old sick woman, who was too vain to let you see her die. I have enjoyed my little joke and now, because you were always a good audience, you shall enjoy it too, and we'll have a last laugh together. If you had come back you would have spoilt it—remember that, Biddy—for now I know that you can stand on your own feet, which is the only way to live.

"Here is the nucleus of your antique business. Yes, I have

*spied upon you and don't deny it, as you strolled among
my treasures, saying nothing, but speaking none the less ...
you and your old rose box. Now why, I have often wondered, did you not recommend your gift? Was it merely
good manners, or were you, too, spying on me to discover
just how much this queer old woman, your grandmother
(I like the title), knew or did not know? An amusing question ...I must think it out. I bought the little stool I leave
you from a man named Dawes in Dover Street. You may
have heard of him. It was discovered and brought to him,
he told me, by a girl of twenty-one, with eyes in her head
and a mind behind them. He seemed taken with the chit.
You will see he is a courtly man, and I know him to be
honest as men go.*

"Do you as you wish with the things, my dear. Samuel
Dawes will help you, if you so desire, and I am happy to
leave them in your hands.

"M. O. B. Devonshire."